THE TREASURE OF
SAVAGE ISLAND

THE
TREASURE OF
SAVAGE ISLAND

LENORE HART

DUTTON CHILDREN'S BOOKS

DUTTON CHILDREN'S BOOKS
A division of Penguin Young Readers Group

Published by the Penguin Group

Penguin Group (USA) Inc., 375 Hudson Street, New York, New York 10014, U.S.A.

Penguin Group (Canada), 90 Eglinton Avenue East, Suite 700, Toronto, Ontario, Canada M4P 2Y3
(a division of Pearson Penguin Canada Inc.)

Penguin Books Ltd, 80 Strand, London WC2R 0RL, England

Penguin Ireland, 25 St Stephen's Green, Dublin 2, Ireland (a division of Penguin Books Ltd)

Penguin Group (Australia), 250 Camberwell Road, Camberwell, Victoria 3124, Australia
(a division of Pearson Australia Group Pty Ltd)

Penguin Books India Pvt Ltd, 11 Community Centre, Panchsheel Park,
New Delhi - 110 017, India

Penguin Group (NZ), Cnr Airborne and Rosedale Roads, Albany, Auckland 1310,
New Zealand (a division of Pearson New Zealand Ltd)

Penguin Books (South Africa) (Pty) Ltd, 24 Sturdee Avenue, Rosebank, Johannesburg 2196,
South Africa

Penguin Books Ltd, Registered Offices: 80 Strand, London WC2R 0RL, England

This book is a work of fiction. Names, characters, places, and incidents are
either the product of the author's imagination or are used fictitiously, and
any resemblance to actual persons, living or dead, business establishments,
events, or locales is entirely coincidental.

The publisher does not have any control over and does not assume any responsibility
for author or third-party websites or their content.

CIP Data is available.

Published in the United States by Dutton Children's Books,
a division of Penguin Young Readers Group
345 Hudson Street, New York, New York 10014
www.penguin.com/youngreaders

Designed by Jason Henry

Printed in USA • First Edition
ISBN 0-525-47092-1

2   4   6   8   10   9   7   5   3   1

For Naia, again

ACKNOWLEDGMENTS

THIS AUTHOR owes a thousand and one thanks to many people, but here is the short list: Miles Barnes, who verified historical details, and Ina Birch, who gave the manuscript a thorough proofreading. Janet Perry and Sheri Reynolds saw an early draft of the novel and gave back their usual gift of insightful comments. So did editors Alissa Heyman, Michele Coppola, and Sarah Pope, with the later version. The Virginia Commission for the Arts provided generous support in conjunction with the Virginia Center for the Creative Arts at Mt. San Angelo—a peerless haven for writers and artists. But again, my deepest gratitude goes to my husband, novelist David Poyer, for trading stories and providing love and support every day.

CONTENTS

THE TREASURE OF
SAVAGE ISLAND

A TYGER AND A STOWAWAY

WHEN RAFE FINALLY REACHED THE DOCKS on the Chowan River, he stopped running. Stopped in his tracks, panting, amazed at the noise and commotion at the pier. Sailors shouted from ship to ship. Deckhands heaved boxes and crates over the rails, to crash on the planks below. Snorting beef cows clattered down the ramp of a large schooner. Sheep bleated and pigs squealed, all amid the salty stink of seawater and heaps of fish heads rotting under the sun.

Rafe suspected his own smell was hardly sweet—a mix of sweat and dirt from long nights of running. And even longer days of hiding in barns and sheds, since he'd laid down his hoe and crawled like a snake between two rows of corn, all the way to the edge of the woods. Then he'd leaped up and started running, and hadn't stopped since. He meant to leave Penland Plantation, and soon all of North Carolina, far behind.

For many weeks he'd slept in ditches and under bushes, till dust and mud crusted his skin and clothes. He'd eaten late berries and windfall nuts, stolen food from smokehouses and cellars. One desperate night he'd wrestled an old, half-toothless dog for the scraps in its bowl, until a woman had shouted from the back stoop. Then he'd started running once again.

He had stopped to wash himself in a creek before he got to Edenton. Now bits of dried dirt he'd missed were cracking, flaking off under this strangely warm October sun.

"Look you, boy! Outta my way," snarled a red-faced man lugging two heavy sacks. He pushed past Rafe, knocked him down. He tensed, ready to spring up again and run. But the man stomped past without a glance.

So Rafe took a deep breath, got up, and walked on. If he seemed not worth noticing, he might be safe for a while. Besides, all around him other dark-skinned children rushed about the waterfront. Men and women, too. They carried market baskets full of bread and vegetables, or balanced timbers on their shoulders. A little toffee-colored girl in slave calico wore a dozen trussed white chickens like a live, squawking shawl. A barefoot boy herded a spotted pig, slashing at its backside with a peeled branch. Rafe looked away, tried not to wince. He could all too easily imagine each blow on his own throbbing back.

Farther down the waterfront, ships were unloading barrels of flour, salt, and sugar. Pipes of brandy, kegs of butter. A whiskey cask tumbled off a handcart and smashed on the pavement, amid curses and shouts. Down one ramp trotted several fine Arabian horses, including a dapple gray just like the one Rafe's master rode, back home. The sleek animals whinnied and balked as if, after a sea voyage, solid land felt strange beneath their hooves. Their grooms clucked and whistled, leading them like exotic princes through a motley crowd of peddlers and gawkers.

Most of the wharf was noisy and bright, colorful as a festival. But at a pier set off all by itself, a black-painted brig was unloading another cargo, one with less spirit than any of the livestock he'd seen. Rafe halted near its plank as a staggering, ragged, miserable assortment of human beings emerged. They were naked, their dark skin covered with sea sores, crusted with dried filth and vomit. Some glanced about with eyes slitted against the bright sun, faces twisted with fear. But most looked down dully, beaten and uncaring. The stench that moved with them was so strong Rafe could almost see it hanging on the air.

He backed off, not wanting to see any more. Or to have to imagine what horrors these captured Africans had endured. He already knew what lay ahead for them: the same thing he was running from.

Before he turned away, a boy his age looked up, right into his eyes. Rafe shivered, as if the slave had suddenly recognized him. He was trapped for a frozen moment by the African's anguished stare before he could turn and run the other way.

He made himself slow down again, for running boys attracted attention. So he slowed to a stroll, trying to look unconcerned as he glanced at each ship. To relax his face into the bored mask of a lazy boy putting off some errand for Mistuss.

But Rafe's only errand was his own. What he wanted was a ship, one loaded and ready to leave.

Nearer the end of the pier a smallish brig was tied up. Its figurehead was weather-beaten, the paint so faded he could barely tell the wooden carving on the prow was actually a woman. Her hands were splintered to stumps, her nose worn flat. Beside her, in peeling fancy letters of faded red and gold, the ship's name scrolled:

TYGER

Rafe walked past the brig, yawned, then shoved his hands in his pockets and crossed the street. He leaned against the wall of a tavern, in the shadow of its hanging sign. The rough tabby masonry prickled through his shirt. His feet were blistered bloody. He shifted, but it was impossible to get comfortable.

A white woman approached. Her nostrils flared when she glanced his way. She opened the tavern's door and hurried inside. A warm gust from within carried the yeasty scent of baking bread. Rafe's stomach growled. All he'd had to eat the last two days was a handful of wizened, leftover summer blueberries.

As he watched, several seamen left the brigantine. Before they reached the pier, another sailor called down after them: "Be back at sunup, or we make for Boston port without you!"

Boston. The word he'd waited for, longed for, a magic incantation. There were no slaves in Boston. There he'd be free.

He waited until a few more men left the ship, then slowly approached the gangplank. Aside from one disgusted-looking sailor swabbing the foredeck, no one was about. Rafe took a deep breath and scurried up the plank.

He knew little about ships. Only what he'd learned from eavesdropping while young Master William had his lessons in the plantation's overheated nursery while the big mahogany mantel clock ticked off the hours. He could still feel the scratchy patterned wool rug beneath his bare feet. And a pang of something, almost homesickness. Except he could recall even more clearly the sight of his mother whipped bloody in the pantry. And the dull ache in his own back, where unhealed wounds still stuck to his shirt.

He had to hide . . . perhaps in a cargo hold. Had to find a place out of sight for as many days as it took to reach Boston port. But now the deckhand was coming, mumbling curses as he dragged his swab over the planks, toward Rafe. In a moment he'd be discovered. Taken. And the slave catchers would be called to bring him back.

A dead rat lay near Rafe's feet, stiff and bloated, covered with flies. He grabbed its naked tail, then slung the carcass hard as he could up toward the foredeck. The rat landed with a thump behind a pile of coiled lines. The sailor dropped his mop and went to investigate the sound. Rafe darted toward the aft hatch.

He crouched at the opening. It was very dark down there. Darker than the box where captured runaways were always sweated. And full of . . . who knew what. But footsteps were approaching again. He gripped the rails of the ladder, panicked, and lost his grip, then fell down the hatch, making a hard, hurtful landing on his back.

For a moment he struggled to draw in the breath that the

fall had knocked out of him. When he could breathe again, the air smelled of mildew and scum and damp anchor lines. And the sweetness of molasses, which must be inside the barrels he'd landed next to. He rolled to his knees, then stood, wincing, and leaned his face for a moment against a bulkhead.

So cool it was down there, he could hardly believe that topside folks were still sweating out an Indian summer, as the mistress used to call it. Right now some other slave boy or girl would be manning the ropes that swung the huge fans, cooling the masters of the Penland Plantation. A job Rafe's arm muscles knew all too well. He shivered in the damp dark.

"I'm not afraid," he whispered.

Heavy footsteps paused overhead. Then a deep, gruff voice said, "Dirty weather offshore, they say."

A second voice replied in flat, clipped tones Rafe didn't recognize. "Don't matter to the Old Man. He'll drive the sticks outta her."

Then the hatch slammed, the hold went black. At last no one could see him. He didn't have to pretend anymore. He crouched suddenly, weeping in terror, alone in the dark.

2

A SHIPWRECK
ON THE BANDY

MOLLY SAVAGE SAT UP SUDDENLY in her rope bed, under the steep, slanted ceiling of the Hog's Head Tavern's attic. A storm was battering like hard fists at the tiny window over her bed, but what had waked her was the sound of running footsteps and shouts from below. She huddled under the quilt again, hoping to go back to sleep. But the hoarse voice of Mrs. Ben, the tavern owner, was calling up the stairs.

"Ever'body outside, an' down to the beach! You, too, girl. There's a ship nigh, a-breakin' itself up, out on the Bandy."

A shipwreck! Molly threw back the covers and yanked her woolen dress over her shift, wondering, as she fumbled with the buttons, how the widow always seemed to be the first to know such things. Every man, woman, and child on Savage Island would be out on the beach tonight. She forced the last wooden button closed at the neck of her dress, then listened in the dark. No sound from across the attic, where normally her father would be snoring. He must already be up and gone.

In the three years since her mother had died, he rarely slept a full night anyhow. He had nightmares. He'd once told her he'd always had them—ever since he'd run off to the war against the British as a boy. Sometimes at night he cursed or cried out, fighting with the bedcovers as if for his very life. He'd been a soldier in the Continental Army at thirteen, and by the time he was her own age, fifteen, he'd been wounded, seen horrors. He never liked to speak of the war, nor of her mother's death.

Molly lowered her bare feet to the icy boards and groped under the bed for her shoes, thinking she'd do better to sleep in the stable with Old Janey the horse and Miranda the nanny goat and—

Something shoved roughly at the middle of her back.

"Ephraim!" She'd sneaked the baby goat into bed for extra warmth. Now the kid butted free of the covers and stood blinking in the dim light.

"Come on," she whispered, scooping him up. "I'll get you back to the shed."

She opened the loft's trapdoor and peered down. Quiet below. She could probably carry him on her shoulders through the pub with no one the wiser. But she'd learned to be careful, for the widow wouldn't like to see a goat inside the tavern. Downstairs stank of wet ashes and stale smoke and sour ale. Molly slipped quickly through the pantry and outside. Miranda the nanny goat bleated sleepily and nuzzled Molly's ear as she laid Ephraim gently on the straw in their pen. Then she secured the gate, ran through the still-darkened village of cottages and sheds and scrubby garden plots, and down the long wooded lane to the beach.

As she burst onto the beach, a gust of wind knocked her off

her feet. She sprawled on the damp ground, flying sand and icy spray stinging tears from her eyes. She grabbed a myrtle branch, pulled herself upright again, and looked around.

For a fearful moment it seemed she'd stumbled into a scene from a terrible fairy tale, where dark misshapen things leaped and shouted through flickering light and shadow. But she could put names to all the soot-blackened faces she saw. Except, where was her father?

"Pa!" she shouted.

She couldn't see him in the milling, shoving crowd, though the whole population of the island was fewer than twenty-five people. But each and every one, wrapped in cloaks and capes and old blankets, was rushing about, screaming conflicting orders, arguing and waving their arms. In the flare of bonfires, people she'd known all her life looked jack-o'-lantern strange, their faces orange masks with dark hollow eyes and turned-down mouths.

The big fires on the beach were meant to warn any ship back before it ran aground on the deadly shoals of the Bandy. But it was already too late. Through wind-whipped rags of scudding fog she could see points of distant lights swinging crazily. She heard the splintering of a grounded ship's backbone. And worse, above gunshot cracks of breaking oak, above the crash and thud of drumming waves and the banshee shriek of the gale, faint shouts came. Screams for help.

Oh, mercy, she thought.

If it had been daytime, the island's watermen might've dragged one of the big log canoes into the surf to pull survivors in. But it was the middle of the night and, outside the circle of fires, dark as the inside of a brandy keg. Only madmen would row out into such a blow for strangers. But even madmen would never make it back through such wild surf.

The whole town might shout and curse and run into one another in the dark, but nothing in the world could save that doomed ship or the souls she carried. Still, Molly watched hopefully in the cold until her frozen fingers clattered numbly together like sticks of winter wood. Until she could no longer tell if the wind or her own shivers shook her body. She edged to the nearest fire, held out her hands to the glow. But the heat was snatched away like a warm scarf in the teeth of a bad dog.

At last her father ran past, face striped with black soot and runnels of sweat. She grabbed at his coat. "I'm here, Pa. Can I—"

"Run along back to the inn, Moll," he yelled over his shoulder, then turned around and heaved a dead stump, which flew cartwheeling onto the blaze.

"Let me help! I can carry wood."

He shook his head. "Get on now, princess, before you turn to a block of ice." He leaped back as the fire spat sparks, then rushed off into the dark again.

Molly sighed, and clamped her frozen hands under her arms. She was no princess, and she hadn't been a little girl for a long time. In fact, she stood taller than her mother ever had, straining her hand-me-down skirts and long-sleeved blouses at the seams. *I'm fifteen now, Pa. Not five,* she wanted to say. He never seemed to remember. Just as he never seemed to remember to visit his wife's narrow grave on the other side of the island. Sometimes Molly felt she was the only one who missed Caroline Savage. Her mother's name, and Molly's resemblance to her, were no longer mentioned.

If Molly forgot, and spoke of some little thing Ma used to do or say, Pa's face would close up like a slammed door. So she'd learned to keep her memories to herself. It felt to her as if he didn't want to remember, and didn't want Molly to, either. Somehow that made her feel as if her mother had died all over again. And this time, had left no trace she'd existed.

But then Molly also recalled how he'd sit up nights, unable to sleep. No, he wasn't really hard-hearted, or forgetful. He still grieved, but only on the inside, where no one else could see.

She watched him heave another huge chunk of ship timber to sizzle in the blaze of bonfire. *He loved Ma, all right,* she thought. *So much he can't bear to even think of how it used to be, when she was alive.*

She wiggled numb toes, sorry she hadn't stopped to pull on her woolen stockings. These old boots pinched her feet. They'd been her mother's, too, but Molly had inherited her father's big hands and feet. The fine Spanish shoe leather had cracked, the soles were nearly worn through. Not likely she'd get new ones anytime soon. Since her father had lost the Hog's Head Tavern in a card game with old Ben Pruitt five years earlier, they were penniless as beggars.

And Mr. Pruitt had taken their tavern, for he was a canny businessman. He'd let them stay on, though, and paid decent wages for odd jobs. But his widow, Mrs. Ben, pried away every brown cent as payment for their room, and meals that often consisted of stale bread and watery porridge. Their miserable attic with the flour-sieve walls leaked cold in winter, but held heat in summer like an oven.

Molly turned away from the fire and trudged back up the marl path to the Hog's Head, crushed oyster shells crunching underfoot. As she walked she recalled the nightmare she'd had earlier. She'd sat at the kitchen table while her mother—alive again and smiling—was setting a huge platter of roasted turkey and buttered sweet potatoes in front of her. But before she could taste a bite, even a sliver of the crisp, crackling skin, a figure in black rushed in, sleeves flapping like a crow's wings.

Mrs. Ben. The widow had snatched the platter and flung it out the window, steaming bird and all. Then shouted, "I'm your mother now! No time to eat, Molly Savage. Work to be done." She'd tossed her a huge broom, one Molly couldn't lift no matter how she heaved and sweated.

"Well, but for all that, it was just a dream," Molly muttered as she tugged the inn's heavy front door open. Mrs. Ben was already back from the beach. She'd opened the pub so cold, wet townspeople might straggle in to warm themselves with a pint and a smoke.

"Look sharp," the widow snapped when she saw Molly. "There's work enough to keep three girls busy tonight."

"Yes'm," Molly mumbled. She picked up a hot poker from the fireplace and thrust its glowing end into each mug of rum toddy Mrs. Ben slammed on the counter. Molly wrinkled her nose as alcohol fumes rose. Mrs. Ben pointed at a table of laughing old men. Molly lifted the heavy tray and staggered over.

She began setting the toddies carefully in front of each man, but her half-frozen fingers still couldn't feel the cups. She inched around the table, praying not to spill a drop, half listening to the codgers jawing and cackling.

"Yeah, recall in '69, the wreck o' that packet. Whattuz she called?" mumbled a bearded man with one eye. Tim Tuttle, the net mender.

"Oh, aye. *Anastasia,* out of New York. Found her stern board in a clump of marsh grass next morning. All hands lost," wheezed his companion, Doc Drummond. He was naught but an herb seller, yet the islanders gave him a medical title and visited him when they were ill.

"Now, didn't she spill some fine goods? A whole bolt of China silk, spoilt by the saltwater. My missus never got over that."

They howled with laughter. Molly carefully lifted the third mug, but hesitated with it just inches from the table planks as bewhiskered Hank Blodgett said, "Mayhap this 'un carries Spanish gold. Eh, gennelmen?"

There was a moment's reverent silence, along with squinted eyes, slowly licked lips.

Then Mr. Tuttle scoffed. "Naw. They're blockaded tight. I'll be bound she's a Britisher, off her course to Canada."

Doc Drummond slammed a hairy fist on the tabletop. "A limey man o' war, more like. Spying redcoats! We sent 'em packing in '81, but mark my words—they've come creeping back on their rosy bellies to haunt us."

"Aye. No doubt. But here's Miss Moll, the innkeeper's beautiful daughter."

Molly made a face, but laughed all the same.

"She's bound to be a rich lady one day, boys," said Hank, winking, lifting a grizzled eyebrow. "You know I heard tell a golden treasure was hid somewhere near this very house, before the war ended. Mayhap you'll find it all one day, and swan off to Richmond in a golden boat, eh, girl?"

But just then Mrs. Ben waved impatiently. Molly's shoulder prickled; she'd gotten a pinch the night before for spilling the cream. She quickly lowered the third mug and grabbed the last one. But her fingers must've finally thawed, for this time the heated pottery scorched her thumb. She shrieked and the mug slipped, splashed, bounced off the table, and smashed to bits on the floor.

"Drat it all, girl. I didn't want a bath in the stuff," cried old Drummond, grinning as he wrung out his coattail.

One of his friends snorted. "Why not? Be your first proper washup all year, Doc."

They roared and slapped the table as Molly scrambled under it to pick up the shattered crockery, bumping her head on the thick carved legs and the wooden rims of chair seats. She wrinkled her nose at the smell of wet wool and stale sweat and old men's ancient boot leather. Then she heard Mrs. Ben's quick, angry steps.

Molly gathered the thick shards, backed out, and stood.

The landlady's face was every bit as red at that moment as it had been in Molly's nightmare. But instead of screaming or cursing or spitting, the widow raised a quick hand and slapped Molly's face. The men barely glanced up at the sound, then fell to talking as if nothing had happened.

Gritting her teeth, lips tight, Molly gathered the broken cup in her skirt. Tears burned beneath her eyelids, but she wouldn't spill them in front of anyone. She touched her burning cheek, staring after the woman's stiff, outraged back. *Why,* she thought, *does she hate me so?*

Mr. Blodgett cried, "Well, if the poor souls all perish, those stuffs'll do 'em no earthly good, fellows. Gold or no, reckon we must check the shore at dawn, eh?"

In the kitchen Molly dumped the broken crockery into the little wagon used to haul trash to the Heap. But all she could think of was Spanish gold, gleaming mounds of it, shimmering so it lit the dark of a ship's hold. Ringing like harness bells as waves rocked the vessel.

She rushed back to take the next tray. Mrs. Ben glanced at her with less of a scowl then, and slid a half-filled mug of cider Molly's way. "Here," she said gruffly. "Warm yourself while you're at it."

Startled, Molly bobbed her head in thanks and took the mug. It was the closest to an apology she'd ever gotten from the widow. The woman wasn't always a witch, true. Still, her strange, shifting moods kept a body feeling on dangerous ground most of the time.

As for the gold . . . surely heavy coins would sink, not wash ashore. She blinked, lifting a tray of foaming ales to her shoulder. Still, even a few such coins might buy back the tavern. Or at least buy them a way off the Island. The Savage family had lived here a hundred years and more, since her great-great-grandfather had floated timbers on a raft all the way from Maryland to build this little tavern.

They still owned the land, three hundred worthless acres of marsh grass and scrub trees and myrtle bushes old Grandda Jedidiah had proudly named Savage Island. But not a cent of rent money was to be had from it, since her grandfather had given free leases to any who'd settle on the island and make themselves useful, as shopkeeper or waterman or tradesman. No farmers had stayed, though, for the thin, salty soil gave back little in the way of crops. That was the way it had been, the way it still was.

She returned and set her empty tray down, then set to wiping the counter well away from Mrs. Ben. Spanish gold or English, who cared where it came from? She supposed only a simpleton would believe golden treasure would just wash ashore.

Still, she'd be out on the beach at dawn, too. Just in case.

3

A HELLHOLE
ON THE WATER

RAFE LAY TREMBLING IN THE DARK for a long time. Finally he must've slept, for he woke to movement, to fearful creakings and crunching and groanings, what he guessed at last must be the thump of waves breaking against the hull. The pounding sounded so loud, and it set everything around him to quivering. He thought at first they'd hit rocks and were sinking. Then from beneath the thuds came a dull metallic clanking; a giant might've been chained beyond the wall. After a while, he understood it must only be the anchor swinging against the side.

At first he had stared hard into the blackness before him, sure his eyes would eventually adjust and he'd be able to make out shapes, at least. He'd waved his own hands in front of his face, but still saw nothing. He felt starved; perhaps he could see if one of the casks held food. But the dark never lessened, and at last he became so sick from all the rocking and pitching he didn't care about eating or drinking. Only spent most of his time lying down, and the rest heaving and gagging, though nothing came up. He couldn't bear to think of food then, and the bilgewater stink in the hold made the thought of drinking even plain water seem sickening.

But after what felt like days, though he had no way to tell how much time had passed, he was so hungry and thirsty he knew he had to find water, and something to eat. He waited until the thin line of light that was an edge of the hatch cover disappeared. Then it must be night, and perhaps safe to come out if he was very careful. He felt for the bottom rung of the ladder, then lifted the hatch cover an inch or two. He peered in every direction but saw nothing—no passing feet, no sailors swinging dirty mops. He heard no voices. So at last he opened the hatch and slid out onto the deck.

He began to think someone or something was looking out for him after all. For there, next to a coil of lines, sat a tin plate with a slice of bread and two salted herrings. He was just reaching for it when his head exploded with pain. The world again grew dark, and fell away to nothing.

He woke groggy and fuddled, to a light like the midday sun shining in his eyes.

"Get up," rasped a deep voice.

The light lowered and he saw it was only a lantern. Rafe rolled onto his hands and knees, then pushed painfully to his feet. His head ached horribly. The rocking of the boat had grown worse, so bad he reeled and pitched as if a storm had blown up. Then fell, face-first, into a second sickening darkness.

* * *

He dreamed a huge, angry cat was sharpening its claws on his bare skin.

"Caught him with old Tom's plate," said a distant voice through his nightmare. "Stealing the cat's grub."

Rafe woke suddenly, fearfully, to the harsh yet delicious smell of boiled coffee. He turned his head, then nearly screamed. A large, bewhiskered man was staring at him with one bulging, bloodshot eye. The man sat across from him in a sort of cabin. Looking about, Rafe saw he was now in a tiny room with a frighteningly low ceiling, fitted with rough-hewn table and chair and bunk. The man did indeed have only one eye; that was no dream. The other was nothing but an empty pit of scar tissue.

" 'Bout time you woke," he grunted, as if Rafe were late for some appointment.

Rafe pulled himself up, swallowing back a new urge to vomit, and a terrible metallic taste that coated his mouth. His tongue was so dry it felt furry.

"Cat," he croaked, wanting to stop its claws tearing at his bare skin. When the big man frowned and looked puzzled, Rafe felt all about him and then realized the scratching must come from the short, thick blanket someone had thrown over him. Amazing any covering could be more uncomfortable than the wool scraps grudgingly doled out to the slaves back home at Penland, but this miserable stinking blanket was. Anyway, there was no cat in sight.

Above the bed a tiny round window was open. Through it

flowed a salty breeze heavy with the scent of wet rope and rotted weeds and more bilgewater. His stomach lurched again.

"Drink this," said the man, who'd gotten up without Rafe noticing. He thrust a tin mug under his nose. The steam rising off the black liquid inside smelled incredibly delicious. Rafe grabbed the mug and took a sip. Very hot, but he swallowed it, then took another sip before he looked around again. Through an open door streamed a wavering shaft of sunlight. He gulped more coffee. The light was suddenly blocked, and Rafe looked up.

A thin, stooped man ducked through the hatchway. His red hair was shot with gray, and a scowl etched deep in his weathered face. "Enjoying my bunk?" he said.

Though this one was not as bulky or as ugly as the scarred, one-eyed man, Rafe felt more afraid of him and his quiet, oily voice. So he only nodded, then tried to say, "Thank you." His garbled croak set both men to laughing.

"Aye, it's a real African," said the thin man. "It don't speak words."

Despite his fear, that made Rafe angry. He tried harder. "I said . . . thank . . . thank you."

The red-haired man scowled. "Ah, but you din't say *sir*. When you talk to us, always say that. Specially to me. For I'm captain of this ship."

"Thank you . . . sir," Rafe added, feeling heat in his face. He swallowed the last of the coffee. Now what would happen to him? These men might be headed for Boston, but how they felt about runaways was anyone's guess. He'd heard escaped slaves sometimes got turned in and sent back by people in free states as well.

"So what shall we do with it?" asked the thin man.

"We might could use a cabin boy," said the bigger man slowly.

"I wan't asking *you*," snapped the captain, stroking the ratty, goatish beard on his outthrust chin.

The coffee Rafe had drunk began to churn in his belly. Before he could lean over, he vomited it onto the bunk and over the blanket.

"Bloody dog!" shouted the captain. His hand shot out like a striking snake and caught Rafe on the side of the head. "Out of here. Go on!"

"Where?" Rafe gasped, choking. "Go where?"

"Forward, you idiot!"

Before he could climb to his feet, the man shoved and kicked him out the door, into the dazzling light of day.

The bad-tempered man was indeed captain of the *Tyger*. His name was Ross, and he didn't grow any more pleasant as the ship sailed through the Albemarle Sound and north up the Carolina coast. Rafe did get a bit more used to the rolling and rocking, and finally felt well enough to eat. He got hard biscuits and salt pork, and sat and ate them with white men. Also a brown one in blue britches with a gold ring in one ear, who spoke no English. And a yellow-skinned fellow who wore only a cloth wrapped around him instead of proper britches, and said nothing at all.

The rest of the crew looked ordinary. Though they came

from both North and South, none seemed to find Rafe's presence remarkable. No one asked how he'd suddenly appeared among them. Their manners were appalling, though.

No wonder they have to live out on a ship, he thought. *They'd never be allowed in a decent house.* Their wet, openmouthed chewing, their unwashed stink, the eternal scratching and spitting and nose picking made the field hands back at Penland seem like princes and ladies.

The captain cared where he'd come from, though. He told Rafe he knew he must be a runaway. And that he had the choice of being turned in for a reward at the next port or working for his passage until they reached Boston. "Then," the man said, "I mought let you go. Or keep you a bit longer. Good hands getting harder to find."

What choice did he have? By night he slept in the cabin hole on a pile of rags and frayed lines. It was a storage place full of old rope ends, heavy glass floats that rolled about, broken lamps, and torn sails. For some reason it was coated with fish scales, too, though this was not a fishing vessel. By day he worked with the crew, tarring ratlines. Or worse, picking junk—pulling apart hemp rope until his fingers bled, then mashing the rough fibers into felt to stuff the deck seams. And washing the deck, rubbing its planks to satin until his knuckles were raw, with an infernal thing called a holystone.

A week into the voyage a squall blew up and stayed with them. Then Rafe got so sick again the captain sent him down into the hole in disgust. There he rolled with each plunge and jerk and rearing of the ship, gagging and retching and clutching his belly, wishing he could die and make an end to it. The wind howled while the men outside skated and tripped and slid across the soaked deck; shouting, screaming into the wind and at one another like crazed seagulls. Waves washed over the sides, cold seawater trickled into his hellish little cave of misery.

That was where he was lying when the ship ran aground, broke apart, and dumped him overboard like a bit of rubbish. He clutched at a broken spar and rode up a wave before it slammed him down again hard. So hard he saw stars layered over the ones already shining down from between raggedy gray clouds. Then a second wave washed over his head and he saw nothing at all.

MOLLY FINDS
SOMETHING ASTONISHING

BEFORE THE SUN HAD FULLY RISEN, Molly pulled on her dress and shoes and rushed out of the tavern. She ran down the narrow road that was silvered with fish scales and lined with drying nets and trays of newly salted toadfish. In passing, she waved at old Mrs. Meeker, the only islander too weak and frail to go down to the water anymore. Then she crossed the beach and splashed into the cold water. It swirled around her knees as she tucked up her skirts and waded deeper. For a dark, mysterious cask was floating her way. She grabbed hold and leaned over, trying to read the letters stamped on the side as it bobbed next to her.

"*S . . . A . . . L . . .* salt," she whispered. "And then *B . . . E . . .* oh, it's salt *beef!*"

Thank heaven her mother had insisted she learn to read, and had made Molly labor over the old primer kept from her years as a teacher in Baltimore. Few other islanders could read, or do more than scratch out their own names. Nor did they seem to care for books or what was in them.

Molly read the two lovely words again, then danced a clumsy jig in the shallows. She hugged the soggy barrel, half as big as she was. No matter; she could float it out, then roll it home. Her stomach rumbled, her mouth watered at the thought of good salty chunks of beef tightly packed inside. She and Pa hadn't tasted real meat in ages, so it was treasure enough for her.

"I'll thank you to take your thievin' hands off'n that," someone shouted behind her.

Molly froze; it was the widow's voice. She looked wildly around. Too late to escape. Not ten feet away Hank Blodgett clung stubbornly to one side of a wooden crate. On the far side the widow, wide heavy skirts tied up to her knees, tugged at the same crate with one hand and slapped Blodgett's arms with the other. Neither was looking Molly's way.

"I saw it first, woman. It's mine clear and rightful." Blodgett staggered as Mrs. Ben pummeled his narrow chest.

"No, it's not." She gave a mighty jerk, her hair tumbled from its pins, and the crate broke apart. Silver knives and forks sparkled as they tumbled into the foaming water like diving fish.

"Cursed she-devil!" old Blodgett cried. Mrs. Ben shrieked as if someone had just died. They both plunged their arms underwater and groped about in the sand.

Molly hurried to splash away before they noticed. Otherwise they'd be hauling on her and her find next. She passed other neighbors scrambling to gather the flotsam: smashed crates, waterlogged bolts of calico, stoppered jugs and nail kegs and planks; even a small tin coffin. Stuff was still washing ashore from the wreckage of the doomed merchantman. Out on the Bandy, its mainmast, which had whipped back and forth crazily the night before, jutted motionless as a huge needle jammed into a pincushion.

She slogged through the shallows, shoving the cask before her. Seagulls wheeled and shrieked as if they, too, demanded a share. The cask seemed to grow heavier and heavier, but she dared not stop. There were too many folks out. Some had undoubtedly come across the water from the Eastern Shore, a narrow spit of land trapped between the broad Chesapeake Bay and the sea islands like this one. The fires on the beach the night before would've drawn them like moths to a lantern. Molly knew little of the Shore, or the rest of Virginia, but she was sure those folks were bound to be as thieving and greedy as the gulls.

She stumbled over a sunken log, slimy and slick, but caught herself just before she went under. "Oh, drat! And bother everything," she panted. She struggled to her feet again, tugging at her skirt, which had hooked on a driftwood branch. She was soaked and shivering. But the Heap, her destination, was just around the marsh-grassy bend. And as she waded against the current and pushed at the stubborn cask, she grew warmer, until finally she was sweating as if summer had suddenly come back again.

The Heap seemed impossibly distant. She grunted and shoved at the barrel, looking around, hoping no one was watching. A few yards off, three laughing men were trying to land a huge floating crate. Molly hurried by, glad they were intent on their own treasure and not hers.

A shipwreck was always a strange mix of funeral and festival, perhaps a bit like public hanging days on the mainland. Though the sailors had probably done no crime to be so cruelly punished. Just bad luck and bad weather. The few survivors had been fed and warmed up, and would soon be taken across in a fishing boat to the Virginia mainland by one of the watermen.

In the early dawn hours, only two bodies had washed ashore.

The women of the village had solemnly borne them off, spreading an old sail over the still forms they'd laid well away from the spoils. The poor souls would be properly buried later, Molly knew, in the same tiny graveyard where her mother lay.

She'd caught a glimpse of the dead men before the sail settled over their faces like a dingy shroud. One was old and thin and sour-looking, with scraggly, graying red hair and beard. The other was young, and had damp blond curls plastered to his forehead. He might've been only sleeping on the damp sand, his face smooth and unlined as if he were enjoying pleasant dreams. Molly wondered if he'd had a sweetheart back home, or a baby. A daughter who would wonder, and miss him.

But even that sad sight hadn't made her feel bad long, because she was terribly hungry. Thinking of how good the salt beef would taste brought water to her mouth. She'd keep to the far side of the island and wait a bit. When everyone had had a chance at the flotsam, then she'd risk rolling her treasure up to the Hog's Head.

Two years earlier she'd found a lovely wooden tray all painted with flowers, and had run with it up the winding shell path toward the inn. But someone had pushed her from behind and snatched it away. By the time she'd gotten to her feet again, both tray and thief had vanished. All she could do was limp home with a skinned knee, empty-handed.

If her father were along this morning, he could carry the keg on one shoulder; he was strong enough. But he'd be manning the counter at the Hog's Head, for Mrs. Ben never left it unattended. She'd remarked more than once that if she did, something was bound to go missing. The widow knew how to get things, and how to hang on to them. No woman had ever been able to bring old bachelor Pruitt to the marriage altar until she'd come along. But like Molly's mother, Ben Pruitt hadn't lived through the sickness four years earlier. Now the widow had to count her pennies all alone.

Her father would never make money, Molly thought. Once he might have dreamed of great wealth, like the treasures in the stories he'd told when she was small. But he'd also loved to play at cards. His fondness for wagers and gambling had cost them the Hog's Head, the family business. Now she sometimes wondered if they wouldn't be better off leaving the island, trying their luck on the mainland, over in Virginia or Maryland. But the few times she'd suggested this, he had gotten angry and stomped out of the room. Ned Savage was stuck smart as a barnacle to this island, glued like an oyster to its rocky bed. If better fortune was needed, it seemed it would be up to her to make it. For he seemed content to be held in thrall to the widow, who'd inherited the tavern and all the other holdings that'd belonged to the late Mr. Pruitt.

Molly sighed and shoved at the keg even harder. She loved her father, but Ned Savage would be stepping on a long white beard before he earned enough as waiter, handyman, and general dogsbody to pay off the fearsome debts he'd run up at cards, losing to others as well.

A dead fish floated by, its gimlet eye giving her a pop-eyed look of surprise. Molly wrinkled her nose and sidestepped. "Mercy, what a stink." She cupped one hand over her face, but kept the other firmly on the cask. Actually that fish had looked fairly fresh. The stench was no doubt blowing from the Heap.

Slipping, lunging, and panting, she rolled and shoved the cask through the last few feet of water until she could lodge it behind a stump in a bunch of cordgrass. Then she picked her way around the marshy edges of a driftwood pile festooned with fish heads, shattered clam and oyster shells, rotting cabbage and blackened potatoes, all piled higgledy-piggledy in the saw-edged weeds.

A scrawny hog, its ribs sharp enough to scrub laundry on, narrowed its beady black eyes, as if she'd come to fight it for the offal. It glared, then snorted up at the airborne gang of screeching gulls that hovered above. After another warning grunt, the hog returned to his stinking breakfast.

The Heap was a garbage mound where islanders dumped smashed crockery, broken tools, spoiled food, or any dead animals that floated up. The idea being, her father had long ago explained, that the ocean's tide was supposed to carry all the nasty stuff away. Somehow it never quite did. So the wind blew the reek of rotten meat and decaying turnip tops and staring fish heads right into her face.

"Phew," she gasped. Then she stopped and waited, listening. She'd heard a sound. Not the pig this time, but something else. It certainly didn't sound human.

"Likely just flies," she said loudly, and the sound of her own voice made her feel braver. Except in coldest winter, hundreds of insects buzzed around the Heap. Yes, flies, that was all.

But there it was again. Not an insect buzzing, but lower, more of a whimper. A stray dog, ashore from the shipwreck? Not likely, unless it was a champion swimmer. The eerie sound made her neck and arms prickle. She backed up a step, but then a new thought occurred to her. Ephraim, the baby goat, was always squeezing out the bottom of his pen through a gap in the slats.

And here were jagged smashed bottles, broken dishes, snarled rope, and other traps to maim or choke a foolish kid. If he were hurt, Molly's heart would break. And Mrs. Ben would make sure the rest of her hurt as well.

"Ephraim?" She whistled the way she did when she led him and the nanny goat back to their shed behind the tavern. She mustn't make much noise; some folks couldn't stop sticking their noses in at the worst possible times. Old Joshua Turner or some other layabout would be happy to carry a tale to Mrs. Ben, hoping to be rewarded with a free pint.

"Ephraim," she whispered. "Come out."

Molly pushed a little farther into the fouled mess. "Faugh," she exclaimed, and pulled the hem of her skirt up over her nose, but the smell was still dreadful. Her stomach no longer growled for beef. Instead, it churned like the stormy Bandy.

Dead branches, sweetbriar thorns, shards of oyster shell, and prickly severed crab legs plucked and pinched at her like sharp fingernails.

The next moan was louder, and her arms rose all in goose bumps. Could the Heap be haunted? But she'd been here in all types of weather; it was nothing but old garbage. What sorry sort of ghost would haunt a trash pile?

She called louder, "Ephraim!" Then she glanced over her shoulder, toward the beach. In the distance dark figures scurried over the creamy sand like beetles on a dead seagull. No one turned her way, or shouted.

She was listening instead of looking, and almost stepped on him. At the last moment she saw the foot, like a brown club of driftwood against dead grass and salt foam. Her gaze traveled up, past an ankle, a thin dark calf, a scabbed knobby knee, and a ragged hem of wet, tan cloth. All dark, sodden with seawater. The body had been flung on the sand like a bolt of wave-tossed cloth.

A boy, she thought, staring with wonder at brown arms and legs that poked like twigs from the rags of a long white shirt and rough pantaloons.

He rolled his head weakly in her direction, and Molly gasped. A long pale smear of mud on his cheek stood out like paint against smooth, dark skin. *He's like an Indian,* she thought. Or could he be an African? Well, he was almost that dark. . . .

His eyes fluttered open. The whites were bloodshot, the lids swollen, lashes caked with salt. And he was looking right at her.

"Oh!" She stepped back. A hard finger of something she hoped was only driftwood poked her back.

The boy's cracked lips, rimmed white with dried salt, moved. No sound came out. His large eyes were dark, too, almost black. Nothing like the blue or hazel ones she saw every day in the Hog's Head or passed on the shell-paved lane that was the island's main thoroughfare. His lashes were long and thick, and he stared from beneath them with mingled hope and dread. This boy was clearly helpless, and that touched and reassured Molly.

"Lie still. Don't move. You'll snare yourself worse." She stooped to tug a fetter of seaweed and frayed rope off his wrist. She moved slowly, carefully, to untangle snarls of sea grass and ship's line. She avoided looking at him directly, wanting time to think.

His head sank back and he closed his eyes again. Oh, he was a sorry sight, halfway drowned. But he was not dead, like the other two from the wrecked ship.

She felt a nudge of pleasure as she picked bits of wrack and seaweed from his face and thick, curly hair. Of all the scavengers out combing the beach this morning, only Molly Savage had discovered a survivor.

5

A PROBLEM NAMED RAFE

YOU'D BEST LIE STILL," said Molly to the boy. Though it seemed silly to say when he was already stretched out there on the sand. He was so thin and starved-looking, covered with bruises and scratches, as if he'd been dragged through bramble bushes before that ship had coughed him up ashore, after the wreck. She brushed gritty sand and dried salt from one arm. Beneath it his skin felt soft, as soft as her own. That surprised her. She'd always thought dark skin might feel different: rough, maybe, like bark.

At her touch, his eyes snapped open again. He rolled to one side and tried to rise on all fours, but fell back, trembling like a fresh-born calf.

"Who are you?" she asked. "Where'd you come from?"

The boy shook his head. He moaned and retched up a little seawater.

"If you don't lie still," she ordered again, trying to sound stern as Mrs. Ben, "I'll . . . I'll have to go get someone."

He collapsed onto his back again, but shot her a rebellious look that said he was more exhausted than obedient. His face had taken on a grayish tint. Molly's mother, on her sickbed, had looked that way. For death, she knew, always crept in. Stealing away first color, then life.

Alarmed, Molly tapped his cheek with her fingertips. "You aren't dying?" she whispered.

The boy shook his head feebly. "No. Just . . . feel like it. Belly full . . . saltwater. And that bad *stink.*"

"It's just the Heap," she said, surprised. She'd been mesmerized by her discovery and forgotten all about the hundred years' reek surrounding them.

"Oh." He clamped his lips tight on a gag.

"What's your name?" she asked.

"My . . . I'm Rafe."

"Just Rafe. But no other, no proper name?"

He frowned and nodded, as if it took great concentration to answer the simplest question. Sweat beaded on his face, and she wiped it away with the hem of her skirt.

"Rafe," she murmured. It was a common enough name. "Well, of course, you aren't from around here." Then a worrisome thought struck her. "Unless you be a slave?"

One night, when she was only ten, two runaways had landed a leaky scow on Savage Island. One was shot and killed while raiding Hank Blodgett's smokehouse, and slave chasers arrived soon after. Molly had been outside the tavern the following morning, sweeping, when they'd dragged the other away.

She had known well enough by then that slaves were deemed property, like goats and cows. She'd never had reason to think much on it before. No islander had ever owned slaves.

The captured man she had seen was weighted down with iron chains. His face and back and legs were bleeding. That was bad enough. But as he'd passed by, he'd turned such a despairing gaze on Molly that she'd dropped her broom, burst into tears, and run into the tavern.

Later, from a front window, she saw the bounty hunters come back for the body of the dead slave. They had carried it slung between them like a sack of meal. One was whistling a cheerful tune.

Molly had asked her father why the dead slave hadn't been buried on the island.

"Got to turn him in, like a fox pelt, do they want to get paid. 'Sides, we keep no colored graveyard here."

Still she'd stood there, waiting for him not only to explain it all, but somehow to make these things seem right. Until Ned Savage had finally shaken his head. Then pressed his lips into a knife-thin line and set to splitting shingles again.

So now, when the boy didn't answer immediately, Molly asked again. "Be you slave or free, boy?"

Something flickered in his gaze at those words. Maybe only the sudden reflection of the sun, just out again from behind a fading storm cloud, had seemed to cast a furtive gleam there.

"Me, a slave?" The boy snorted, then coughed again. He gasped and took a slow, deep breath. "I'm no man's slave. Just a . . . a sailor. Cabin boy from the *Tyger*. Brigantine bound for Boston."

Cabin boy on a ship named *Tyger*. What could be more exciting, more different from her life? This boy could visit far-off places, like the ones written of in books, or whispered of in tales told around a fireplace to a ring of rapt faces. . . . She was suddenly envious of this wet, ragged, miserable boy. And a little resentful, though her troubles were certainly none of his fault.

Besides, she wasn't bound to believe him. "You look young to be a sailor."

"It was . . . my first voyage."

"Hmm," she said thoughtfully, "hereabouts a person of your color would be taken for a slave."

A dry click in his throat as he swallowed, then licked cracked lips. "Where . . . is here?"

"You've washed ashore on Savage Island."

He seemed to mull that over. "Never heard of such place."

"It's just off the Eastern Shore."

"You mean, off the coast of Virginia," he whispered, suddenly looking downcast. "No farther north?"

She shook her head.

"Ah," he said, then was silent.

"If you still live, does the place matter?" she asked. "Some of your shipmates were less fortunate." Besides, the boy still hadn't completely answered her question.

"I . . . that is, *we* were bound for Boston," he said a bit gruffly. "Thought we'd got farther along, is all."

She shrugged. "Well, you didn't. But come now, I should be getting you up to the tavern so's you can get warm. We'll pry a bite to eat from Mrs. Ben."

"No!" He sat up suddenly, gripping her arm. "I mean . . . not if I'd be taken for a slave. As *you* say."

"You surely talk nothing like one," she admitted. Not that she'd know much of that, but the boy did speak very well, as if he'd been schooled. And slaves weren't allowed to learn reading and writing, much less take lessons. "Besides," she said, "with your sailing papers—"

"Oh, but I lost those in the wreck," he said quickly. Not meeting her gaze, but still gripping her arm.

"Let go. You're hurting me." Something was wrong; he'd suddenly gone wary as a snared muskrat. When he looked surprised and released her arm, she went on. "If you've no papers, that could cause trouble. For then what's to prove you're free after all? They do hunt runaways hereabouts."

"I'm no runaway. I told you I'm a free man."

"So you said." But certainly no man, not yet. Molly wasn't sure how she felt about the rest. A slave belonged to his master, and owed him obedience; that was the way of it. The law said so. Even the preacher who sailed out to the island once a month had deemed this arrangement the will of the Lord, in one tediously long sermon. But this boy Rafe seemed young to have run away and found his own way out to sea. So perhaps he was telling the truth.

In any case, it felt strange to talk to a person so close to her in years. Even if he was male, and brown-skinned at that. The only other children on the island were the grimy little Keller boys, seven-year-old twin demons of mischief; pie stealers, floor muckers, notorious chicken-house thieves. Other than that, at the moment there was only Hank Blodgett's new granddaughter, barely two months old.

"How old are you?" she asked suddenly.

He hesitated a few moments, then blurted out, "Fourteen— no, fifteen years, come next month."

The same nearly as her own age. Odd he'd had to think about it, though. To figure up before he said. Perhaps that meant he might indeed be a runaway. Oh, but she hoped not. For then wouldn't she have to hand him over to the same fate that frightened, dark-skinned man in chains had received? When her mother had still been alive, she'd said it seemed wrong to treat human beings so. "Worse than beasts," she'd insisted. "It's not a Christian thing to subdue any creature so cruelly."

Her father had shifted uneasily and insisted that such was not for them to judge.

"But you know what they'll do to the poor soul, Ned," her ma had persisted.

"Aye. Whip the running right out of him. Then, if that don't do the trick, break his foot," said her father. "Or mayhap chop it off so then he can run no more. And what can we do about any of that, eh?" But when he shook his head, he'd seemed more sad than angry.

Her mother had gone back to the kitchen then, and kept silent. But Molly hadn't been able to stop picturing the shackled man who'd looked at her so despairingly. Her stubborn mind kept imagining him chained in a dark shed, one foot chopped off like kindling, the bleeding stump bound up with dirty linen. It seemed as bad an end as in the most terrible fairy tale she'd ever heard.

Yet it was the law, her father said.

After that night, she'd decided secretly that the law must be both a fearful and a cruel thing. But then, laws were made in far-off Richmond, by rich men who sat in judgment, wearing powdered wigs and velvet coats. Not in scruffy backwaters like Savage Island.

She glanced down at Rafe again. She, too, often dreamed of running away from her station in life, from the boredom of the island, the harsh tongue of Mrs. Ben. Who, come to that, nearly owned them, both Molly and her father.

That disturbing thought made up her mind. Even if this boy was a slave, she wouldn't send him to the ax. If his life had been terrible enough to run away from, what right had she to send him back to it?

"This is what we shall do," she said, standing abruptly, dusting damp sand off her skirt. "There's an empty root cellar over the way. No one uses it now. A storm after the war washed away part of the beach. They had to move the main house, the old Hog's Head Tavern, up inland with the rest of the cottages. Then the cellar was too far, and anyhow too damp for good storage. But you could stay inside there until—"

She broke off, at a loss. *Until what?* What could she do with this strange boy, this dark-skinned Rafe?

"Until we decide exactly what to do," he put in, sounding wary, but hopeful.

We, he'd said. "Well, yes. I'll think of something bymeby," she replied, trying to hold the upper hand. It was her island, after all. Not his.

He nodded silently, then closed his eyes again.

Now that she'd committed to a plan, she wondered what she was doing, keeping secrets for a stranger. She'd have to find or steal food, or tell a lie to the widow to wheedle something from the pantry. She might have to lie to her father as well. Though perhaps if no one asked straight out about Rafe, it wouldn't be a sin if she didn't confess his existence straightaway. That seemed fair, if keeping silent meant he was saved from punishment and torture. Still, she knew her father would not approve.

But her mother might, had she still been alive. Molly felt tears burn behind her eyes and shook her head. That hadn't happened in a long time. She'd thought she was used to getting along without a mother's guidance. She took a deep breath. "Come. Follow me, Rafe."

He rolled to his feet unsteadily, staggering as if his legs thought they were still crossing a rolling deck. His feet looked rough, hardened, even tougher than her own. Molly never wore shoes, except during the worst cold of winter. Summers, her tough soles barely felt the thin cutting edges of crushed shells on the common path, or the sharpness of fallen burrs or whip-sharp cordgrass. But this boy's feet looked even more hardened; padded with calluses, cracked deeply in places.

When she looked up again, he was watching her, too.

Could life on board a ship toughen skin to such abused

leather as that? She couldn't imagine how. But what was more important at the moment was getting him out of sight. So she turned away and led him to a crudely timbered opening cut into a packed mound of clay and sand. The root cellar dug long ago by old Grandda Jedidiah.

"In here." She picked up a dry myrtle branch, thrust it ahead of them into the dark opening, and swept it about briskly. Dozens of tiny brown fiddlers scuttled out sideways, waving their claws angrily at the unwanted housecleaning.

Rafe looked after the little crabs doubtfully, obviously shivering in the cold breeze off the water.

"Here you'll be out of sight," she explained. "And it's warmer out of the wind. I'll bring down some things later. Food, and a blanket." Though how she'd get these out under Mrs. Ben's nose—well, she'd manage.

"I'm so thirsty," he said suddenly.

Of course; she ought to have thought of that. "Well, see the pond over there, under the trees?" She pointed. "The water tastes a bit nasty. Still it's sweet, not salt."

She followed. Watched as the boy knelt and drank. He made a face at the first swallow, but soon was crouched, greedily scooping up handful after handful.

"Don't gulp so," she chided. "You'll sick it all up again." This was indeed a strange situation, she thought. She felt protective, as if he were a child and she the parent. So was that what saving a life did, make you responsible for the person ever after?

She worried that it might.

At last his thirst seemed quenched, and she said, "Come on over here, now. Help me break into this cask. I'll leave you some good salt beef. You must be hungry as well."

They slogged back through the shallows to where she'd lodged the cask in the weeds.

"You're very good to help me," he said suddenly, stiffly, reaching out as if to touch her hand. Without thinking, she pulled back a little. Her face grew hot when she saw that he, too, had hesitated. As if he didn't want to touch her, either. She folded her arms and shook her head. "Only what any good Christian would do." The self-righteous sound of her own voice made her feel prim and silly.

"Not all of them," the boy said with sudden bitterness. She glanced over curiously, but he'd already turned away, was bending over the cask. "How do you open this thing?"

"Here." She crouched to direct him. "Let's see . . . take up that piece of broken shovel there. . . ."

As they worked, already she felt a dull nudge of regret: of having leaped too fast because she was impatient and didn't want to look first. Just as her father often said. Maybe the boy was right. What sort of trouble had she gotten herself into now?

6

RAFE LOOKS BACK, AT LAST

AFTER THE GIRL LEFT, Rafe lay on the sandy floor of the root cellar for a long while. But it was hard to rest when you were worried, when you expected any moment to be betrayed or discovered.

He'd have to trust her for the time being, but he wouldn't tell his true story. For one thing, she seemed to talk a great deal. What might she do, who might she tell if she knew he was no cabin boy at all, but an escaped slave from the great house of Penland Plantation, and its thousand acres of tobacco and cotton?

No, he'd keep that to himself. Back at Penland, older slaves had sometimes claimed there were white folks who actually believed slavery was wrong. That these people would even help runaways escape north. He didn't know if that was true. Maybe this girl was already at home and telling her people about him. Why, already she knew his name, and he hadn't even thought to ask hers.

Still, what choice did he have except to trust her? He didn't know this place, this deserted coast, or how to get away from it. An island, she'd said! And he had no boat. Even a strong boy couldn't very well swim to Boston. He was not strong, at least not at the moment. And he'd never thought himself much of a swimmer anyhow, except to paddle a bit around the pond behind the slave quarters at Penland. Perhaps that was what had saved his life. How he'd survived the wreck at all was a mystery.

He thought even living in a stinking hole like this one would be better than being sent back to the plantation. But how long could a lone black boy stay on a tiny island before someone saw him? Rafe curled up into a ball, wishing he could get warm. He'd gotten used to many hardships on the run, but he still hated the cold. At Penland, in the winter, they laid blazing fires in the big brick-and-marble fireplaces. The one in the parlor was so tall he could stand upright in it and not even graze his head. There were flannel sheets and soft wool blankets and thick socks knitted by Delia, the seamstress. . . .

Penland had been his home since birth. He'd grown up side by side with William Carter Pennington, the master and mistress's son. Pale, sickly Will was their only living child. Rafe's mother had wet-nursed him when Mistress Pennington had been ill, after the birth.

William and Rafe played in the big, sunny nursery and slept in the same room, Rafe on a pallet at the foot of William's four-poster bed. They were always together, almost like brothers. Almost . . . except when Master Will turned six and started lessons, Rafe was told to wait outside, away from the door, and was not allowed to watch or listen. But William had thrown a fit until Rafe was allowed to stay. So he kept to the back corner of the nursery and pretended not to be interested.

But he did listen. And he learned letters and numbers and the histories of far-off places. And the most wonderful stories.

His mother warned him to keep this new learning to himself. "That stuff not for you," she said. "You fill your head with such, and it become a burden. A danger."

He didn't see how that could be so. Big Master Thomas seemed fond of him; he'd been the one who'd insisted Rafe be raised in the house, not out in the slave quarters where all the other dark-skinned children shouted and played and quarreled, barefoot and half-naked. Why, Master Thomas gave Rafe pats on the shoulder and as many barley-sugar treats as he did his own son, Will.

But by the time Rafe was three, he understood Mistress hated the sight of him. Anytime he came into a room, she ordered him out. If he walked by, she swept her skirts aside, as if he were a large muddy dog. But he was nearly eight before he finally found out why.

One afternoon, after lunch, Rafe had run down the stairs to retrieve a ball Will had pitched over the banister. He'd snatched up the red-and-white-striped toy and was on his way back up to the nursery when he heard muffled shrieks and cries coming from the back of the house. He froze for a moment, terrified.

But when nothing bad happened to him, at last his curiosity overcame his fear, and he followed the terrible sounds to the kitchen. Then to the pantry, where he pushed the door open to see what was wrong. He stopped on the threshold, for there stood his mother, stretched on tiptoe, her wrists tied to the same beam that held the smoked ham and bacon. And there was Mistress, flogging his mother with a cowhide whip and cursing like the men out in the fields. Worse, for she was calling his mother terrible, ugly names.

Rafe had seen house slaves slapped before—for breaking a dish or looking a white guest in the face. That was not unusual. But his mother had been lashed so hard blood ran down her back. Penny-size spots of it had splashed the wood floor right at his feet. He looked at these, and a sudden, unexpected heat seeped through his clothes. He realized he'd wet himself, that he stood in a shameful puddle, wanting to run, yet unable to move. Not toward them, or away. He wanted to grab the flicking black cowhide whip, but he was too afraid of Mistress. Too weak, too cowardly to protect his mother.

Mistress Pennington kept shouting. She either didn't see him, or didn't care if he heard. ". . . and you live in my house, under my roof, you black harlot! My innocent son must eat and sleep with this misbegotten thing you call a child! You mock me, the boy's very face mocks me. And my own husband allows it!"

Rafe dropped Will's ball, and it rolled through the open pantry door, right up to the mistress's ankles. Both women looked down at him. The mistress with hate in her eyes, his mother with either sadness or resignation in hers. But judging by their otherwise blank faces, neither one seemed to really know who he was. Only then could Rafe turn and run out of the kitchen, down the hall, and out the front, while Will called impatiently over the railing at him to *fetch the ball, fetch it right away!*

That night he sat on the edge of his mother's pallet in the attic as Delia dipped a rag into a bowl of warm water, bathing the wounds on his mother's back and shoulders. Rafe watched the water turn pink as she dipped and wrung, dipped and wrung, and he asked why the mistress hated them so much.

"Mistress believe Old Marster Thomas care more for me, more for you, than for his own wife and son," said his mother dully. Delia, who was humming, only nodded.

"Well, does he?"

His mother sighed, and didn't answer for a moment. At last she said, "You live in his house almost good as a white boy. Like a brother to Young Marster."

Rafe thought of Will's thin white arms, his blond curls. "We don't look the same. I don't see how we could be brothers."

She laughed then, but it wasn't a happy sound. "Yes, baby. You is." She sighed again and reached out to pull him to her. "You is, for all the good it do you."

"Lord, yes," muttered Delia. She picked up the pan of rusty-looking water and rose to go.

Rafe had turned away then, too, and gone up to the room he shared with Will. He didn't want to hear any more. All that time he hadn't understood, but after that he did. Of course he was different from William, anyone could see that. Much darker in skin and hair, because they had different mothers. Yet Rafe was just as much a part of the master as William, for they shared the same father. Except no one was ever allowed to say so.

After a few days, his shock at what the mistress had done faded. He'd expected more terrible things to follow: to be dragged to the pantry and beaten at the very least. Or perhaps the master would scold Mistress. But none of those things happened. He went on living in the big house, and played and ate and slept with Will. And when his mother and Mistress passed in the halls, they behaved as if the awful scene in the pantry had never happened.

Gradually, an idea came to him: Since he was the master's son, no real harm would ever come. And then, even more gradually, this one: Perhaps some day he, too, might be a master. Then he'd free his mother and all the other house slaves. And, of course, the poor raggedy ones working barefoot under a hot sun or in coldest weather morning till night, picking and hoeing and raking and cleaning. He *was* different, though, and always would be. He already wore nice clothes, and lived in the big house.

The doctor was occasionally called to Penland, and these times the somber bearded man spoke of young William's health as if it were a problem beyond solving. For the boy was sickly, and often had to lie down and rest, while Rafe could've run and played for hours yet.

"Poor chile. Might not live to grow up," said Rafe's mother once. She had nursed little Will until he was three, and was still fond of him. Almost, Rafe thought resentfully, as if she were *his* mother, too.

But Rafe was strong. He never got sick, and he knew all the lessons as well as Will. No—better. Of course the tutor never gave him pen and paper. But later, when they went out in the yard to play, Rafe made Will watch and correct him as he drew out the same sums and alphabet letters with a stick, in the dirt. Rafe was the one who could recall the stories of Greeks and dragons and strange gods and heroes best. Will had headaches. He hated sitting still at his desk. But he liked to hear Rafe retell the stories from the schoolmaster's books.

"You tell 'em. You do it better," he always said with satisfaction. And then Rafe could bargain for more writing-out of longer words, or of simple sums in the dirt, all the while holding a story over the other boy's head like a dangling treat. He knew better than to tell stories or work any sums when grownups were about, though. And he told Will that he must never mention any of this to the mistress.

"Then she would send me away, and make you spend all your time on numbers," whispered Rafe.

Will had blanched at the thought and quickly agreed.

None of the slaves who labored in the fields like farm animals could read or write. Their skin was burned black under the Carolina sun. They went barefoot and half-naked, even in winter. Shuffled and bowed, and looked at the ground when any white person was near.

Rafe had nothing in common with them. He wore leather shoes like the master's own son. That fact alone somehow seemed proof of his special place. So he decided to wait, to learn all he could. Then if sickly young William was called by his Maker, well, that would be a sad thing. But Rafe would still be there, son of the same father.

Thinking back on all this as he lay on damp sand in a hole-in-the-ground cellar on an island he'd never heard of, Rafe smiled bitterly in the dark. What a good joke it had all been. On him.

MRS. BEN'S
STRANGE PROPOSAL

TWO DAYS AFTER THE BOY WASHED UP on the beach, Molly was swinging a wheat-straw broom back and forth across each step of the short staircase leading to the Hog's Head's two modest back rooms. Sometimes a waterman or duck hunter stayed over in the smaller one. The larger had been her parents' bedroom. But now it was Mrs. Ben who slept in the carved rope bed generations of Savages, Molly included, had been birthed in.

Before picking up the broom, she'd stripped the high, carved wooden bed and changed the widow's linens. As she worked she'd imagined a number of childish but satisfying acts of revenge, such as leaving a surprise under the bedclothes. Not dirt or sand; she'd be blamed for that. A large hairy spider, perhaps. But she hadn't. Instead she'd only tugged the smooth white sheets tight as a miser's pockets at the corners, shoving the ends under the crackling corn-husk mattress. She stood back and surveyed the expanse of ironed, sun-bleached linens, the creaseless stretch of quilt. Now let Mrs. Ben call her Mistress Lazy Bones!

The scent of browning popovers drifted up the stairs, teasing a loud growl from her stomach.

"Oh, hush," she whispered. It would be the two-day-old bread she and her father would get later. Not the warm fresh stuff . . . which she'd better not forget to take out of the oven in a few minutes or the popovers would burn. She'd have to sneak some of her own stale loaf to Rafe later. He couldn't eat nothing but salt beef for long.

What was she going to do about the boy? Get him off the island, of course, but how? She was astonished someone hadn't stumbled onto him already. Impossible to keep secrets long on Savage Island, where everyone lived in one another's pockets. No, she supposed she'd have to tell her father after all. To get his help, and soon.

The night past she'd managed to smuggle out a piece of chicken only partly gnawed by a tavern guest, along with some crumbled corn bread. Inside the root cellar, by the guttering light of a pitiful candle stub, she'd checked the clean rag bandage she'd wrapped around Rafe's middle. His ribs still pained him; he must have been bashed smartly against something on his rough journey between ship and island. He still refused to tell much of himself, and when she'd tried to pry more out of him, he'd interrupted to recite a tale about a pirate captain named Sinbad and an Egyptian princess. At least it was one she'd never heard. But Molly was sure he was hiding something.

When the boy finally did get away, he'd sail off in another ship, and no doubt have more adventures. While she'd still be here at the inn, sweeping and serving, dodging Mrs. Ben's slaps and curses. She wished she'd been born male. As far as she could see, women and girls got a bad bargain, nothing but cooking and cleaning and caring for animals and babies. While men and boys slipped away to have fun, to go places, to do battle for glory and prizes. To make their own fates.

She took a deep breath. The air was fragrant with yeasty baked bread. She sighed, and swallowed back the hopeful watering of her mouth. Then picked up the broom and began whisking cobwebs from the dusty corners of the steps, violently, as if she, too, were doing battle, but with an unseen enemy. No matter how often she swept, the same spiders—or perhaps their next of kin—were back the following day, spinning new webs so quickly Molly was sure it was just for spite. She wondered if the tiny beasties weren't in league with Mrs. Ben to keep her eternally housebound.

When she heard the murmur of a woman's voice coming near, she swung the broom all the harder, stopping only to pull sticky strands of web from the straws. But the voice came no closer, so the widow had halted just around the corner, behind the stairwell where Molly stood.

She kept sweeping, more quietly, intrigued when she heard her own name. She leaned out of the stairway a little, to hear more.

"Did you give thought to my proposition?"

Mrs. Ben sounded different. Her words pitched lower, the tone more confiding than threatening. Almost friendly. Wheedling, as if she wanted the person she was talking to to think well of her, or perhaps even wanted to please them. Molly's mind reeled at that idea, though she supposed it could happen.

To anyone but her, that is.

The answer was rumbled in a deeper voice: her father's. But he was practically whispering; she couldn't make out all the words.

When Mrs. Ben broke in again, louder, Molly had no difficulty hearing. "It's time you thought of remarrying. It's been years since your wife passed away. And your dear child has need of a mother."

The broom almost slipped from Molly's hands. She forced it to make a few halfhearted swipes back and forth across the lower step. Of all the men in the village, why had the widow chosen to matchmake for Ned Savage? Oh yes—and his *dear child*.

Until then, Molly had assumed the widow hated children, all children. But perhaps it was only Molly she disliked. She dug the broom into a particularly dirty corner.

Her father said something else, quietly, as if he wanted no one to hear. Molly could make nothing out of it.

"But, Mr. Savage, you'd be my wedded husband then. And as such, free of debt."

Molly stopped sweeping altogether then and sat down hard on the second step. The good wife the woman was proposing to marry to her father was the widow herself! Suddenly Molly couldn't catch her breath.

But that couldn't be right. Her father would never marry Mrs. Ben. Once, while serving ales in the tavern, she'd heard

Doc Drummond whisper to old Mr. Blodgett to be careful. "She might spike a man's breakfast ale with arsenic, that 'un," he'd said, inclining his head at the widow, who was counting pennies behind the counter.

Of course Doc and Hank grinned, and there'd been much winking and guffawing. Molly had supposed it was a joke. In many of those told by her elders, she still saw neither sense nor humor. Besides, she knew for fact that Mr. Pruitt had been a sickly soul who'd taken ill like so many others that year of the lung sickness, and died of a coughing fit.

But how could her father even listen to a woman who'd treated them so badly? Who'd inherited away everything they'd ever owned? For, years back, when old Ben Pruitt was ailing, it seemed he was on the verge of forgiving Ned Savage the old card debt. But Mrs. Ben had objected, had harried and nagged her sick husband day and night, even in public, until he'd changed his mind. Now she was queening it in their house, in their kitchen, even in their bed, while feeding them on leftovers. And even so, begrudging every mouthful.

Molly hauled herself up, hands trembling, gripping the stair rail hard. What would her father answer? He never spoke ill of Mrs. Ben to her, though she noticed he always set his lips in a thin line at the end of the month when the widow dropped a few coppers in his hand. His pay, less expenses. Still, Molly could read it in the slope of his shoulders as he split shingles or stacked kindling. Ned Savage hated Mrs. Ben as much as she did.

Surely he wouldn't marry the widow, so black and spider-like. True, she supposed his money worries would be over. For who'd ever heard of a wife charging her husband for food and shelter and clothing?

Perhaps he'd even have a little left over to gamble at the table with Doc Drummond and Mr. Blodgett and the others who came to the tavern to laugh and swear and slap their cards down with black disgust, or chortling glee. He could play again, instead of watching from the corner. A small comfort, knowing the widow would never allow him to stake the Hog's Head on the turn of a card again.

Pa has always dearly loved a glass of beer and a game of chance, she thought. *But which does he love better?* She gripped the railing tighter. *Drinking and gaming—or me?*

He was speaking again. *Say it loud, Pa,* Molly prayed. *Tell her the only woman you ever loved is lying in the little cemetery on the sea side of the island. Tell her your only daughter, Molly, is all the company you need.*

She leaned out farther, trying to hear. So intent was she on his murmured reply, deciding her whole future, that another ominous sound—the crack of wood—came to her faintly, as if a tree had fallen outside in the woods. But suddenly, while her hands still gripped the railing, her toes were no longer firmly planted on the worn step. By then it was too late to do anything but hang on to the useless rail as she fell.

The pain of landing on the brick floor was nothing compared to the fear that shot through her when she looked up and saw the widow and her father gaping down at her, their mouths identical *O*s.

"Molly!" her father finally exclaimed. "What on God's earth?" He glanced from her to Mrs. Ben, then reached out to touch her face, her shoulder, to check for injury.

The widow's scowl smoothed away so quickly Molly wondered if she'd imagined it. Instead of screaming or dealing out the slap Molly expected, Mrs. Ben only sighed and shook her head. "You see, Ned? The girl's clumsy as a drunkard. No wonder she's a patchwork quilt of black-and-blue. Running wild around the island without a mother's guiding hand. She needs that hand, and a firm one it must be, too."

Her father knelt and lifted her from the wreckage. "Whatever happened? What a turn you gave us, my girl. But all's well? Nothing broken?"

Because he was bending over her, Molly couldn't see the widow's face. But she could hear her shoe leather tapping the bricks. Then Mrs. Ben turned and threw her parting words like darts over her shoulder, before she strode away into the tavern room.

"That railing will have to be replaced, Mr. Savage. The cost of the nails and wood shan't come out of my pocket."

Before she closed her eyes in shame, Molly saw the loving look in her father's eyes replaced with worry. How could she burden him with a runaway boy as well? No. Rafe was a problem she'd managed to get into by herself. She alone would have to find the answer.

He pulled her to her feet.

"I wish I had that treasure," she said fiercely.

"What's that?" her father asked, looking surprised. "Treasure? What treasure?"

So he had forgotten even that. "The redcoat story you used to tell me, Pa," she said. "That tale of gold being hid hereabouts, maybe even right in the tavern."

He laughed, and for a moment Molly saw the old Ned Savage, her young, handsome father, who used to swing her around in his arms till she'd screamed with delight. Who used to take her out in the boat; who had patiently taught her to sail the shallow waters of the Shore islands with her eyes shut.

"Aye, so I did. But you were little then, Moll. And that redcoat gold was never found, you know that."

After the Revolution, when the colonists had fought England for six years and the defeated British were finally fleeing, two men wrapped head to toe in cloaks had stopped at the Hog's Head. They'd paid to stay over, but kept out of the tavern room, talking to no one. Late that night the noise of a terrible row came from the upstairs room where they slept. Molly's grandfather was away fighting with General Washington. As was her father, though still a boy. So it was left to her frightened grandmother to climb the stairs and pound on the guest-room door.

When she did, the story went, it burst open and a man ran out, pushing past so hard he threw her to the floor. He bolted down the stairs, out the door, and was never seen again. Inside the room she found the other, lying in a great pool of blood.

Before he died, he'd whispered to Molly's astonished grandmother, "The gold. Where did he hide . . . the gold?"

The man had struggled to say more, but he'd already bled his life away. He died in Grandmother Savage's arms. And when the few men left on the island climbed the stairs to lift and carry him away, the dark cloak fell back . . . to reveal his blood-soaked uniform was British navy blue. The man was buried in the little graveyard, beneath a plain wood cross. But no gold was ever found. The redcoat gold was the only story of interest Molly had ever heard connected with the island, for it was in truth a very dull place.

"That's naught but a bedtime tale," her father said, settling on the lowest step, pulling her down beside him. "There was no treasure. My pa and his brother fairly took this place apart, even the paneling. I looked around myself, years back." He sighed. "A dying man might say anything, Moll. If we had any gold about, do you think I'd have let the tavern fall away from us?"

She settled her head on his shoulder. "No, Pa. But perhaps you could tell me a story again—just a short one."

He was silent for so long at last she became alarmed, and raised her head to look at him. "Sorry, girl," he said in a low, sorrowful voice. "They all seem to have left me."

And so they sat like that for a while, without speaking. Not jumping up to milk the goat or chop firewood for Mrs. Ben. As if not so much time had passed, and she was still a child, and they both were happy enough again just to be content in each other's company. As if things had not changed, as they always seemed to, for the worse.

PIRATES AND PRINCESSES

THE GIRL CAME AGAIN THAT EVENING, to check his wounds. Rafe knew her name was Molly now; she'd told him so. But he didn't call her by it. He didn't want to think of her as having a name, or a family and friends. He couldn't afford to be familiar, to trust her too much.

"Hold still," she said each time he flinched. "You're a worse baby than Ephraim."

She shook her head and went back to wrapping a new bandage tightly around his ribs. By the poor light of the candle stub she'd smuggled out, he saw the bruises on his arms and legs were fading, from deep red and purple to shades of yellow and brown and green that reminded him of spoiled fruit. She wanted to press on his ribs, to check their healing, but he'd refused to take off his shirt, only allowed her to wind the new bandage on over it.

For if she saw the old scars from the wounds the cowhide whip had branded on his back, she'd know he had lied. Each time she pulled to tighten the cloth she was winding, he had to grit his teeth to keep from screaming. All the old lash marks hadn't really healed. His back might be festering. Or did slave stripes simply carry pain and humiliation longer than was usual?

"I'm sure not a soul has seen me," he said, trying not to sound worried. "I keep to the cellar all day, but—"

"Hold still!" she said again as he jerked away.

"Ah, but it hurts," he said at last, gritting his teeth, hissing at the pain. As she tugged the last knot tight he moaned. "Ow! Must you truss me up like a roasting hen?"

"I have to bind it snug or those ribs won't heal proper," she said firmly. "Of course if you weren't so modest, if I could only see them . . ."

He shook his head.

She knew about ribs, she'd explained, from the time someone called Doc had bandaged her father's. He'd cracked them falling from the roof of the tavern trying to replace rotted shingles. "Pa cursed and complained even more than you. But Doc only cursed him back, then poured a draft of ale laced with poppy juice down his throat to quiet him."

"You have no such remedies, I see," he said sullenly.

She shook her head and made a regretful face. "No. You'll simply have to bear it. There." She patted the last knot. "I predict you'll be good as new in a few weeks."

From the pain in his side, he doubted it. But he worried then he'd spoke too sharply. He must keep this girl on his side. At Penland, the only way he'd ever found to do that was to entertain and distract the person whose sympathy he needed—

whether it was his mother, or the cook, or the master himself who was angry with him. "Don't think me ungrateful. You make a good doctor."

She snorted at that. "What a notion."

Certainly he knew it was ridiculous. Women were allowed to treat only toothache and chills and such. To dole out herb teas. A few were skilled enough to deliver babies. At Penland, the mistress saw to slave ailments, even delivered babies when the black midwife couldn't be reached. But wealthy families like the Penningtons preferred to pay the higher fees of a physician. And those were men, and always would be.

But then the girl grinned. "Though it's true Doc is getting old, and some deaf."

"Then what—will you take his place one day?"

She stared, and finally laughed aloud at that. "I hope we'll be gone from here before then, my father and I. But enough talk of doctors." She paused to tuck in a trailing tag-end of cloth. "If you like to tell stories," she said in an odd, subdued voice, without looking up, "you can pay me with one."

Rafe couldn't seem to stop himself from goading her, though. "Don't you think a good doctor should demand cash from her patients? How'll you make enough money otherwise to leave?"

"Oh, and I suppose you can pay," she snapped. "With pirate gold, no doubt."

Her annoyed look told him he had pushed too far. Maybe she was growing tired of helping him, of keeping him a secret. He decided to launch into a tale, if only to change the subject.

"Strange you should mention gold. When I was a prince on the Barbary Coast, I had gold enough to buy a thousand doctors. But no one in my beautiful country ever grew sick or died."

He gazed beyond her, to show he was recalling a rich, colorful paradise. But really what he saw was Penland, the great house and all its inhabitants, black and white, going on about their lives without him.

"When I get off this island I'll revenge myself on the pirates who seized me," he continued. "The thieves stole my throne and enslaved my people. I'll send you a cartload of gold then."

The girl smiled doubtfully. "Well, I won't stand on the beach waiting. Might catch a chill. Or grow so old and sick I'll need doctoring myself."

Neither of them laughed at that. Beneath their uneasy silence, the only sounds were lapping waves, and the gritty scratching of a fiddler crab in one corner of the cellar, digging himself an escape tunnel. Lucky, simple creature, thought Rafe. If only freedom was won so easy.

"Well, then, tell me something different," said Molly abruptly. "I'm tired of captives who stay captured, and gold that stays buried."

Really, he was tired of telling stories to white folks, who took and took but never gave. But this girl, he reminded himself, had helped him. He thought for a moment, then leaned closer and lowered his voice. "What if I told you this Mrs. Ben you speak of is really Blackbeard the pirate—"

"What!" She looked startled, then covered her mouth with one hand, laughing.

"Of course! But in a skirt."

He felt so tired now. He'd like to lie down and sleep.

But the girl nodded and laughed. "Oh yes! I see it. She's got his mean crafty look about the eyes. But what has he—I mean, she, done with her awful curling beard? The one they say she hangs burning fuses from?"

"Made it into a horrible black wig for her head," said Rafe solemnly. They both burst out laughing, and for a moment he, too, meant it.

"Shh," said Molly. "Half the island will turn out to see what all the cackling's about." She laid a hand on his bare arm in warning. When he looked down at it, she bit her lip and quickly drew it away, hiding it in the folds of her skirt.

"Cackling?" said Rafe too loudly, stifling a yawn. "She's not a pirate, but a witch, then."

Suddenly Molly stopped laughing. "She is indeed. Look." She rolled up her sleeve and showed him a bruise that circled her arm, like a bracelet of flat dark pearls. "I suppose my shoulder looks worse, though I can't see. But I feel her marks on me like a brand sometimes."

Rafe frowned. What did she know about brands, or about suffering? She was white, and free, and could claim a father. "Then why doesn't he stop her?"

"Who?"

"Your father. But then, most of them care nothing for their children."

Immediately he saw it had been a mistake to say that out

loud. For the girl scowled and climbed to her knees, rolling her sleeve back down as if ready to go. "The truth is, I didn't tell," she said coldly. "He has worries enough. We could be turned out, and a few bruises are easier to bear than starving."

Rafe might argue that point as well, but thought he'd better not. A muscle in his jaw began to twitch. He got up and paced the dirt floor.

"What ails you, boy?" she asked curiously. "Marks on skin fade. They don't hurt all that much." She snatched a broken broom handle off the floor and waved it like a sword. She looked anxious, as if they'd somehow changed places, and she must now entertain him. "I need no hero to defend me. I'll run the witch through myself!"

She struck an exaggerated military pose, then thrust the stick at her own shadow, which the guttering candle stub had stretched to giant size on the wall. "Take that, you miserable pirate. Skirts or no, I shall pierce your black witchy heart—*if* you truly have one." She spun, then whacked and jabbed at the wall.

Rafe was first slack-jawed at her antics, then, despite himself, amused. Not wanting to, but laughing all the same, and clutching his sore ribs at the pain. This white girl was strange, unlike any other he'd ever met. Finally he gasped, "No more. You're killing me, not the old witch."

With one final stab, the handle broke in two. "Ouch! She's a tough old bird," Molly complained, rubbing her hand, suddenly looking embarrassed. She tossed the remaining half aside. "Never mind a story. They only make you even unhappier at your own fate. Anyhow I must get back; it's true dark now. Won't do for anyone to miss me and come looking."

Rafe stood silently in the doorway of the root cellar as she collected her excuse for leaving the tavern to come down to the Heap so late—the trash wagon she'd hauled there, overflowing, right after dinner. That wagon, or taking the goats out to forage and graze—one or the other had been her excuse to slip out most nights.

But how much longer before someone noticed she was going so regularly, and asked questions—or followed? This end of the island seemed deserted most of the time. Yet someone was bound to stumble on him eventually. Rafe shuddered to think what might happen then.

She bid him good-bye. The empty wagon rattled and bumped behind her as she dragged it back up the beach, dodging wait-a-minute vine and low branches. Finally she turned down the path to the village he'd not seen as yet. By the darkness and the risen moon, it was later than he'd thought. He crawled back inside his hole in the ground, covered himself with the scrap of quilt she'd brought, and lay awake in the dark, listening.

9

BOATS THAT PASS
IN THE MARSH

WHEN MOLLY CAME DOWNSTAIRS the next morning, it was still dark. Mrs. Ben, who was already in the kitchen rolling out biscuit dough, jabbed a floury finger in her direction.

"Ah, at last," she said, as if Molly had been lying in bed till noon. "Hie yourself out to the channel for my onions and such, or you'll miss the bumboat. Then what'll I have to make a stew, eelgrass? Get on with you, now." She thrust a few coppers into Molly's hand. "And don't be profligate with my money, do y'hear?"

"Yes'm," Molly mumbled, yawning. She took up the split-oak basket hanging on the wall and went out sleepily, rumbling within at the lack of breakfast, but still glad to escape for an hour.

Her breath plumed before her in the cold dawn air. How often lately she'd tapped little Ephraim with a stick, to prod him back onto this same path, while his mother plodded slowly down the middle of the shell lane, head lowered, as if she had given up whatever dreams goats might have, and never even *thought* of bolting anymore. Molly sighed.

Most cottages in the village were dark, though one or two showed a miserly flicker of candlelight. The yards all looked the same, neatly swept sand marked out with driftwood or shells. Some with nets hung out to dry. Tom Turner's old yellow hound thumped his tail on the ground as she passed, then lay back, too lazy to bark. Didn't anyone here ever imagine going away to someplace more exciting? How could they be content to spend their whole lives on one tiny hump of sand in the water, doing the same tiresome tasks?

Down at the water's edge lay a log canoe, hollowed from a felled tree years ago by her grandfather. She'd never met him; he'd died shortly after the war. But many years ago he and his brother had crossed to the Eastern Shore peninsula. They'd found and felled a great tree, its trunk four feet across. One so heavy they couldn't move it, but had to cut away the waste wood with adz and broadax right there where the tree had fallen in the woods. Then, when they were finished, they'd pushed the great log canoe they'd made into a tidewater creek and brought it home to Savage Island. Her father had rigged the mast and sail himself. He'd meant the boat mainly for errands, but had decided to teach Molly to sail as well.

She'd practiced in the shallows, raising and lowering the sail, wrestling with the tiller till she got the feel of it. Basking in her father's praise when she could finally rig it up on her own and actually make it go where she wanted.

"You're a fine sailor, Moll," he'd said when she was ten or eleven. "No boy or man could do better."

Soon she knew the mazy backwater passages around the island as well as the freckles on her arms. Though now her time in the boat was spent not improving her sailing skills or watching the antics of otters and waterfowl, but haggling over the price of vegetables. Then hauling hard on the sheet or poling like mad to get back before low tide made for a long, hard pull over razor-sharp oyster beds.

She pushed out into the shallows as the sun rose over her shoulder and turned the silvery marsh grass and the flat water beyond to pink and red and orange. A deer bolted back into the woods, tail flashing like clean laundry on a windy day. A fat gray muskrat slid off the bank and disappeared with a plop below the cloudy surface. Round the bend a pair of bold otters popped up to play tag, splashing and tumbling before her bow.

As the sky lightened to rose, then pale gold, then finally blue, she rounded the curve toward the channel. Just in time. For there, a few hundred yards out, a couple of bumboats were passing. Francis Ley, a pimply young man from one of the mainland farms, was in the nearest. He rowed out with produce twice a week to peddle up and down the coast.

Mild, slow-moving Francis normally sailed nodding over the tiller, or rowed the vegetable-heaped skiff as if he were about to fall asleep and slide overboard. Today, however, he was staring around, unusually alert.

When she hailed him and pulled up alongside, he looked her up and down, swallowing several times, his prominent Adam's apple bobbing like a fishing cork.

"H-have you heard the n-news, then, Moll," he said, the words tumbling out in what was, for Francis, great haste.

He'd never been very talkative. Perhaps that came of spending long hours alone in the boat. But it seemed to Molly that lately Francis had seemed awfully glad to see her. The week before she'd had to cut him short and pole off, the buzz of his drawled words pursuing her like lazy, droning bees.

As she drew alongside he stared at her as if she'd sprouted feathers to wing it over the marsh. His look made her uneasy, though she couldn't tell why. She'd known Francis since she was seven or eight, and he not much older, back when her father had used to bring her out in the boat to buy the vegetables for her mother. Back then, he still used to joke, and tease her. "I'll be bound, that Ley boy's getting sweet on you, Moll. Did y' see those big cow eyes?"

This morning Francis's yearning gaze made her wonder if her father's joke might be coming true. Then she snorted and laid her pole in the thwarts. The idea of being courted by heronlike Francis over a boatload of wilting carrots was too silly to think about.

"I need a head of cabbage, a dozen carrots, lots of potatoes. And six onions, please," Molly said quickly, jingling the coppers in her pocket. Then she recalled his remark. "And what news is that, Francis?"

His darting glances, thick shock of straw-blond hair, and jerking Adam's apple made him look even more like a gawky marsh bird. "Wayland Makeele," he whispered.

"Makeele?" Molly nearly dropped the bunch of crisp, dew-speckled carrots he'd pressed into her hands. "The picaroon? But they caught those pirates months ago!" Everyone knew about picaroons, dreaded pirates of the bay before the war and ever since. And their chief, Wayland Makeele, who'd once nailed a farmer's hand to his own barn door when the man objected to the picaroons' intention to burn it down.

Francis shook his head, spiky crest bobbing. "Not so. Only s-seized his ship. Makeele's raiders been coming in off the bay, raiding plantations again. L-looting and burning. They say he'll head for the seaside now, make his way up to Maryland." He looked around again, as if a murderous gang might be skulking behind the marsh grass and driftwood.

Molly swallowed and glanced around, too. "But Makeele mostly sticks to the western side, to the Chesapeake. He's never bothered with these islands."

"Not so," said Francis. "During the war, old Jonas told me once, the picaroons landed, b-buried a treasure on one. Then cast off, leaving a d-dead man to guard it."

"Oh, Francis," chided Molly. "Old Jonas? He's away with the fairies. Been addled for years."

Still, she supposed she'd heard that tale, too. Makeele, grandson of an old pirate, was feared up and down Virginia's coast and up the Chesapeake Bay, and from Salisbury, Maryland, to the Outer Banks of the Carolinas. His picaroon raiders were unrepentant renegade Tories. The meanest, lowest sea raiders, thieves, and scoundrels. The war was long since over, but they still preyed on remote houses and farms up and down the shores of Maryland and Virginia.

They'd fought and thieved so long for the British, terrorizing and robbing neighbors had become a family trade. Makeele's band was composed of brothers and uncles and cousins. Though some members were said to be Royal Navy deserters, out for bloody vengeance. They'd been a scourge for over twenty years, and perhaps always would be, some folks said.

"Maybe he hasn't come to S-Savage Island yet," said Francis. "But when the F-French took his ship and rearmed it for a patrol vessel, they told the governor the s-state would have to look to its own to protect the creeks and marshes. He's been attacking from b-barges and rafts, then scooting up the creeks to hide, where no state vessel can follow."

"But still." Molly heaved a sack of white potatoes into the bottom of her canoe, then reached for the string of onions dangling from Francis's raw-knuckled hands. "What's to gain here? We have little enough. Certainly no gold."

Why, the thought of Savage Island being *robbed*—for what, fish heads and fraying nets?—was laughable.

"He's after anything he can g-get now," said Francis. Molly suddenly realized he was still holding one of her hands, though she'd already taken the onions and stowed them under the bench. She tugged back, but Francis held fast. His fingers felt cool, damp as seaweed. Callused from years of rowing.

"I'd hate to see any h-harm come to you, Molly Savage," he whispered, so low she had to lean forward to make out the words.

"Francis, what's come over you? Let go my hand."

Still he clung like an oyster to its rocky bed. "I know it's early yet to say so. But I aim to court you proper. Soon you'll be ready to marry."

Molly gasped, snatched her hand away, and picked up her pole. "Don't be a simpleton, Francis. Why, you and I . . . I mean, I'm not even—oh, for mercy's sake!"

She brought the log canoe about quick as she could. She dug in and poled off, too rattled to even consider hoisting the sail. Marry skinny, birdy Francis Ley! The very idea made her laugh.

And yet . . . what if her father and Mrs. Ben *did* wed? Perhaps they'd want her out of the way. They might have more children, give her little half brothers and sisters. She recalled her father's joking comments about Francis. Molly gritted her teeth and dug her pole viciously into the mucky bottom, then gave a mighty push, and the little boat leaped forward. The muffled clink of shifting metal, as her weighted skirt pocket swung against her thigh, reminded her she hadn't handed the widow's coins over to Francis.

She lifted her pole from the water and looked back over her shoulder. Oh, mercy. He was still gazing at her, one hand lifted in forlorn farewell. She took a deep breath and poled on.

10

A VERY EXPENSIVE BOOK

RAFE MUST HAVE SLEPT AT LAST, because suddenly it was growing light outside the cellar. He threw off the scrap of old quilt Molly had brought. His pillow was a folded grain sack, only a bit mildewed, that he'd discovered in a corner of the cellar and dried out in the sun. He'd slept on worse since leaving Penland.

At the plantation he'd had first a slave's pallet, then a real trundle bed with cotton sheets, wool blanket, and even a feather pillow. In the great house he slept surrounded by the warm gleam of polished mahogany paneling and shining oak floors. Above the wainscoting, hand-painted horses and riders galloped across wallpaper fields. He'd dreamed himself into such scenes many a night, back then. He'd even believed he might somehow grow up to inhabit such a place. Until the day Mistress had caught him in the nursery, reading a primer.

Earlier that afternoon he and the young master had gone outside to roll barrel hoops with sticks. Rafe had coaxed William to draw out in the sand the sums the tutor had taught him before lunch. It was the only way Rafe could learn the lessons he couldn't see from the back corner, the place he had to sit while Will was schooled. Sometimes he could slip back to the nursery to read a few lines from the forbidden books on the shelf. But such risky opportunities came seldom.

"Write *sums?*" the younger boy had whined, his lower lip creeping out, his high voice growing sullen. "We came out to play, Rafe. Not study. All those stupid numbers make my head ache."

"But you want to get it all straight. Then when Mr. Epps goes over the lesson tomorrow, you'll be done sooner. We can play even longer."

"Oh, all right," the other boy had grumbled. "But it's not as if you can really *help* me figure, Rafe," he'd added, with a hint of superiority.

"That's right," Rafe had agreed meekly, trying to look bored and uncomprehending as Will began to trace the lesson in the dirt with an oak twig. The boy was only a year younger, but a great deal smaller and shorter. He still needed an afternoon nap. And they weren't allowed to stay outside too long because his pale, freckled skin would burn, then itch and peel for days.

After an hour the cook called them inside for bread and milk. Then William lay down and soon was snoring wheezily. Rafe slipped away to read in the deserted nursery. He'd done it before, and always managed to slip back before anyone noticed or William woke. Everyone knew the mistress also took a nap during this, the hottest part of the day. But Master Thomas would be riding the fields, as was his habit after lunch. He never trusted his overseers not to cheat him for more than a few hours at a time.

The nursery in the afternoon was a beautiful place, a curtained wonderland where dust motes drifted on the still, cool air. Sun glowed through the filter of the gauze drapes kept up at all times to protect the books from fading. It was to Rafe a dreamworld of soft pillows, wheeled and stuffed toys, gleaming oak chairs and tables rubbed daily with lemon oil, of the smells of polished leather and beeswax and India ink.

He chose a green book with gold letters embossed on the spine, then opened it and traced the swirls of color of the marbleized endpapers. Soon he was forming words silently in his mind, whispering aloud the ones he didn't yet know. Gradually he forgot who and where he was, caught up in the tale of a princess who could sleep in only the finest of beds, piled high with down and feathers, or her white, white skin would be bruised as if she'd been beaten. How strange and terrible to be a living thing, yet breakable as a china vase!

He hadn't heard footsteps coming up behind him. But suddenly, just as the princess was tossing and turning in terrible discomfort on at least a hundred goose-down mattresses, Mistress Pennington stood before him. Her hair was twisted up in paper curlers, her face red and sweating, shiny with some greasy concoction. And she was scowling fiercely at Rafe.

"What's in your hand, boy?" she'd said, reaching for the book. Without thinking, Rafe thrust it behind his back. Over the last few years he'd begun to feel certain he was clever, for he knew his numbers and letters better than young Master William. But at that moment he couldn't think of a single word to say to save himself.

Run, he thought. But his feet refused to move.

"Answer me or by God I'll whip you right now," she snapped.

"I . . . was only taking this book up to Will. He wanted—"

"That's Master William to you, boy," said the woman, narrowing her eyes. "You never seem to recall it. Now hand me the book."

Ever since he'd learned to talk, Rafe had been told to call a boy younger and weaker than himself "Master." The same boy who was his half brother. So even though he realized he was in serious trouble, at the mercy of a woman who hated him, he felt angry. But only for a moment. Because anger for a slave is a very dangerous thing. A tempting feeling that could make you forget how to keep silent and agreeable on the outside so you can go on getting by in a white-owned world. So he took a deep breath and only nodded. "Yes'm," he said. Keeping his gaze on the floor, he slowly pulled the book from behind his back and handed it over.

She opened the book and flipped through several pages. Then looked at Rafe again. Her lips twitched, then parted until her teeth showed and the corners of her mouth turned up. It wasn't really a smile.

"You were reading it," she said, sounding pleased.

The punishment for a slave who learned to read was terrible. The law forbade any white man to teach a slave his letters. Rafe's mother had told him how once a slave had been made to stand up on the pillory in the town square while first one then the other ear was cut off. All because he'd been overheard reading aloud the label on a crate of apples.

"I tell it so you know the danger," she'd said. "If you be frightened, you remember."

For a slave, it mattered not *what* was being read—crate label or flour sack or cookbook or primer. Not even the Bible was allowed. So his answer to Mistress Pennington had to be a good one.

"No," he said quickly. "I mean, no, Mistress," he corrected as he caught her frown growing deeper. "I . . . only look at them pictures. I likes pictures. And Young Master William . . . he show them to me sometime."

Her laugh was like the bark of an ugly dog. A cold, thoughtless sound that had made Rafe shiver even though it was June. "Liar," she said. "It has no pictures, only small decorations. I know what I saw. You mean to contradict me, boy?"

He had grown a great deal the last year. Now he was as tall as Mistress Pennington. Perhaps he was strong enough to shove her down and run away. But then what? He reminded himself to keep his gaze on the polished boards of the nursery floor. "No'm, Mistress."

"Go to Master William's room and stay there till you're called. We'll see what your master has to say about this new wickedness."

So he went back to the room and sat stiffly on his cot, like a horse thief waiting to be hanged. When Will woke and asked what was the matter, Rafe said he was sick. That the young master should go back to the tutor this afternoon without him. He didn't tell what'd happened, even though the boy looked worried and kept asking. Will did like him, Rafe knew that. But probably only because he didn't know any other boys. Any white boys. None lived close enough to be his friend. Besides, even Will sometimes reminded Rafe to call him "Master." Even when they were alone. He sounded too much like the mistress when he did that. To Rafe, that only proved Will was no more his friend than any other white person.

Anyway, what could such a sick, pale weakling do to help, even if he wanted to?

No one came for hours. By the growing shadows outside and his growling stomach, dinnertime had come and gone. William didn't return either. Finally, as the sun was setting, a frightened-looking housemaid named Kessie knocked on the nursery door.

"Massa, he call for you," she whispered, looking at Rafe with wide, shocked eyes, as if he were a ghost already.

He followed her down the stairs and to the library. Master Thomas stood before the fireplace, staring at the embers. When he saw them in the doorway he cleared his throat and waved them in, then began to pace. The master always did that when they were in the same room, as if the sight of Rafe made him nervous. The mistress sat calmly in a slipper chair with flowered cushions, embroidering, head bent over her work. This time she didn't order Rafe out. She only glanced up and told Kessie to go. The girl fled as if she were being chased by hounds.

"Now look here, boy," said the master, lifting a finely-molded bronze figure of a stallion, inspecting it closely, as if wondering how it'd appeared on his desk. He carried the horse as he paced, weighing it in one hand. "You were caught reading a book. Do you deny it?"

Rafe hesitated. He wanted to say, *You're my father, but you deny it. Why shouldn't both your sons learn to read and write?*

He could just imagine what sort of punishment that would earn him. Ever since he'd found out who his father was, he'd dreamed this stocky, red-cheeked man would someday clap a hand on his shoulder, would call him by his name. Then he'd be as good as William. He'd stand next to Thomas Pennington, even take his place as the eldest.

In that foolish daydream Master Thomas came to Rafe with joyful tears in his eyes and held out his arms. "You shall be Master after me," he always said. And then Rafe would free his mother, and all the slaves on the place. Sometimes at night, Rafe dreamed young William fell ill and died. Sometimes . . . sometimes Rafe even killed him. He didn't like to recall that, when he woke.

A fantasy, not a pretty one. The real world was here in this room, with the man who would never admit he'd fathered him. With the woman who'd probably like to bury Rafe and his mother both in the little graveyard plot for slaves only, behind the rows of cabins. To put them under the ground, marked only by a pair of crooked lath crosses, and forget them.

The master stopped pacing and his cheeks grew redder. He glanced at his wife, whose mouth was pursed, as if she'd bitten into an orange and found it sour.

"I said, do you deny it?" he asked again.

"No, Master," said Rafe. "Sir."

The man looked uneasy. "Ah. Well, then . . . it ain't acceptable. You know that letters and ciphering . . . these things are forbidden."

"For heaven's sake. Just *tell* the boy," said the mistress, throwing her embroidery down in her lap.

"For this transgression, you'll no longer stay in the house or share a room with Master William," Pennington said suddenly. "You got to live now in one of the slave-quarter cabins. And starting tomorrow, work as a field hand, with the others in the cotton."

The mistress made an impatient gesture.

"You and . . . your mother, too, of course."

The master actually looked guilty, or at least unhappy, at this last part. But then Rafe finally took in the words. *Work in the fields. With the others. Out in the cotton.* But he and his mother had always lived in the big house! Worked and slept there, and ate in the huge gleaming kitchen with Sally the cook and Delia the seamstress and the other house slaves.

"Lord God, them field hands is nothing but trash," Sally liked to say. "Uh-uh. Too dirty and stupid to be let in past the front door."

"But, Master." Rafe clasped his trembling hands behind his back. He kept his eyes carefully downcast. "My mother didn't . . . she done you no wrong. I was the one—"

"How dare you talk back to the master of this place," said the mistress softly, as if she were too proper ever to raise her voice, even to a slave. "You see, Mr. Pennington! The insolent boy needs a whipping." She folded her arms, then softened her gaze when she glanced at her husband, as if she, too, were bound by some cast-iron rules of submission. "Though that would be your decision, of course. After all, he *is* . . . your responsibility."

Master Thomas stopped his pacing at last. He slammed the bronze horse back on the desk, snatched up his hat. "Enough." He gritted the words out between clenched teeth. "Do as you like, madam. I'm going out." Then he stalked from the room.

"But where to?" she called after him.

"To hell," Rafe thought he heard the master shout, before the door slammed behind him.

"Go on out to the stables, boy," said Mistress Pennington, calmly picking up her embroidery again and threading a needle with blue silk. "Directly to Mr. Snow the overseer. He'll know what to do with you."

And when he stumbled into the stables, out behind the big house, Rafe found that it was true. There stood Mr. Snow, cowhide whip in hand. He was indeed expecting him.

11

SACRIFICES AND LIES

B Y AFTERNOON MOLLY WAS STANDING over a copper pot of boiling white linens, stirring, forever stirring. Sweat dripped into her eyes. Her hair matted, then stuck to her neck. Her face felt parboiled.

Ha, she thought. *Even Francis might be put off if he could see me now.*

Her arms felt like she'd been stirring for hours, but stains from gravy and port still spotted the swirling cloth. She wished diners at the Hog's Head would spend more time getting their food from fork to mouth, and drink from cup to lip, and less dribbling on the table.

She wiped away the beads of sweat that kept dripping into her smarting eyes. Then she hauled harder on the wooden paddle, sending Mrs. Ben's best napkins whirling crazily through the boiling water. If it had been fair weather, she'd at least be outside in the cool air. But a steady drizzle had set in after she returned from the bumboat. It had doused the fire in the yard. So then she had to come inside and do the wash in the steaming confines of the tavern's kitchen.

Even through the layers of skirt and shift and petticoat, she felt the rounded edges of the four coppers still in her pocket. As she leaned over the hot woodstove, the metal disks had warmed, until each coin seemed to burn through the cloth separately, all the way to her skin. Why hadn't she returned them to the widow?

When she'd come in carrying the load of vegetables, and Mrs. Ben said tersely, "Change?" Molly had simply shrugged and braced herself for curses. But the woman had only clicked her tongue in annoyance, then turned back to mince-pie making. So after a moment Molly had slipped out of the kitchen, gliding carefully, scarcely breathing lest the coins give a telltale jingle in her pocket.

The satisfying, solid heft of a pocket heavy with coin made her feel oddly lighthearted. She kept slipping a hand in her pocket to feel the pleasingly round edges, to trace the outlines of the figures embossed on both sides of the coins.

Money, the problem was always money. Where to get it, and how. She used to make a little cash netting crabs. She'd pole the log canoe through the marshes, dragging a bit of spoiled meat or a gristly bone on a line to attract the greedy blues. They were easy enough to scoop up in her old net. She had sold quite a few to the bumboats, until Mrs. Ben found out. Then the widow had said, "Use the Hog's Head's boat, girl, and my net, and the profits are mine."

Molly had clenched her fists, wanting to shout: *But it's my dad's own boat! The net was my granddad's before him—he made it!*

But talking back would only gain her a slapped cheek or a pulled ear. So she kept quiet but vowed never to net a crab again. And even that small source of income had gone.

She'd give the money back to Francis if he asked for it. If not . . . *well, the widow owes us at least this much,* she thought. *I'm sure she cheats us at every turn.*

Somewhere between boat and tavern Molly had decided the pennies were a sign. A start, however small, toward freedom. Still, she felt guilt nagging at her. Her mother had been a gentle woman. "You're too kind by half to everybody, Caroline," Pa used to say. But she had never put up with two things—stealing and lying.

Now, Molly thought, *I've done both—and more than once.* She hadn't told her father about Rafe; she'd taken food to feed him. And now, she'd kept money that didn't belong to her. Well then, she'd pay the widow back someday. But she could think of no way to make amends for lying to her father. Now that she'd withheld the truth for several days, it seemed impossible to reveal it. Where to begin?

"Still at that bloody wash pot?" shouted the widow from the tavern room. "God's body, hurry up. I need the brass polished yet."

Impatient steps thudded her way. The widow thrust her flushed face around the corner. "A taproom full of thirsty duck hunters. And here's you, daydreaming over the stove."

"No, ma'am," said Molly. "It's just these aren't done yet." She lift a corner of stained, dripping cloth with the ladle.

"Well, throw in more bluing," snapped the widow, coming

closer to look at the spotted linens. "Oh, and I'll be needing fresh mint for sauce. There's one good clump not yet withered up, in the nook by the stable wall."

"Yes, Mrs. Ben." As Molly climbed down off the stool, her sleeve caught on one of the pot handles. Hot water sloshed, missing her, but it soaked the widow's boots.

"Wretched, clumsy girl," said Mrs. Ben. "Guests coming and you've ruined my best pair of shoes."

"What guests?" Molly asked. Visitors from off the island seldom came in the late fall.

The widow's face mottled red. "Never you mind." She grabbed Molly's arm and pushed her toward the stove. "No one need know my business. Swear you won't mention it to a soul. Not even your father."

Molly thought the widow was about to put her hand in the flame. She could almost feel her palm blistering.

"Swear, I said!"

"Ouch, I swear," gasped Molly, who'd only been curious. What matter if a few folks stayed at the inn? Mrs. Ben must be going mad.

"What's afoot here?" said a new voice curiously. Her father's.

The widow dropped Molly's arm as if it were hot as the flame. "Nothing at all, Mr. Savage. Merely instructing your daughter in useful household skills."

He smiled. "Good, good. Always well to know such, eh, Molly?"

She stared at him. *God's blood,* she thought. *Is he blind? Or just . . .* it suddenly came clear to her then. He didn't hate the widow at all. Perhaps even liked her, and did intend to marry the woman. So he'd come to care about Mrs. Ben more than his daughter. Maybe even forget his dead wife, who lay—

"Well, on with you then, dear," said the widow cheerfully. "Gather up that mint. Season'll wither into January at this rate." The woman all but pushed her out the door, smiling broadly all the while at Ned Savage.

"That's my girl, Moll," he said, patting her shoulder as if she were five years old. Molly bit back a curse and rushed out gripping the basket handle, wishing it were someone's neck.

The spell of warm days was clearly over. The near-wintry air cooled her throbbing palm and her burning forehead. She wiped her flushed face on one sleeve, blotting away the dampness that was mingled sweat and tears. Where was this blasted mint growing, anyhow? She looked around the foundations of the stable.

Mint jelly seemed an odd thing to make, too. Not the usual season for it, which was spring. Extravagant for the spare table the widow usually set. You didn't serve mint with baked fish or chicken stew. In fact, the only dish Molly knew that called for mint was roasted spring lamb. A few farmers kept sheep across the water, mostly for wool. But there were no sheep, much less lambs, on Savage Island at the moment.

As she passed the lean-to stable, the goats bleated. "Hush, you beggars. I've no crusts nor sugar lump today."

She finally found a leggy, straggling stand of mint by the far wall. Yes, with mint, only lamb. Lamb, or . . .

Or baby goat?

Ephraim, she thought. Her throat closed upon a lump until she couldn't breathe or swallow. She ripped blindly at the green, fragrant stalks. *Oh, not the little one.*

Molly threw the bunch of mint to the ground, ran into the stable, and hugged the kid so tightly he struggled and bleated. She dried her tears on his soft warm neck, and the straw dust made her sneeze. Ephraim licked her earlobes, then nosed hopefully in her pockets. She let go, and he trotted off to pester his mother, who'd decided to wean him.

Why would the widow suddenly give up a whole goat to guests? She was too stingy for that. Molly got up, brushing bits of straw from her skirt. Still, she'd better keep a close watch on the stable from now on. Though what could she do—steal the kid? Hide him away? Rafe's cellar would get mighty crowded after a while.

The kitchen was empty when Molly returned. She washed and chopped mint leaves, set them in a pot to boil, then went out into the tavern room. She'd barely come in when the widow rushed over and shoved some rags into her hands. "Do the brass."

Honestly, the woman was a wreck, as nervy and anxious as . . . as a bride. But Molly didn't want to think of that. She began rubbing the taps behind the bar. The smell of sour ale was choking. An empty barrel stood off to the side, waiting for her to roll it out back.

If only she had some money, more than a few miserable coppers. Ephraim was the closest thing she'd ever had to a pet, for the widow wouldn't allow a dog, or even a cat. "Cats track in dirt and shed hair. They get in the cream. They're bad luck," she'd recited when Molly had timidly suggested they take one of Hank Blodgett's kittens to keep down the mice. Mrs. Ben preferred to poison the tiny rodents instead. Molly hated it when she heard their agonized squeaks break the stillness in the middle of the night.

No, Mrs. Ben counted it a great foolishness to feed cat or dog or bird simply for the pleasure of their company. *In a way,* Molly thought bitterly, *I can see why.* All the widow's table scraps went to feed her father and her. So perhaps *they* were her pets—or simply her fools. *A fool and his money are soon parted.* Come to think of it, the widow was very fond of that saying.

All right, she was exaggerating. But how else might she find them more money? Around the tavern, perhaps under the tables, dropped by customers who'd had too much ale? Well, she'd never happened on any before. Perhaps the next time she went out for vegetables, if Francis Ley—

She stopped rubbing the brass, shocked. Here she was plotting to trick honest folks out of their rightfully earned money. Folks she knew. Was she no better than the widow, then?

The wicked always have excuses for the ill they do. Her mother had been fond of *that* saying. She'd once caught Molly when she was six with a sack of sugar, squeezed into the cupboard beneath the dry sink, eating handfuls of it after she'd been told not to. The sugar had been meant to bake a cake for a sick neighbor, and Molly supposed she'd been told that, too. Her face had burned with shame. It burned again now as she felt the hard copper disks press into her hip when she leaned over the counter to polish the brass fittings.

But all those years ago, wiping away Molly's tears, her mother had also said, "You know better, darling, you're good at heart. You'll always know what's right thanks to your own conscience."

Her conscience was prodding her hard just then. The only worse thought was what might happen if she went to the widow and confessed. She'd taken food from the woman's pantry for Rafe. And a blanket. And what was more, she planned to take more victuals tonight.

Mrs. Ben called out to a departing waterman, startling Molly out of her reverie. When the widow glanced her way, she scrubbed twice as hard. Anything to avoid those piercing black eyes that sometimes seemed to read her mind.

If this Rafe hadn't come along . . . not that she wished him drowned. But for the sake of a stranger, she'd broken the law. Deceived people. It was not his fault, but this troublesome boy had given her more, much more, to worry about.

Her mother must be looking down from heaven, disappointed at the way her only child was turning out. Molly's hand slowed until the rag lay still. *But you never told me what to do if you were gone, Ma,* she thought bitterly. *Never explained how I might save myself from poverty, or people who were not too good for this world like you.* For a moment Molly wished it hadn't been her mother who had died, but someone, anyone else. Even if it had to be her father.

"No," she suddenly said aloud, and the widow looked up curiously. Molly polished harder.

What kind of girl would wish her own father dead? Would cry for a baby goat, plan to lie and cheat to save it, yet begrudge the same mercy to a human being? To her father or to Rafe. Oh, it was all so complicated.

She'd heard slavery talk in the tavern; there'd been some heated arguments, too. Once Hank Blodgett had broken his cane over the head of a visiting waterman. A terrible brawl had followed, until the widow waded in with her broom, clobbering heads right and left. She'd had Ned Savage toss both men out on their ears.

"Slaves are property," the vanquished waterman had shouted again from where he lay in a puddle, wringing out his ruined hat. "Meant to serve us. They haven't the *brains* to be free. Any fool knows that."

The widow, dusting her hands, retorted, "I'll not spare a broken chair on fools, slave or free. On your way, before I set the hired man on you!"

Molly couldn't help but admire the widow that night, the woman's hair and skirts flying as she'd bravely and matter-of-factly dealt with a bunch of rough, shouting, brawling men. While her father had hung back, waiting to see what would come of the fracas. Only stepping in when the widow ordered it. But then wasn't Pa nearly a slave himself?

That day the runaways had been hauled off by the bounty hunters, her parents had argued about the nature of slavery. She'd been sent to bed but had crept out onto the stairs to listen, curious, because they seldom ever seemed to disagree.

Her mother said, "The Africans are innocent, Ned. Childlike and ignorant. Surely God meant for us to enlighten, not enslave them like beasts."

"I've enslaved no one," her father had retorted. "But perhaps ignorant savagery is the reason they're kept safely on plantations, instead of taking honest work from white men."

His words had made sense to her then. She'd gathered that dark-skinned people were different. Not as good or as smart or as trustworthy.

And yet . . . Rafe knew more stories than her father, and could write his letters in the sand with a stick. Slaves were never allowed schooling, it was a crime that brought terrible punishment. So how could the boy be a slave? Her father had had to work from an early age, he'd never got an education. When he needed to sign anything, he only made his mark on the paper. He couldn't write his own name. She'd thought to show him how once, years back, thinking he'd be pleased to gain such a wonderful skill. But he'd turned away angrily, and only later had she understood why. He was too proud to be instructed like a child, by his own daughter.

She rubbed at the brass savagely, until its bright gleam stung her eyes. She *would* find a way to get the boy off this island. Slave or free, she envied him a chance to start anew in a different place.

She fell to polishing the last piece Mrs. Ben had set out, the huge carving platter. A lovely oval of silver. Molly had always taken pleasure in the way it shined up. But this time she realized with a shudder it was the only plate big enough to hold a large main dish. Something just the size of a roasted baby goat.

12

A PRINCE'S RANSOM

THIS TIME RAFE HEARD THE GIRL coming before he saw her. "Whoa there, Ephraim," she called, using her stick to nudge the wayward goat back onto the path.

She seemed distracted, and nearly stepped on some scurrying fiddler crabs. Scarcely bigger than spiders, the creatures scattered at her approach, waving their claws, darting between her feet and the goats' hooves. One by one the agitated fiddlers popped down holes in the sand, out of sight.

If only it were so easy to escape trouble, thought Rafe.

She almost took the turn for the beach instead. Rafe frowned. What if a fisherman or net mender was about, noticed her, and remarked on it to someone else? But she clucked to the goats and turned back, taking the side path that led to the Heap. Rafe ducked back inside the cellar, not wanting her to know he'd been watching.

She whistled a greeting as she approached the root cellar, the secret signal they'd agreed upon. When Rafe stuck his head out, Ephraim bounded forward, skidding the last few feet into the doorway. There he lost his footing and fell in a tangle of skinny legs at Rafe's feet.

Rafe nearly laughed, but then sobered when he saw Molly's face. "Have they found me out? Is someone coming?"

She shook her head and plopped down in the sand beside him. "We need a plan to get you off this island. And money. How else will you make your way north?"

"And I have none. Can't work since I . . . have no freedman papers. Without them, I'm in danger anywhere south."

She nodded. "We've no boat, no fortune, no relatives on the mainland. Even if we had, I don't know that they'd agree to help. How will we manage it?"

He gazed off over the water. The girl's turn of mind worried him. She might give up; and then she might tell someone about the burden he saw now he'd become. All he could think was to fall back on the old remedy: to speak of safer things. To distract her; to entertain and change the subject to a more lighthearted one.

"I was marooned once before, on Ocracoke Island," he said suddenly.

Molly stared at him. "Not the wreckers' lair? Oh. This is another of your made-up stories."

"Not just a story," Rafe said solemnly, crossing his heart, keeping his expression sober. "The ghost of Blackbeard himself came ashore to check on a chest of gold buried years before."

"Oh, bother," she said. "It *is* a story." Still she scooted closer, playing the part of attentive audience. "I suppose that you . . . I mean, the boy in the story . . . was horribly scared?"

"Why fear pirates, especially dead ones? I have Spanish

blood in me. Takes more than a pirate to scare such a boy. Pirates are cowardly dogs, in any case."

"Maybe so," she said doubtfully. "But living or dead, I'd still fear digging up their gold, no matter how I wanted it. In stories, one pirate is always killed and buried with the treasure to protect it. An angry ghost set as a guard."

"What of that?" He stood and strode about, waving his arms. "If we could get there, I'd dig it up."

She scowled. "Well, we can't get there, or anywhere else, far as I can see." She crushed a bleached, brittle scallop shell between her fingers. "'Tis a pity the redcoat gold is only a tale. It would be in reach and do us some good."

He frowned, puzzled. "What is redcoat gold?"

She told him the story then—of shouts and blows, and a pool of blood, and a dying man's confession to her own grandmother.

"Perhaps the picaroons took this gold," he said slowly. "You said they were in league with the British. For surely pirates have set foot on every island around here. Even now they could be plotting to come back, and—"

"Makeele," whispered Molly.

"What?"

"The picaroon. Francis Ley, a boy I know, he thinks Makeele might come here soon."

"So it must be for the gold," Rafe mused.

But the girl shook her head hard, as if to dislodge the very thought. "No! No, I'm sure it's more likely they'd come to sift through the wonderful Heap," she said, wrinkling her nose. "Our great stinking treasure trove."

He laughed then, relieved that her mood was lightening.

"No," she said again, as if arguing with herself. "The only thing of worth on Savage Island, with all its sand and crabs and mosquitoes, is a bit of livestock, a couple of boats . . . and the people, of course. But then again, maybe not all of them."

Rafe stopped at that, and glared at her. "What did you say?"

She looked puzzled. "About what?"

"That some people might be worth nothing." He realized he'd clenched his hands into fists, and made himself relax again. No good to get angry, to make her angry in turn. He was dependent on her goodwill as much as he'd depended on the goodwill of his masters at Penland.

She looked at him in surprise. "I only meant I place no great store by Mrs. Ben. But my father is a good man. Most of the folks here are good."

"Oh, are they? And if I came out of hiding," said Rafe slowly, "what would these good folks do?"

She looked away, and dug a stick into the soft sand. She seemed troubled, as if she were struggling with some bad memory. What she said next chilled his bones. "Once a slave was shot dead here. Of course, he'd sneaked up to a house in the dark of night, and surprised a man. Mr. Blodgett had only seen a dark shape skulking about near the chicken coop, and since he'd been in the war, thought the British had come again."

Rafe sprang to his feet. "So you think a bunch of chickens are worth a slave's life?"

She got up, too, facing him. "That's not what I said! He didn't even know the man he shot was a slave, or why he was sneaking about the cottage, until—oh, I don't know what they might do about you," she admitted at last. "Send for the sheriff from Eastville, perhaps. Thinking you must be someone's property."

He kept staring down at her. Waiting. He would not let her evade the answer. His life depended on it. He had to know where she stood.

"It *is* the law," she said at last, looking miserable. "And we didn't make such laws here." But she couldn't meet his demanding gaze.

He nodded slowly. He'd expected such an answer. Most folks, even good ones, couldn't be bothered to help if it meant inconvenience for them. He was certain now the old slaves had lied. No white person would ever really help a black one. Why should they?

Molly was speaking again. "But you're *not* a slave, you said. Are you sure you have no other proof?"

This change of direction brought him up sharp. For it was true that he'd not exactly told the girl the truth of things. It was also true she could be in terrible trouble for the few things she'd already done for him.

Suddenly it was his turn to avoid her gaze. "No, none."

He sat down again, feeling as glum as she looked. Molly did the same, and made a halfhearted attempt to speak of other things. But neither could find a way to bring back a jesting mood. She stood again and snatched up her walking stick. "I must get back to the inn." She whistled up the goats.

He supposed if he'd asked, she might've lingered. She had done so before, and it wasn't really late. But he didn't say a word. Suddenly he felt as trapped as he had at Penland. And he had no one here to blame but the girl, even though he knew it wasn't her fault. So he only nodded. Then he climbed back into the dark root cellar that had briefly felt like freedom, but now seemed to be turning into another sort of prison.

Of course, he reminded himself, he'd once been locked in a much smaller, darker place—the box at Penland reserved for sweating the mischief out of captured runaways and other miscreants.

Luther Snow had smiled when he'd showed Rafe the braided leather whip, as if it was a toy he might find pretty. The overseer had taken away Rafe's shoes, tied his hands together, and slid a thick stick of firewood between his hands and knees. And then, with many quick, well-practiced strokes, he'd beaten him bloody. Fifty lashes, and Snow had ordered Rafe to count each one aloud.

"Since you such a smart boy," he'd said, drawing his arm back for the first stroke, "you keep track. Or we got to start over."

When Snow untied him, Rafe collapsed at the man's feet. But he was jerked up, dragged by the arms across the kitchen yard. The knees of his pants snagged on sharp pebbles, tore on tree roots. Until, with a satisfied grunt, Snow heaved him headfirst into a squat box full of the coppery stench of old sweat and blood and fear. Rafe lay on its dirt floor gasping, staring into a darkness so heavy it seemed to press down on him.

Afterward, someone pulled him out of the hot, airless box, half-conscious, fainting. Then Rafe lay on his stomach on a pallet, in one of the small, dusty slave cabins lining the wide lane in a double row. Soon his mother had come. She'd bathed his torn, bleeding back with clean rags and water and said softly, "Now you 'most a man. You see how it is. They got no pity for you, even if you share their blood. Can't be Young Master's playmate all your days."

He'd buried his head in his arms and refused to answer. He hated Mistress and Old Master for sending him to this filthy hole to live. One square room, no bigger than a shed or a smokehouse. One door, one window without glass, a hole cut in one of the logs that made up the walls. Light shone through chinks between the logs. His new bed was a patched pallet on the hard-packed dirt floor. No cover, no sheets. Already, beneath the unbelievable pain of his lacerated back, he felt things crawling. Biting. Some small, like fleas. Others larger.

He hated his mother, too. The woman who was sponging blood lovingly and gently from his back. She was the wrong color. Why had she brought him into this world if there was no rightful place for him?

But most of all he thought of the morning, when he'd have to pick up a hoe and join the lines of field slaves herded out to the cotton and corn like cattle. The house slaves, most of them lighter-skinned, who worked and slept in the big house, always looked down on the field hands. Laughed at their ragged clothes, their dirty, bare feet that had never worn shoes. At their black faces shining with sweat, streaked with clay and dust.

And he'd joined in the laughter and jokes, knowing he was better, too. But out here he could no longer pretend to be different.

"I'll run away," he said suddenly.

"Don't talk fool," said his mother sharply. "You not grown yet."

"But you are. Come with me," he said. "We'll go . . . up north." He had no plan yet, but would think of one. He was clever enough. Through the open windows each summer he'd heard the slave songs. The ones that the fat cook and the thin, wide-eyed laundress whispered were codes for escaping to freedom. North, the Promised Land. You just followed something . . . a star called a drinking gourd—

His mother stroked his arm. "This pass. Mistuss, she all worked up. But we be back in the big house by and by."

He hated her calm acceptance. "I won't go back there. Don't you want a place to live that is yours, your own? Maybe work for pay, be your own master?"

But his mother was staring down as if he'd lost his mind. "Don't know nothing 'bout that. At Penland they feed their nigras good. We get nice hand-me-down clothes, a nice place to live. Junkanoo, and cake every Christmas. The biggest place in three counties! The biggest great house, too. Hundreds of miles of woods and snakes and patrollers out there, baby. Only a fool try to get past all that. Just get dragged back and whipped to death. Here, on a day off, you can fish, or trap—"

As she went on and on, outlining the superior joys of the big plantation, he'd felt it for her then, too. The same contempt and dread he'd felt looking at the field hands. She was a coward, ignorant. A house slave. A tame black pet.

And she was his mother. Well, no one had let him choose his birth, or his parents.

The next morning when the overseer whistled, Rafe's mother prodded him awake. He stumbled out of the cabin, bent nearly double, stiff and sore. His back felt as if it had been set on fire and stamped out. He took up a hoe and followed the others in a long line to a huge field. There they would chop cotton from sunrise to sunset, with an hour to rest at noon and an hour at dinnertime.

As he worked, he avoided looking at the others or talking to them.

But they noticed him.

"You all like it down here?" asked the thin, sweating man next to him. "Ain't nothing like that big house, huh?"

When Rafe didn't answer, the others all laughed. They turned away from him and went back to chopping, row after row. In the next field, women plowed barefoot alongside the men, their muscles straining, sweat running down their necks. He saw his mother was one of them.

He fainted around noon. The overseer nudged him awake with the toe of one boot. "Get up, boy. Now."

And thinking of the black snake whip, the thin, three-foot

cowhide strip that whistled through the air before it struck, he had gotten up.

At lunch and dinner the slaves ate crouched at long wooden dishes like shallow troughs. Slobbering pigs, thought Rafe, and turned away. But by dinnertime he was so hungry he pushed his way in and snatched up food with the rest. And so tired, he slept as soon as he lay down on the thin hard pallet.

All his days went on just like that. He saw them stretched before him, endless as the rows of cotton plants and cornstalks in Master's fields. Until at last, he'd decided to leave it all behind. Even his mother.

He had been sure then that he'd show them all. And no matter what happened now, even if he died somewhere on the road to Boston, no one could deny that he'd surely come a long, long way from Penland.

13

A FORTUNE
ON TWO FEET

MOLLY SERVED SHEPHERD'S PIE and fried fish that night to Mrs. Ben's two regulars, Doc Drummond and Hank Blodgett. Joining them were two watermen from Cape Charles, who'd decided to sit out an evening squall. A stranger dined alone at the remaining table. The man was well turned out in fine wool trousers and an embroidered waistcoat. He'd announced that he was on his way from Snow Hill, Maryland, to Wilmington, North Carolina. "On a slave-buying trip," he remarked casually, yet loudly enough to make sure everyone in the place heard. "I got a nice little farm up the county."

Doc leaned over and invited him to sit at their table. Molly feared there might be another row if Hank and this Marylandman got to arguing the merits of the slave question. As she served them a round of ales, the farmer kept grumbling.

"It flattens a man's purse just to buy a single witless field hand these days." He snatched the ale before she'd properly set it down, and sucked foam off the top, smacking his lips.

Then he gave Molly a long up-and-down look, one she didn't much care for.

He turned from his rude appraisal, wiped his mouth on the back of his hand, and went on as if she'd never appeared. "And then, when a body shows up to collect the fine specimen advertised, the black wretch is spavined as an old horse, mean as a snake, and sporting enough cowhide scars on his back to prove him a troublemaker and a runaway."

"Oh, aye," said Doc Drummond, nodding as if he bought and sold fifty slaves a week himself. "What scandalous price they quote ye for the sorry devil?"

The farmer picked up his mug, then slammed it down again. Molly, sidling around the table, saw Mrs. Ben frown at this abuse of the tavern's pottery. "Five hundred dollars. In gold!" the man snapped.

Doc shook his head. Hank Blodgett tsked. But Molly had seen the glint of surprise in both men's eyes. She, too, was amazed. A man on Savage Island might not see so much cash in his entire lifetime. That must be what drove the slave chasers to their work—greed. A big reward. But she'd seen their quarry's bloodied face and desperate eyes. Molly didn't think any amount of gold would be worth such misery. Or being kept awake by nightmares, not to mention a bad conscience.

The supper hour passed without any uproar, though. Then Hank and Doc rose from their table and ambled home. Mrs. Ben did the receipts and counted money while Molly washed dishes in a bucket in the kitchen. Her father came in to help, scraping the blackened cast-iron pots and pans. He hung each back carefully on its iron hook. Molly was surprised; that wasn't usually a chore he took on. He chatted away, too, which was also odd. Her father wasn't normally much for small talk.

"What'd you get up to today, then?" he said.

"Well . . . not so much." She couldn't mention Rafe, and otherwise it'd been the same as any day. "Took the goats out. Did some wash. You know."

He lingered even after he was done, getting in the way. She got the feeling he had something else to say. It made her first curious, then uneasy. But when she finally asked outright, he only shook his head. "No . . . nothing."

He turned away and went to trim the wicks of the oil lamps, then outside to see to Janey the horse and the goats.

Molly wrung out a wet rag and wiped down all the counters and tables, yawning. How late it was; she felt exhausted. Then her hand stopped circling the last pitted pine tabletop. She was so tired, she'd forgotten Rafe. He'd be very hungry. She'd saved some cold pone from her dinner, and even managed to wrap a large piece of fried bluefish the loud farmer from Maryland had scornfully pushed aside on his plate. The crisp, greasy bundle still faintly warmed her pocket.

The farmer would be sleeping in the small guest room. As she'd served him a last glass of rum in the tavern, he'd complained of indigestion, muttered oaths about the scarcity of lamps.

"I can't abide a lumpy mattress," he said loudly, throwing a meaningful glance Mrs. Ben's way. The widow didn't say a word, only pursed her lips, took up a guttering candle, and led the belching, grumbling man up the stairs.

So now would be a good time to go to Rafe. Molly was done with chores, and it was near time to be getting to bed. If she was quick about it, Pa would assume she'd gone to use the privy. She slipped out the kitchen door and ran down the path. She couldn't be long, or her father or Mrs. Ben might come searching.

The cottages looked as if everyone had turned in, for fishermen get up long before the sun does. All the windows were shuttered or dark, the smoke from chimneys thinning to pale gray threads. She finally slowed down, panting, when she reached the edge of the woods, and listened. No sounds in the night woods but the scuff of her own bare feet, the skitter of loose shells, the buzz of the few hardy insects left this late in the year, the lone eerie hoot of an owl, and the hushing sound of waves lapping the beach beyond the trees. Otherwise all was so still that, as she walked on, she heard the pennies clinking in her pocket.

A poor hoard indeed, compared to the price of a slave. Five hundred dollars. In gold! She could not picture it except as a dazzling yellow tower. Surely no one would carry that much money all the way from Maryland. But then the farmer had said he hadn't brought the cash along on his person. No one on this island would rob him, but a traveler had to be cautious.

Molly hadn't realized a slave was a fortune walking on two legs. She was poor, but still fortunate not to have been born African on a far-off continent. Or on a plantation where she, too, could be bought and sold for her labors, like a milk cow or a pair of boots.

She shivered in the chill of the salt-tinged breeze and rubbed her arms briskly. They were nearly bare under the worn shawl. The danger Rafe was in struck her anew, and she shivered all the more. She was in trouble, too, for helping. Of course, if he was not a runaway, as he'd assured her, she wasn't breaking any law. But who knew what terrible things might happen until he got new papers or made his way to the free states. Massachusetts, or Vermont, or one of the others in New England. They might as well be on the moon, as far north as that was.

Any person who wished to make his fortune need only take him by force and sell him. For five hundred dollars in gold! He was no scarred, spavined runaway but a strong, healthy boy. Did cleverness add to his worth? He knew tales of princes and dragons, wise foxes and talking wolves, spiders who played tricks on people. He had nearly convinced her there was pirate plunder to be had for the digging.

Of course she didn't believe. He only told her lies and pretty tales to make sure she helped. Digging holes in the sand would never free them from debt, or save Ephraim from the roasting pan. Rafe himself was the only real fortune around. Worth more than enough to free Molly and her father from Savage Island and servitude at the Hog's Head.

Molly kicked hard at a shell in the path. *Five hundred dollars.*

An islander might not hesitate to turn Rafe over to men like those slave catchers. Or some fat, smug farmer like the one snoring in the guest-room bed. Might indeed consider selling the boy like a farm animal. She had only to say the word, and she'd be free of that secret burden. Might even be rewarded for upholding the law.

No. It was not only wicked, but impossible.

She hurried on, catching the fresh breath of seawater mingled with rank whiffs from the Heap. A three-quarters moon had followed the storm. Pale and shiny as a fish scale, it sparkled off the water, gilding the ugly bulges and piles of the Heap into something nearly beautiful.

Molly whistled a greeting as she hurried up to the root cellar.

The boy peered from the doorway fearfully at first. Then crawled out, rubbing his eyes, looking tousled and sleepy. "How nice that crash I heard in the bushes was you," he said. "And not a drunken fisherman or a man-eating beast."

He did look genuinely pleased to see her this time. Molly's hastily eaten dinner felt leaden then, heavy with guilt. She handed him the pilfered bread and fish silently.

"Will you stay a bit?" he asked, unwrapping the bundle.

She shook her head, backing away. "No, it's late. They'll miss me."

"Oh, it's fish." The delight in his voice scalded her. "Thanks! Mayhap you'll come back in the morning? I thought to look at some of the fishing boats tonight, to see if one might be large enough to go north in."

He couldn't take one of the watermen's boats. It was their living. But she didn't want to discourage him. . . . Oh, what a hypocrite she was. "No, I don't . . . that is . . . I don't know. Perhaps."

He'd started to take a bite, but lowered it and looked at her again. "What's wrong? Does someone suspect, or—"

"No, it's nothing." She turned before he could ask anything else, and fled up the path. She stopped at the edge of the village, panting. Ahead the tavern was dark now. Her father and Mrs. Ben must be upstairs, asleep. She hurried across the clearing and down the narrow sandy lane again. Stepping lightly, hoping the crunch of shells wouldn't wake folks in the cottages she passed. She'd make a quick trip to the privy and then slip quietly up the stairs and into bed.

But as she rounded the corner of the inn, she ran smack into something. A solid, though yielding mass that said "Oof," and reached down to imprison her in strong arms.

Molly's scream was muffled, her face pressed tight to scratchy, heavy cloth. She beat the thing wildly with her fists, until her father's voice said, "Whoa, Molly. I've been looking all about. Where've you been?"

"I, uh—just to the privy, Pa." Not exactly a lie; she had been headed there next.

"Are you not feeling well?"

"No, indeed, I'm fine."

"Yet you run like the ghost of Blackbeard is after you."

Her laugh came out as strangled choke. "No, Pa. I just—

heard a noise outside, when . . . I went to check on the goats. Then the privy . . . a noise spooked me, and I guess I ran."

He raised an eyebrow, but only said, "Ah. And Ephraim and Miranda are safe and sound? So all's well, then."

Molly nodded. "So, good night," she said quickly. "I'll be up soon." She started for the privy behind the stable.

Her father caught her arm again. "Wait. I have some news."

He led her over to the back steps, and they sat down side by side.

"What, Pa?" She pretended to yawn, wondering if somehow he'd learned about Rafe. She sat straighter, watching him anxiously.

Once they were seated, he seemed at a loss where to begin. He took off his cap, turned it in his hands, staring down as if he'd never set eyes on it before. Then he cleared his throat and finally said, "It's like this, Molly. I'm just a man."

Molly stared at him, puzzled. "I know that, Pa."

"What I mean is, you must be missing having a mother as well. To look after you."

"Well . . . yes, I do. I miss her dreadfully. Don't you?"

"Aye, that I do." He cleared his throat again and rubbed one eye. "But she's gone from us. She'll not be back in this life. And . . . you need guidance. A mother's hand."

Now Molly saw where all this was leading, for those had been Mrs. Ben's words exactly: *She needs that hand, and a firm one it must be, too.*

"No," she protested, "I don't—"

"Hear me out, Moll. I know I've never been a good provider, God forgive me. Nor much of a father to you lately, much less ma and pa combined. But a chance has come my way to change our fortunes. To provide things you need."

"Please, Pa. Don't do this."

He went on in a rush, as if she hadn't even spoken. "You could have decent clothes. Two parents to look after you. Maybe even go to a young ladies' school, somewhere like Baltimore. Your ma would've liked that. As things stand now, if anything should happen to me, why, then you—"

His voice cracked and he fell silent, staring off across the yard. As if he were seeing Molly, alone and orphaned, huddled in a doorway, ragged and cold and starving.

She opened her mouth to protest again, but he held up one hand and went on in a rush. "So that is why, come Sunday next, Mrs. Pruitt and I will be wed."

Molly leaped up to face him. "No! You will not. Why— she's nothing like Ma. Not, not nearly . . . good enough for you."

He sat stiffly, looking into the distance. He spoke stiffly, too, not meeting her eyes, reciting as if words written for the purpose had appeared hanging in the air behind her. "It's only natural for a girl to miss her mother. And to resent a new stepmother. But I do all this for your own good, girl. For the good of us both."

"But you can't marry the widow! Listen. She—she beats me, Pa. And pinches my arms and curses me. She's a cruel, and wicked—"

Ned Savage stood up. "Beats you? But you've never said a word of such before. Why accuse her now? Unless . . . oh, I see. You've always been a stubborn one, and I never sought to break your spirit. Thought a bit of gumption might help you along, maid, for life's hard. But there comes a point when you must leave off, Molly. When having things your own way only does harm."

"But you can't marry that harridan, that scold . . . that . . . that greedy, black-hearted witch!"

Her father flinched. His face contorted, and she saw him get up, but didn't realize he was drawing back his hand until the slap that followed rang in her ears like a gunshot. The blow itself was not so bad. She'd had worse hurts tumbling out of trees, or scraping her knees in a fall. Certainly worse punishments from Mrs. Ben. It was just that her father had never struck her before.

She bit her lip. *Whatever happens, I won't cry.* She'd told herself this before, too. But her father had never been the cause of it . . . till now.

Ned Savage was looking down at the ground, twisting his hat again, but harder, as if he meant to kill it. He sounded both determined and bewildered as he said, "You mustn't speak so of the woman who'll be my wife and your new mother. You cannot tell your own father what he must and must not do. You're a child, and shall do as you're told."

"I've done as I was told all my life!" she shouted. "And what good has come of it?"

He recoiled as if she were not his daughter but a snake striking out at him.

She didn't care. "I'll tell you what good! I have no mother, true, and I wonder sometimes if she didn't die of shame. Our home no longer belongs to us because my father cared more for a deck of cards than for her, or me. You're the one who should be told what to do! The one with less good sense than a goat."

She stopped then, panting, expecting another slap at the very least. But her father only sighed. Set his rumpled hat back on his head, and turned to go. Then he hesitated. "Before God, it's the truth. I haven't been much good, not to anyone," he said over his shoulder, in a low voice. "Don't think you're the only one to see it." Then, a bit louder, "It's late. We must be up early tomorrow."

He reached out as if to stroke her face, but drew the hand back, fingers clenched, and walked off, disappearing into the back of the inn.

Molly stood a moment longer, until the door shut, then she ran into the stable. Ephraim and Miranda were settled for the night in fresh hay. She flung herself down between them, for comfort, thinking she would cry here, where no one else could see. Her eyes burned and stung, but now, when it was safe to do so, she still could not cry. Perhaps she never would be able to again. She felt wrung dry, like an old rag. So she sat up and drew Ephraim onto her lap, hugged and petted him, rubbed her burning face on his soft-furred back. He bleated and snuggled his head beneath her arm, as if he understood what she was suffering.

She hugged him to her chest and got up from the straw. "Good night, Miranda," she whispered. "I'll bring your baby back in the morning."

Upstairs Ned Savage was already in bed, breathing softly but evenly—apparently asleep. She came in quietly, for the last thing she wanted was to wake him. She eased Ephraim under the covers of her own bed and slid in after. She wished she could hide the little goat upstairs until Mrs. Ben got tired of looking and changed her menu. But the widow would hear his hooves clattering over the attic boards. For a moment Molly considered taking him down to the Heap, hiding him there with Rafe. But if Mrs. Ben called for a thorough search, then both boy and goat might be found.

She lay back, exhausted, but couldn't sleep. Her thoughts circled as fruitlessly as black crows over a barren winter field. Rafe would be discovered. Ephraim would be killed and eaten. She'd be forced to serve the meal, no doubt. Her father would marry a horrible woman, and Mrs. Ben would be her stepmother.

And she, Molly Savage, was helpless to stop any of it.

What if she ran away, too, perhaps along with Rafe? They could take the log canoe, follow the coast north. And then . . . but at this point her mind balked. What would an unschooled girl do to support herself? Work was given to grown men. The few women unlucky enough to have no husbands or fathers or brothers to support them scratched out pennies by pricking their fingers spinning wool all day or painting china with silly bunches of flowers. She'd been warned of the dreadful fate awaiting girls cast adrift in cities like Boston or New York. She shivered, and hugged Ephraim closer. And she . . . she'd never been off this island. At least, no farther than the Eastern Shore peninsula. Between it and the Virginia mainland lay the broad Chesapeake Bay. Why, she'd never even been as far as Norfolk!

What choices did she have? Eventually, to marry pimply Francis Ley. He'd said he'd like to court her, when she felt ready.

But she did not *want* to marry Francis.

Oh yes. It all came back to money. With enough of it you could do anything, whether you were young or old, male or female. And she had just four pennies in her pocket.

But if you sold the boy as a slave.

She inhaled sharply, for those words had sounded all too clearly in her mind. So clearly she'd thought for a moment someone else in the room had spoken. And the wheedling voice seemed familiar as her own, yet not quite hers. Older, colder sounding. Almost . . . evil. She pulled the covers up to her neck, feeling foolish yet still frightened. How horrible the voice had sounded, as if it came from a mouth not quite human, not quite serpent.

Yes, you could. You could sell him.

Molly squeezed her eyes shut. But her mind worked on; for it needed no permission to keep spinning . . . and it supposed that, on the Eastern Shore, any number of farmers would be pleased to buy such a strong, healthy, clever boy. If she just convinced them he was hers to sell. After all, Rafe owed her his life. Without her help, he'd be dead now. Or like the man she'd seen led away in chains, beaten, bloodied, half-dead in body and soul . . .

Could she betray Rafe, to save her father and herself from this drudging life? Dear Lord. She was actually considering it.

Perhaps the boy did owe her a good deal. Yet she'd chosen to help. All her life she'd heard folks say Negroes, especially slaves, were simple, childish brutes. Mere dumb property. But she knew now Rafe was none of those things, so she couldn't convince herself he was no more a thinking creature than a draft horse or a milk cow. Which must mean . . . that there were others like him, still enslaved and worked like animals, beaten, too. So how could she even accept the idea of slavery ever again?

Her head began to hurt, and she put her hands on both sides and squeezed to stop the throbbing. "Nothing I can do," she muttered. "Nothing at all."

She might have to watch her father marry Mrs. Ben. But she'd never call that woman "mother." Nor would she stand by as Ephraim was slaughtered and cooked for the wedding feast! For Mrs. Ben's "special guest" was most likely the preacher from the mainland.

Molly sat up suddenly. To get the reverend here in time, the widow would've had to send word to him a while back. He was not brought out all this way on a whim, a drop of the hat. So she'd planned this wedding, had known it would happen long ago. . . .

Molly squeezed Ephraim until he struggled in alarm. "I'll stop it," she whispered to the dark, her breath a pale puff of fog in the cold attic. "Somehow, this plan of hers will not come to pass."

14

THE TROUBLE WITH BOATS

RAFE LAY AWAKE IN THE DARK after Molly Savage left. He still trusted the girl, though not enough to tell his true situation. Yes, she seemed friendly, even sympathetic, but he couldn't let his guard down. The color of her skin was enough reason. What would this white girl do once she knew he'd lied?

As the night dragged, he worried on and on, his mind churning out black thoughts. Why had Molly acted so strange? What had it meant, the way she'd run away up the path, when he'd only said . . .

Maybe she'd changed her mind, and was giving him away that very moment to someone on the island.

He sat up suddenly, sweating, though cold air was blowing through the entrance to the cellar. Scrambled up, and rushed outside. The moon was under a cloud. No stars pricked the great black tablecloth of sky. He couldn't go back inside; he felt trapped in there. So he began walking quickly, toward the water. He'd seen the boats there.

It was low tide. At water's edge, Rafe stood with cold lapping at his bare feet until they prickled, then went numb. He stared out over the endless stretch of water where the *Tyger* had perished. If this was the east end of the island, then to the right, that was the ocean. On the other side of it lay a country called England. He'd seen maps in the nursery schoolroom, had pored over them in secret while Will took his naps. But how to get from here to there? He turned away abruptly and began walking along in the shallow water. That way, he'd leave no telltale footprints. Such tricks had become natural, by then.

After a while the sound of the lapping waves receded. More grass and reeds and humps of ever-present myrtle bushes thrust out of the damp sticky mud, and he had to move up, out of the water.

And just ahead, in a cleared patch of marsh, lay . . . a boat.

Not much of one, though. A rough-hewn sort of dinghy, with a detached, splintered-looking mast and a patched, folded sail. He stepped over the side and into the bottom, then nearly leaped out again in terror, until he realized the slimy wet coil under his feet was a line, not a sleeping snake. He'd learned a little on the *Tyger,* the few days he'd been aboard her. But they'd kept him caulking seams and scraping paint, not manning sails or wheels. They'd had a great brass compass, too, though the captain had seemed to rely more on winds and stars than anything. Any one of the men off that ship could probably sail this pitiful boat with one hand.

Any one but him.

He picked up a line, grabbed up the mast in the other hand, and tried to fit it into a socketlike contraption in the bottom.

He lost his balance, slipped and nearly fell in the marsh, but at last managed to set it in place. But then, when he attempted to raise the sail, the lines snarled. Then the mast fell, striking him a hard blow on the head. He struggled with it again, panting and cursing as if he wrestled a human opponent.

Just as he'd almost got it right again, he heard voices. At least two. One was singing loudly as if the owner had had a drop too much. And both voices, the laughter, the singing, all were coming his way.

In a panic, he wrestled the mast back down to the thwarts with sweating hands, then hastily coiled the line. The sails he only had time to stuff back inside, and hope the owners, if that's who they were, would think the wind had disturbed them. For now he heard the footsteps closing in, crackling through the dry grasses and drier shells. Rafe leaped over the side and ran as fast as he could, hoping the tide would cover his footprints before first light.

When he arrived back at the cellar, gasping and out of breath, he had a terrible pain in his side. He stood for a moment at the entrance, puffing and blowing like a winded horse. Then he threw himself inside the dark hole and huddled there, straining his ears in case more footsteps were coming. . . . Because this time they'd be coming for him.

So it seemed he had no choice. He knew nothing much useful about boats. And couldn't swim to Boston, much less far-off England. He didn't even rightly know just where either place was. Even if he could take a boat, wouldn't its owner raise an alarm? And if he was spotted in it, a stolen craft . . . Or went the wrong way, landed back in slave territory, back at Penland . . .

No. He'd just have to be careful. To sleep with one eye and one ear alert to any trouble. This stinking hole might be tiresome and damp. There were times, more and more often, when he wanted to burst out of it, simply to run around crazily in broad daylight, shouting aloud. To smell something sweet and fresh, something other than the rank gleanings of the Heap.

Still, at the moment it smelled sweeter by far than the big brick house with white trim and broad porch, cleaned top to bottom each day by slaves, scented with lemon oil and lavender sachets. The expensive, handworked, lace curtains might've been brought all the way from France to frame its windows. But any place was better, if it was away from there.

15

A RESTLESS NIGHT
AT THE TAVERN

WHEN MOLLY WOKE, her father was snoring in his bed. It had to be very late, but perhaps just the time to talk seriously to Rafe about leaving. And to find out if she might go along. She slipped carefully from under the covers, leaving the little goat asleep. He loved the warmth, so he wouldn't be going anywhere soon.

No need to dress. She'd left everything on. The trick was to get downstairs without making the stairs creak, or the widow might fly out of her room and swoop down on her. Molly couldn't say she was going to the privy again. Under every bed was a chamber pot for middle-of-the-night use.

So she stepped down slowly, putting her weight on the very edge of each tread, where the stair was least likely to sag or creak. It felt like creeping down a mountain, but at last she reached the first floor, sweat prickling her skin. To her left lay the kitchen; she might as well take some provisions along.

She hacked a chunk of bread from the crusty brown loaf left out for the morning's breakfast, added dried figs, a thick rind of cheese, and wrapped it all in a flour-sack towel. Then she pulled her shawl around her shoulders and concealed the package beneath it.

She grasped the back-door latch with two fingers and prepared to slip out into the dark. But as she lifted the latch there came a creak, as if the house had shifted, turned over in its sleep. She waited and held her breath.

Silence.

Again she moved to slip out into the dark, and again the noise came. This time louder. She heard the distinct creak of the second warped stair. Then footsteps slowly crossing the floor toward the kitchen—toward her. In a panic, she ducked back into the pantry, through the half-open door, and crouched behind a flour barrel.

From there she could see nothing, but heard stealthy footsteps cross the scullery. Then the click of the latch as someone softly, firmly closed the kitchen door.

She waited a moment, to be sure the nightwalker was gone. She drew slow deep breaths to let her hammering heart slow its pounding. It must've been Mrs. Ben, bound for the privy. Or perhaps Pa. But he was a big man who never walked lightly. Well, she'd better hurry and make her way to Rafe before the whole household started walking in its sleep. She poked her head out, saw no one, and stepped across the kitchen floor. As she closed the kitchen door behind her, a cold breeze curled around her ankles and lifted the corners of her shawl. The air was filled with the smell of wood smoke, the faint rustle of unseen creatures in the woods.

She ran tiptoe up the lane, past the lopsided cottage of Doc

Drummond, the shingled, pitch-roofed one of Old Tim the net maker. Past the cold-shriveled geraniums on the porch of little Mrs. Meeker's one-room shanty, and the scrubby but well-hoed garden of Hank Blodgett's wife. All the houses were dark, though a trail of smoke still threaded from Doc's chimney.

She followed the path to the woods, where wind whipped the rustling trees and sent fingers of ice poking through the thin wool of her dress. Then she realized why she was shivering; she'd dropped her shawl somewhere back on the path. Molly hugged the bundle of food to her chest, glad Ephraim was still warming the covers for her return. *I'm a smuggler,* she thought with some satisfaction. *I roam the night, and no one sees. I don't need a shawl. I don't need anything.*

But *smuggler* was just another word for a thief.

She shook her head free of such unwelcome thoughts and hurried on, looking down to avoid snaking roots or fallen branches. The lost-soul moan of the wind said a nor'easter might be on the way. She ran faster, anxious to get the food to Rafe and run back to her safe, somewhat warm room.

As she rounded a bend in the path, she saw something through the overhanging branches of a willow, outlined in silvery moonlight. A dark shape looming. She clapped a hand over her mouth, a bit too late to muffle her gasp. The shadowy figure didn't pause or give any sign of hearing, it simply moved on ahead. And in a patch of moonlight Molly recognized the familiar billow of her father's old army cloak, swaying, whipped by wind off the water.

But that made no sense. He'd been sound asleep in bed when she'd left. Had he somehow raced out the front while she'd been busy in the back, scavenging a meal for Rafe? She didn't see how he could've beaten her down the stairs and out the door. But perhaps it had been he, not the widow, who'd passed by the pantry where she'd hid like a dormouse. Perhaps he'd waked, missed her, and been worried.

But then why walk out so far to look without once calling her name? She started forward again, wondering whether it would be best to let him know she was there, or remain hidden and hope he returned to bed.

She went on quietly as she could, following. Now she might be forced to tell her father about Rafe. She kept his dark silhouette in sight, careful not to lessen the distance between them. As the path curved again, her father stopped. Molly saw him fumble with something, a line tied about a tree. Then she heard a soft whinny.

Up ahead, old Janey was tethered to an oak just off the path.

What in the world! Molly wondered. Taking a moonlight trot? Now that made no earthly sense at all.

And as the dark figure led the horse along, toward the beach, doubts filled her mind. Surely her father wouldn't pull on the lead in such an awkward, jerky way. He knew horses, had handled a good many for General Washington's army during the war. Janey had been his for seventeen years; he'd had her since before Molly had been born. He knew the horse's ways as well as his own and would never get in the way, stumble too close to her feet, or drag on the halter so awkwardly.

Man and horse did not turn toward the Heap, which was good, at least for Rafe's sake. Instead, they followed the path straight on to the beach. Where woods gave way to scrub, then cordgrass and sand, Molly hung back, crouched in the shadows of the trees. The figure pulled a lantern from beneath the flapping cape, lit and hung it from the harness around Janey's neck. Then it turned and slowly led the docile old mare along the shoreline.

As Molly watched their dark shapes move away, she became certain it was not her father after all. The way the figure moved was wrong, and the shoulders were less broad. When the moon emerged the sand gleamed like an opal, dotted here and there with wrack and dark bits of seaweed. But it wasn't until the lantern swung back and forth like a lighted bell that she understood suddenly what was afoot. Then she was terror-struck, clutching the razor-edged beach grass in handfuls, not caring that it cut her hands.

Her father had told other tales besides fairy romances and the high adventures of kings. When she was younger he'd thrilled and sometimes frightened her with sea stories of the infamous cowards called shipwreckers. Some who'd plied their deadly trade as close as the Outer Banks of the Carolinas. Lantern and horse was the very ploy dishonest men used to lead ships onto shoals, for the bobbing light appeared from a distance to rise and fall as if hung on the mast of a ship at safe anchor. Then passing sailors would mistake the killing shoals for a safe harbor.

Once the doomed ships were lured aground, wreckers and their families scavenged, even grew wealthy from the goods that washed ashore. Ocracoke Island to the south sheltered a notorious clan of such villains and was still avoided and feared by sailors.

Her father had said bitterly, "Bad men care nothing for right or wrong, or the lives of crew or passengers they send to the bottom. And if any survived the night," he said, lowering his voice to a whisper, "they did not last the morning."

"Ned," her mother had said reprovingly, when she'd looked in on them. "Don't frighten the child so."

That long-ago night Molly had hidden beneath her covers and begged Pa to let her sleep with a candle lit. He'd looked sorry then and vowed never to tell such grisly tales again. For a long while she'd dreamed of black-haired pirates clothed to look like simple fisherman. But they dragged human beings from the sea instead of fish.

If any ship out tonight saw the light bobbing on Janey's neck, they'd turn trustingly toward it, and then the curved teeth of the Bandy would tear their planks asunder. Run aground on that huge horseshoe of sand and oyster shell, they'd be mired first, then beaten to pieces if the wind was high. The goods they carried would be washed ashore.

As would the people, alive or dead.

So it couldn't be her father out there with Janey. He was good at heart, though he might take a drink too many. But he'd never hurt others in such a cowardly way. Just because he dearly loved a game of dice or cards—

Enough to wager all you had, that dreaded voice whispered back in her mind.

"Not all," she said aloud, wanting to drown it out.

Yes, all he had. Except his daughter. But perhaps next time . . .

She would have to find out for herself. Molly ducked back into the scrubby, wind-twisted pines, ducked under branches and past hanging vines all along the edge of the woods. Snapping twigs as dry as old bones. Panting, feet slipping and sinking in the soft sand. Hoping the nightwalker wouldn't hear her coming over the crash of the waves.

The moon went in again, under cloud cover. Hot tears whipped from her eyes, streaked her face, not all of them made by the stinging salt wind. She darted out onto the beach, the loose wet sand dragging at her feet like a bog. She crept closer, until, had she dared, she could've grasped the hem of the cloak.

"Wait," she said, and touched one arm.

The figure started, gave a muffled cry, and let go of Janey's bridle. The horse whinnied and shied away, splashing in the shallows. The moon edged out and the hood of the cloak fell back. And Molly stared up into the white, startled face of Mrs. Ben.

A scream choked halfway up her throat. She dropped the bundle of food meant for Rafe. Then she turned and ran, panting as if the devil himself had jumped onto Janey's back and galloped close on her heels.

She burst out of the woods, ran around the house to the back, and wrenched the kitchen door open. Pounded up the stairs, heedless now of what racket she made. Got back into bed, and jerked the covers up. Only then did she think to look over at her father's side of the attic, listening for the steady drone of his snore. She heard nothing but the sigh of wind at the shutters, and the usual ticks and creaks of settling wood.

"Pa," she whispered. "We should leave this place."

After a moment, his voice came from across the room. "Stay in bed nights, Moll," he said. "Sometimes . . . things you don't understand . . . they're best left alone."

She heard in his words not concern or anger, but only resignation.

He must know, she thought. *About the wrecking, about Mrs. Ben. And yet he hasn't told a soul.*

"I never thought you were a coward," she whispered back, her voice breaking.

A rustle of covers as he shifted. Sighed deeply. "Now you know it, then," he said. "Weak men need propping up. Otherwise they don't live up to what's expected of them."

What did he mean? Had all his pride died along with Caroline Savage? Molly held still in the dark, waiting for him to say more. When he was silent, she prayed for sleep to come. Turning away, she pressed her face into the thin, prickly, feather pillow. Finally exhaustion sent her into a nightmare world, where dark figures passed up and down, up and down, their long, knobby fingers cupped around glowing, flickering lights.

16

UNINVITED
AND UNEXPECTED

THE SUN SLANTING INTO THE ROOT CELLAR woke Rafe. He'd lain awake most of the night, too worried, too hungry, to sleep. Dozing off only to jerk awake again. So it seemed that just as he'd fallen deeply asleep at last, the first light of dawn roused him. He yawned and stretched, and his stomach growled loudly.

"Quiet, belly. No one's going to feed you for a long time yet."

He looked out cautiously before he left the cellar and made his way to the spring, the same way he did each morning. But this day he was so tired he nearly forgot to glance over toward the beach, to make sure he had no unwelcome company.

Halfway across the clearing he did remember. And when he looked out over the broadwater, he saw it wasn't the flat empty stretch that greeted him most other mornings. He saw that even this early, before the usual fishing dories and log canoes had gone out and turned seaward, a long skiff and two rafts were approaching. Realizing belatedly how exposed he was, Rafe crouched behind a fallen tree, hoping they hadn't been close enough yet to see him.

How odd that they were coming in rather than going out. From what he'd seen, watermen were generally heading out this time of day, not returning. And even in the afternoons, when all the fishing boats returned, none ever put in at the Heap.

A few minutes later, the first craft beached. Only then, when Rafe finally got a good look at the motley sailors dragging it ashore, did a new, sharp fear drive all other worries from his mind. The sailors who made fast their boats were scruffy, dirty-looking water rats in bedraggled velvet coats, epaulets, tricorn hats. Some were booted, others barefoot. Some wore ragged scarves and torn lace cuffs. But they all carried muskets and powder horns, or cutlasses and knives. These were no watermen at all.

His heart fluttering, beating his ribs like a moth trapped in a lamp chimney, Rafe rose to a crouch in the grass and scrubby bushes. He thought of all the possible things about to happen, of all the people up the lane, just rising to go about their business, thinking this was like any other day. One of them was Molly Savage. But he'd never met the rest. He could return to his hiding place in the cellar with a clear conscience; after all, he was only one boy.

Go back in the cellar, his mind prodded. *There's no help. Nothing you can do.*

These rough-looking men weren't likely to sift through a garbage heap when a sleeping village lay unaware and ripe for plunder. Still, instead of moving toward the cellar hole, and safety, he hesitated another moment, tensed like a deer about to spring away and run for its life.

"The hell with it," said Rafe. He took one last deep breath, then bolted into the trees, keeping as low to the ground as he could. Somehow, he had to find Molly Savage. He had to tell her that it had happened just as her friend Francis had predicted after all.

The picaroons had landed.

17

A THIEF IN THE HOUSE

THERE'S A THIEF IN THE HOUSE!" cawed the crows circling Molly in her dream. "A thief, a thief. Everyone downstairs!"

She lunged up from the covers with a gasp, feeling she hadn't slept at all. But the faint pinkish glow of just-breaking dawn showed it was indeed time to rise. Such a strange dream, she thought.

"*Everyone* means you, too, girl!" Mrs. Ben flung her voice like a slap up the stairwell, and Molly jumped, then scrambled from bed. She pushed Ephraim under the quilt again, bribing him with some crumbs of corn pone left in her pocket. She was still wearing her clothes from the night before, though her boots, coated with sand, lay beside the bed. Then she recalled why, and felt even more afraid. What would the widow do? Molly could threaten to tell someone, but who would take her word over Mrs. Ben's? Perhaps not even her father, now. He wouldn't want bad things said about his soon-to-be wife.

On his side of the attic, Pa sat up, yawned, and began pulling on his shirt. He didn't look over at her, and she wondered if he'd slept at all. For a moment she wanted to go to him, to put her arms around him and hear him say all would turn out fine.

Well, it was too late for that. She was no longer little, with a child's easily cured fears. Besides, he didn't look as if he thought all *would* be well, either.

The widow was shouting again. Without another glance at her father, Molly clattered down the stairs.

She slowed as she reached the last few steps. Mrs. Ben waited at the bottom, face pale and pinched. *I know something that might harm her,* Molly thought. *She must truly hate me now.* Yet with no sheriff or bailiff on the island, there was no law she could go to with an accusation. Besides, she had no proof the widow had been out at the water before. And her father wouldn't want to hear of Mrs. Ben's late wanderings. Or . . . then a different thought struck her. Had he been referring only to the nights when Molly herself had slipped away to bring food to Rafe?

"About time you got down here," snapped Mrs. Ben, tapping her foot at the bottom of the stairs.

Molly heard her father's slower, heavier footsteps descending behind her.

"Yes'm," said Molly, looking at the toes of her boots so the widow wouldn't know she was afraid. "I heard you call."

"Did you, now?" said the widow softly. "Then you know what I want. Hand it over." She thrust out a hand.

"But I . . . what?" Mrs. Ben must have discovered food was missing from the pantry. Then Molly would have to say she'd eaten it all herself. And that she couldn't be expected to spit it back into the woman's outstretched hand.

"You know what I'm talking about, girl. The brooch! Give it back and I'll consider not calling the sheriff."

Bewildered, Molly wanted to spit back some sharp reply. *I'm no thief,* she started to protest. Of course, that wasn't entirely true, was it? She felt her face heating up as she opened her mouth, and prayed to come up with a good answer. For she had no idea what brooch the woman was talking about.

Just then her father reached the bottom of the stairs and broke in. "What's this noise all about?"

Molly was surprised that he actually sounded angry, speaking up to the widow as if she were not in charge of everything, after all.

"Your girl here—"

"Her name is Molly," said Ned Savage.

Mrs. Ben pursed her mouth like a drawstring pouch. "Your . . . *Molly* stole a piece of my jewelry last night. A silver brooch that held a lock of dear, departed Mr. Ben's hair."

Molly despaired then. What matter if she was innocent? She could see how it all would look. Her father knew she'd been out of bed the night before. But surely he wouldn't believe she'd do such a thing!

The widow seemed to sense his hesitation, and pressed on. "So, you know the little sneak was up and about last night." She rounded on Molly. "Do you deny it? No, I thought not. As I was preparing for bed, I found the pin was missing. Heard someone downstairs, moving stealthy-like, going outside. I followed. And found this wretched girl hiding her stolen goods on the beach!"

"That's not right," Molly cried. "She's the one who went out first. I was following *her!*"

The widow cut her off. "I meant to be generous, since she's your daughter, Mr. Savage. But if she has no true notion of right and wrong, perhaps I should send for the sheriff after all. The law can teach her a much-needed lesson."

Molly's hands trembled until she clasped them together in front of her. She'd heard about the jail in Eastville. Nothing to eat but moldy bread and cold bricks of porridge. People died of the chill there, winters, coughing their lives away. Perhaps she'd be clapped in the stocks to be jeered at by strangers. Or whipped at the post. Sometimes thieves were even branded, like cattle.

Who would take her word against a wealthy widow who bragged of connections in Norfolk and Williamsburg? She'd end up imprisoned for a crime she hadn't committed.

There was a crack of thunder, and both Molly and the widow flinched. It seemed the weather inside and out was to be stormy. Then the widow grasped her arm, pressing sharp fingernails into the flesh above her elbow. "Ouch," Molly said. "Let go."

Suddenly her father stood between them. He pried the widow's hand off Molly. "Leave her be," he said sharply.

Mrs. Ben's mouth dropped open. "How dare you!"

"I must dare. She's mine. You'd understand if you ever had a child."

"She's a great grown girl, not a child," snapped the widow. "It's time you see that. Perhaps I have none of my own, but I know a girl needs discipline."

Molly noticed the widow's lips trembling, as if the words had somehow hurt her. As if perhaps she'd once wished for a child, or had lost one. With her hair straggling from its pins, face blotched red, Mrs. Ben looked little like the proper widow she played most times. In fact, she looked as if she might soon cry.

"She's my child," he repeated stubbornly. "And if Moll took your brooch, I should make good the loss."

For a moment Molly felt relief, sweet and comforting as a warm blanket, settle about her shoulders . . . until the meaning of her father's words came clear in her head. He hadn't said he believed her innocent. Only that he should make good the loss.

The widow's lips worked as if she were chewing bitter herbs, until she dragged out a reluctant reply. "Very well, Mr. Savage." Then she glared at Molly as if to say: *Now we are even. Tell on me if you dare, miss.*

But what the widow thought just then mattered little to Molly. Instead she heard the words, over and over, as if a child was repeating them in her ear. *He doesn't believe me. He believes Mrs. Ben. He doesn't believe me, he believes her.*

So now she knew. It would do no good to tell him of the widow's secret doings on the beach, of her walk with Janey, and of the wrecking light. No good to urge him to bring a complaint to the magistrate.

As Mrs. Ben rushed away, her father took Molly's arm gently. Led her to a pub table and settled her in a chair. "Now, daughter," he said. "I know you want to pay off our debt and be shut of worries. But thievery's no way to go about it."

"But, Pa," she said, struggling not to cry. "You know I

wouldn't do such a thing." How galling it was to be nearly a woman, but still treated like a child by everyone. Mrs. Ben was grown, and rich.

Well, she'd just have to make him believe her.

"It wasn't at all like that. She must have the brooch, probably hid it somewhere. I followed her to the woods. She's the one who's a thief. I won't let you marry her—"

"You may be a big girl, but you'll not talk back to me, Molly Savage, as you did last night. As you are now! I've made up my mind to wed. The woman means not to be harsh, only to make you do what's right. And it seems you're up and about nights, doing Lord knows what."

"I didn't steal any . . . any brooch."

He folded his arms. "Then tell me—what is afoot? You know, we're lucky. A harder woman could have us both thrown into jail, or locked us in the poorhouse across the way."

Molly jumped up, and her chair crashed over behind her. "But she's a liar!"

Her father got up, too. And for the second time in less than a day, he drew back his hand as if to strike her.

"So a fist will be the answer I get from now on?" she said.

A startled, shamed look crossed his face. He dropped the hand to his side as if it didn't belong to him. But before he could say whatever it was, threat or apology, the front door of the tavern crashed open. They both turned to look. A figure was silhouetted on the threshold. With the dim, storm-gray light behind him, at first she wasn't sure. But when he stepped inside, she saw it was the boy, soaked and dripping rainwater.

"Rafe!" she gasped. Her father glanced sharply from the figure in the doorway back to Molly.

What in the world was the boy doing? Perhaps hunger or solitude had driven him crazy, and he'd come staggering out like a mad thing. Now she'd never get him off the island. Someone would take him and sell him into slavery.

"Who's there?" Mrs. Ben called from the kitchen. She must've heard the door crash open. Or else she'd been listening all along.

Before Molly could think of an explanation, Rafe darted inside and slammed the door. Rain streamed from his hair and clothes. His breath came hoarse and ragged, as if he'd run full-out all the way from the Heap. But most worrisome of all, his eyes were wide with fear.

"Who are you, boy?" demanded her father.

"Wipe your feet," snapped Mrs. Ben. "Look at the mess you're making."

But when he spoke, all three of them were shocked to silence. "Pirates," he gasped. "They've come ashore. Coming this way!"

Francis had been right, Molly thought. Makeele was back.

"Picaroons, no doubt," said her father. He pushed Rafe aside and started to slide the wooden bar across the door. Then he seemed to think better of it. "Get me the musket. Bolt every door and window but this one," he ordered. "I'll go warn the others."

It was odd, but he looked almost eager. As if he'd welcome a chance to do battle with something solid and simple as a pirate. Something he understood better than his daughter or the widow.

Molly heard him shouting warnings outside, running down the lane and pounding on doors. Soon a commotion of voices rose in the tiny village.

"Makeele, Lord's mercy!" cried Mrs. Ben, turning white as the tablecloth she clutched in her arms. "See to the shutters. This instant!" She turned and ran back to the kitchen.

Molly hurried to do just that, for she knew about pica-roons. They'd steal anything they could carry off, then set fire to houses and outbuildings. They didn't mind hurting people, kidnapping them, or even . . . she knew she ought to move, to leap about bolting windows and shutters, getting the guns as Pa had said. Yet she stood frozen as a winter sapling. What would the pirates do to them? Make Rafe and her father join up, kill them if they refused? And what would they do with a girl like her, who had no money or jewels to take?

Her father's shout, loud in her ear, jolted her back. "Moll! Get my musket and makings. And t'other guns, too. Hop to it, now!"

She looked around wildly, feeling she'd just set foot in the tavern for the first time. For an instant, nothing looked famil-iar. Kegs, chairs, tables—all seemed far away, as if she were peering at them from a great distance.

Her father grabbed her and shook her hard. That rough re-minder brought her back. "Yes, Pa," she gasped, and started in the direction of the storeroom, where the guns lay, oiled and wrapped in felt against the salt air. She grazed her hip on the corner of a table, but even the sharp bruising pain of it seemed far away.

Before she'd gotten across the room, he grabbed her arm again and jerked her back.

"Tell me, short and sweet," he said, keeping his voice low. "Who's the nigra boy? You knew his name."

She felt too frightened to withhold the truth anymore. Yet . . . she looked over at Rafe, who struggled to bolt a shutter that had warped in the heavy rains of last spring. How much could she tell and not doom him?

"He's from . . . from across the water. I've seen him . . . I've talked to him before."

"You mean he's a slave?"

"No!" Molly cried. "I didn't say that."

He wasn't even listening to her! Molly wanted to cover her ears, to make them all stop shouting at once. "No, no, but you see, the morning after the wreck, I—" She stopped, unsure how much to say.

Her father frowned at her, then over at Rafe. "But you knew the boy was here, on the island. For how long?"

"He's not a slave," she cried. "He's free. But we were both afeared that—"

"Ah, never mind all that now," said her father suddenly. She could see he didn't believe her. He turned back to Rafe. "Can you shoot, boy?"

"A bit, yes, sir." But he looked uncertain.

"Well, for the love of God, girl. Go get the guns, then."

Molly's father pushed her. She lifted her skirts and stumbled into a run.

When she returned, lugging a musket under each arm, Mrs. Ben was still nowhere to be seen. *Hiding,* Molly thought, *as we all no doubt should be.* She ran back to the kitchen, latching the shutter on the window there. Only a very small pirate indeed could climb through, but she was taking no chances.

Then, as she slammed down the heavy plank that barred the back door, she recalled the livestock. Ephraim was still up in the attic, but the others . . . she shoved the plank up again, sweating fingers slipping, splinters tearing her palms. She ran out, her father shouting something behind her.

She raced into the stable. "Come on, Miranda," she gasped. But the placid, heavy-bellied nanny only blinked, big golden eyes unperturbed, and resumed chewing her cud.

"Oh, drat you!" cried Molly. "Why can't you move?"

She grabbed Janey's halter and led the mare toward the kitchen door, hoping Miranda would follow.

When she entered with the horse, Molly was glad Mrs. Ben was out of sight. Imagine what the widow would say about barn animals clomping around on her clean floors. She imagined the widow trying to sweep up a mess even as pirates raided the house, and laughed. But the sound was closer to a sob.

Well, I'm the one who has to clean up in any case, she thought, running back to slam and bar the back door again. Miranda's stall door was open, so at least the she-goat could get out if picaroons set the stable on fire.

She tied Janey to a post beneath a beam. The great dappled horse stood calmly in the kitchen, as if she lived there. This might've seemed funny if Molly hadn't been scared out of her wits. Worried the baby goat would tumble down the stairs, she ran up to the attic, then carried Ephraim down. He bleated when Janey nuzzled his head. She shut the half door between kitchen and tavern room so the little goat wouldn't scramble after her.

"What should I do now, Pa?" she asked, panting.

Her father looked grim. "They won't burn the place down around our ears. At least, not until they're sure they can't get in to haul off valuables. But after that—"

He paused to jam a load of powder down the barrel.

"They'll take everything, won't they?"

"If they can. But we won't let them."

She thought again of Miranda. Too late. Already she heard wild cries—howls and yodels and shrieks. Then a thunderous clap from a musket. The loaded gun her father thrust at her felt a good deal heavier than it looked. With shaking hands she passed it over to Rafe. The boy raised it, sighting unsurely down the barrel. Even if he didn't know what to do with it, he looked calm. But then she supposed he'd had opportunities to practice that look.

She heard voices raised outside, then a dull thud. Perhaps a musket ball hitting the tabby wall.

Her father had poked his gun's muzzle through the loop-hole in the shutters. He pulled the trigger, and she heard a fizz, then a loud explosion, smelled the sulfurous stench of burnt powder. He jerked the musket back and reloaded, hands flying back and forth over the pan, powder bag dangling from his teeth. She'd never seen this look on his face before, fierce and wild and determined. He raised the newly primed musket, shoved it out the window, and fired again, teeth bared in a snarl. Perhaps he was imagining brigades of redcoats advancing.

But on the other side of the room, Rafe hadn't fired a shot since she'd handed him the second gun. She crawled across the floor to him. Even in the gloom of the shuttered room she could see that, Spanish blood or no, he was terrified.

She shook his shoulder. "Why don't you shoot?"

"I never . . . I don't know how." He shook his head, looking ashamed.

That old musket . . . it was the one her father had once or twice let her fire in the woods. That'd been years ago, but since then she'd seen him load and fire it many times, at small game. She grabbed the gun, then rose to her knees and poked the barrel out a chink in the shutter. A blur of motion to the left, by the big oak tree. Molly swung that way, closed her eyes, and squeezed the trigger. Then jerked the gun inside, to struggle with powder pouch and shot.

"Help me, it's taking too long," she cried. And Rafe, looking relieved and less shamefaced, grabbed the pouch, loosened the strings, and poured powder. Most of it went into the barrel. She rammed in the wad so quickly the rod nearly pinched off the end of his fingers.

"You're no sailor," she whispered.

He looked away. "No. But my father owns two hundred slaves. Including me."

She stared a moment, but there was no time to gape, to ask questions. She thrust the gun out again and watched for movement. From the Drummonds' cottage across the way, she saw a flash of fire. The others must have holed up in there, for his was the sturdiest house. They were shooting at the pirates, too. She spotted a flirt of white by the stable and fired. This time she didn't shut her eyes. The recoil kicked her shoulder.

Rafe grabbed the gun, and they began the loading process all over again. This time she poured the powder, black and gritty as sooty sand. "So your father's a white man. On a farm?" she whispered.

"A plantation, up Edenton way." Rafe's voice was bitter. "I learned those stories listening to his white son's lessons, sneaking in to read his books."

"But how'd you come to be on a ship?"

"When I ran off, I made it through the woods to the wharves. Meant to pretend to be a ship's boy, but saw no one like me aboard any ships . . . except some Africans being off-loaded from a slaver. I spotted the *Tyger*, stowed away."

Molly wanted to ask a thousand things more, but this wasn't the time. His confession only confirmed what she'd tried to ignore since she'd found him on the beach—that they were both in great trouble. But for the moment, they must only shoot and load, shoot and load.

She peered out a crack in the shutter and saw clearly for the first time the ragged band who threatened them. They darted from tree to tree, howling and shouting curses, trying to rush the tavern, then to surround Doc's cottage. These men wore strange odds and ends—uniform pants, ragged red British army jackets, the homespun gray-brown woolens of farmers. They looked so dirty they must've rubbed charcoal on their black-streaked faces. Some were armed, others weren't. Most were barefoot. This motley dress might've seemed comical, except for the savage looks on their faces, their bared teeth and blood-chilling cries.

One of them, a big ugly man with a scarred face and a bushy black beard, leveled a gun at the tavern. His shot smashed through the shutters right over her head. Molly screamed as fragments of wood showered them. She wasn't hurt, so Rafe took the gun and reloaded as she pulled long splinters from her hair.

When she glanced over, her father was still shooting, loading, shooting. *Pa could use help, too,* she thought. *And where is Mrs. Ben, why isn't she fighting with us?* Molly didn't feel like dying to protect something no longer even theirs. Perhaps instead of risking their lives, they should've just run. Let the pirates have it all.

But then her father shouted and staggered back, clutching his shoulder. His musket clattered to the planks, and he leaned against the wall, face twisted with pain. Through his clenched fingers, thin ribbons of blood soaked his powder-smudged shirt.

"Pa!" Molly thrust the gun at Rafe, not waiting to see if he caught it. She helped her father slide down the wall until he sat propped against it. The bullet had passed clean through his upper arm. She pulled his shirt away and pressed the hem of her skirt to the wound. For a moment she saw a ragged hole, then pulsing blood covered it again and ran down his arm. His sleeve was already soaked red.

She grabbed a napkin and tied it tight around his shoulder, under his arm. The flow slackened but didn't stop.

He grimaced and gritted his teeth. "Tighter."

She pulled the knot snug as he winced. His face was pale. "A one-armed man can only load, Molly girl. You take the musket."

"All right, Pa." She held the gun steady as he poured powder one-handed.

"Where has Lucinda got to?" he asked.

Molly frowned. "Who?"

"That'd be Mrs. Pruitt," he said. "The widow."

Lucinda. She didn't like it much that her father was on first-name terms with Mrs. Ben. Annoyance made her blurt out, "Perhaps she's disguised herself as a jar of preserves in the pantry."

He smiled, one corner of his mouth lifting. "You've a quick wit, Moll. But you don't forgive, do you?"

She took the musket and poked the barrel out, this time from a side window. As she scanned the yard through the loophole, she saw a fat bald pirate driving Miranda across the space between inn and barn. The goat bleated and sidestepped, but the pirate whipped her with a fallen branch. *He has no right to take her,* Molly thought bitterly. She steadied the gun. Just before she pulled the trigger, she recalled the runaway slave killed by Hank Blodgett, when it turned out the man had only been stealing a chicken.

Did she have the right to kill a man for the loss of a goat? She hesitated, then aimed lower and pulled the trigger. The fat man grabbed his leg, roared out a string of foul oaths.

He staggered off, clutching his thigh. Miranda had disappeared. As another pirate came around the corner, she heard a shot. Rafe had hit something, too, she guessed, hearing more yelps and howls. The new man clutched his side, then turned and ran back into the trees, moth-eaten hat forgotten on the ground of the inn yard. Only one pirate was still in view, but before she could shoot again, he ran up and threw a burning torch at the house.

Pa said they'd burn us out, she thought, suddenly panic-stricken. But the flaming torch fell short, lay sizzling in the yard in the rain. Thank the Lord for the weather. She repented of ever cursing the frequent rains they'd had this season, when she'd had to do laundry indoors or slog through a downpour to the Heap.

Miranda reappeared, pursued by the black-bearded pica-roon. He dove at her, and two more pirates came out of the bushes to grab the rope knotted around the goat's neck. One led her off into the smoke thrown off by the guttering torch.

A burst of firing from Doc Drummond's cottage felled one picaroon, then another. With much shouting, the picaroons retreated into the woods.

The silence that followed seemed miraculous. Molly and Rafe reloaded anyway, and waited. After a half hour or so of peace, Hank and Doc emerged from the Drummond cottage. Soon the whole village was in the lane, checking damage to homes, counting livestock. Molly set down the cooling musket and knelt again to tend to her father's wound.

Mrs. Ben reappeared, too, from a hiding place behind the bar. "I was busy latching windows when the shooting began. Are they gone?"

"So it seems," said Ned Savage through gritted teeth.

"God's mercy, your poor shoulder! Though we got off lighter than I expected," said the widow. "But a horse in the kitchen is going too far." She glanced at Molly. "Tend to your father, then that floor, girl."

Then she pointed at Rafe. "What shall we do with the darky boy?" she said rudely, as if he were a piece of furniture and had no ears. "I won't have a runaway slave on the place. That's harboring fugitives."

Molly was about to reply, but then her father surprised her. "Calm yourself, dear Mrs. Pruitt. Turns out the boy is . . . only one of Captain Arnold's slaves from Sweetbriar, across the water. His master asked him to pick up some fish I salted last week. Boy's had bad luck, though, coming this day. Doubtless the pirates have stolen his skiff. He'll be stranded till we get word to Sweetbriar. Don't fret yourself. He can sleep in the stable."

Molly glanced at her father in amazement. What a smooth story he'd just told. And what did it actually mean—did he approve now of her hiding Rafe?

Mrs. Ben looked doubtful. But she was a great respecter of

wealth, and Captain Arnold was a very rich man. "Well, then. He'd better not eat too much in the way of victuals, or his master will owe plenty," she muttered as she turned back to the kitchen.

"At least it's a step up from the Heap," Molly whispered to Rafe.

Mrs. Ben turned back long enough to announce, "I'm going to assess the damage." Then she disappeared into the back.

"Moll, go find out whether anyone else is wounded," said her father. "I'll be fine here for a bit."

Rafe lifted the plank barring the front door, and she ventured out. The first thing she saw was Doc, bending in the lessening drizzle over the still body of Jamie Keller, father of the dreaded twins. The two boys clung to their mother, who was sobbing. So poor brave Jamie had been killed. But not far off lay the bodies of three dead picaroons as well.

Farther down the way Hank was already trading lies with Tim the net maker about the big picaroon that got away. And Mrs. Blodgett was muttering curses as she held up her skirts to stomp out a smoldering patch in her front garden. Their daughter Priscilla rocked her tiny baby in one arm and loudly lamented the shot holes in their good front-room curtains. Tiny Widow Meeker, gray curls slithering from pins, white cap askew, was hobbling around her front garden trying to round up the laying hens, which the pirates had set loose.

"Poor Jamie. A good sort, but what a temper. He charged on out and scared 'em off afore too much damage was done to the rest of us," Doc told Molly, when she came back up the lane. He kicked at the thrown firebrand, now just a charred, sodden stick in the lessening drizzle. "We been right lucky, no question."

"So *you* say. But they'll be back," muttered Hank darkly. "They allus come back."

"Then we'd best have a tot right now," Doc insisted, brightening a bit. "Build up our blood, like."

Hank nodded vigorously. "Aye. To Jamie, rest him."

"You must check on Pa when you do," said Molly anxiously. "He's been hurt as well."

Doc nodded, then turned back to direct the men moving Jamie Keller's body into his cottage. The Widow Keller followed, supported on both sides by women from the village.

Mrs. Ben huffed out into the taproom as Molly was setting up ales for Doc and Hank. "They took my goat," the widow said accusingly.

Molly nearly dropped the mug. She'd forgotten about Miranda. Soon the dirty pirates would be feasting on the poor creature.

"I hold you responsible." Mrs. Ben shook a finger at Molly. "It'll come out of your wages, no mistake."

"My what?"

"You should've looked sharp and brought the nanny inside as well," Mrs. Ben continued. "Now I must trouble to find a new milk goat. Yes, I think you ought to pay for it."

"God's nightshirt!" shouted Ned Savage from the corner.

Mrs. Ben and Molly both fell silent and looked over in astonishment.

"What pay?" he said. "What've you waged the girl, or me, for that matter? Money here is dealt out by one hand and scooped up with the other, before we can sniff the copper. Picaroons stole that goat; Molly didn't leave it out on the beach to wash away. She was defending your precious skin while you were hiding in the cabbages and ales."

"Well, but . . . there's still the matter of the m-missing brooch," Mrs. Ben stammered. Her hands fluttered. She looked, for the first time Molly could recall, uncertain.

"As for that, look about, woman," said Ned. "Perhaps you've misplaced it on your own. Ah, most like it'll turn up, Lucinda," he said, a bit softer.

The widow gaped, but he only stared back, pale and determined. Looking more and more like a homecoming soldier with his bandaged shoulder and soot-streaked face. Something about this must've been both daunting and attractive. For after a shocked moment, Mrs. Ben bustled up to exclaim over his wound, clucking like a worried hen. Then she turned on her heel and went back into the kitchen, vowing to heat up a posset of milk and honey curdled with wine that would heal him in no time.

Molly was amazed. As far as she could recall, no one had ever gotten the last word with Mrs. Ben Pruitt—not even Mr. Pruitt, when he was alive. Yet her father had done so twice in one day.

Without thinking, she bent to hug him. But when she did, he cried out in pain. "Oh, sorry, Pa. Here, let me help you." She got him into a chair. When she stepped back she saw her dress was smeared with his blood.

Doc Drummond came in, accompanied by Hank Blodgett.

"Doc, at last," Molly cried as her father slowly slid from the chair to the floor, unconscious. "Go get your root bag, and be quick!"

As she climbed the stairs carefully balancing a pot of boiling water, Molly smelled the unmistakable odors that always meant Doc Drummond was at work. Rum, stale sweat, green herbs, and horse salve. When she entered the guest room, the first thing she noticed was her father's arm hanging limp over the side of the bed. Mrs. Ben was fussing with a basin, muttering about ruined sheets. But she kept her voice down, and the complaints seemed halfhearted. That scared Molly the most. If even Mrs. Ben was worried . . .

"Pa," she said, rushing over, almost spilling hot water on Doc. "Will he be all right?"

Drummond stood. Gathered his things, stuffing tongs and knives and bandages and cloth packets of herbs in his stained pouch. "Aye, seems so. Gave him a sleeping draft, Moll. I declare, he's hot as a fired pistol. Though the breakbone tea I dosed him with ought to fix that."

"Horse piss," groaned her father. "Old goat poisoned me."

"But if the herbs don't work?" she asked in a low voice, taking up a clean rag, pouring fresh hot water in the basin. She knelt and wiped her father's face. It shone with sweat in the flickering light of the two candles, one their old end-of-the-month stub, the other full size. The widow must indeed be feeling generous . . . or guilty.

Or could it be she truly cared for Ned Savage, despite the way she talked?

Her father muttered something she couldn't make out. He struck out peevishly when she touched the damp cloth to his forehead.

"Then the Lord must step in," said Drummond. "Wound in his shoulder looks not so good, but I seen worse. Now, where's that toddy?" Doc lumbered off toward the stairs. His boots clumped slowly down to the taproom. But even in the dim light, Molly had seen the glitter of tears in his eyes. Doc meant well. But could his potions save her dad?

By early the next day the fever had barely gone down, though her father opened his eyes once and looked at her. Then he slept. By evening it'd risen again, and as she watched him sweat and mutter in his sleep, she knew he might need a real doctor. If so, she'd get one. Somehow. She wiped his face dry again, tucked the blanket around him.

Then she went down the stairs to find Rafe. To explain to him what he must do to help her—if Ned Savage took a turn for the worse. The boy owed her that much.

18

UP FROM THE HEAP

MOLLY NO LONGER HAD TO SNEAK OUT to the Heap to feed Rafe, because now he was assumed by all to be a slave boy from across the water, one the villagers wouldn't be that surprised to see among them—at least for the moment. Rafe had moved into the stable next to the tavern. He slept in the straw with the orphaned baby goat, who was safe, too, for the moment. Since the pirates had also made off with the chickens, Mrs. Ben had declared she wouldn't part with two goats in one week. Not even for a wedding feast. Besides, Mr. Savage was too ill for marriage at the moment.

"We're low on meat," the widow said. She gave Rafe a miserly handful of shot and orders to go out and bag some black duck in the marsh.

The first night he'd stepped inside the stable, he'd simply stood there a moment, reveling in the relief he felt. Marveling he no longer had to hide in a hole in the ground. This must be what it was like to be free, to have your comings and goings taken for granted. Mrs. Ben had given him a threadbare saddle blanket to bed down on. He'd taken it with no complaint, but later Molly had slipped down to hand him a quilt off her own bed.

"You came to warn us, risked yourself. And helped fight off a pack of bloody pirates," she said. "No one should treat you like a beggar come whining for a handout, not even Mrs. Ben."

Rafe had taken the quilt with thanks, but only shrugged in reply. No way he saw to make her understand this stable, this very pile of straw, was preferable to his luxurious old life. He sat and began petting Ephraim, as the girl pulled the lower half of the door shut behind her and set the lantern down a good distance from the straw.

"Sorry you must sleep out here," she said, looking around.

"Oh, but I'm glad for it," he said at last. "Nights out there, I heard such noises. Cricks and cracks, slithering and rustling, as if the woods be filled with snakes and ghosts. Near as bad as the hold of the ship, and its squeaking scurrying rats. I swear, that Heap has haunts walking after dark."

Molly looked skeptical. "I never heard of any such thing."

"Never heard the creaking and splashing of a ghost ship? The voices of her dead crew, come ashore to hunt for treasure?"

"No more wild tales now!" She threw a clump of straw at his head. "Besides, the Heap would be a sorry place to haunt." She pulled her shawl tight around her, and Ephraim rose, bleating, butting his head against the slats of his stall, as if calling for his mother.

"Poor little one," Molly said, glad to turn the talk from dead men and ghosts. She lifted the goat from his pen. "Now he has no ma either." She petted the goat and said without looking at Rafe, "Do you miss your mother?"

He didn't answer, but began to shred a piece of straw. Why did she have to remind him that with each small gain he made came losses? But then it was his mother who'd tried to tell him that was the way of life.

"I do miss mine," she said. "I used to go out and sit by her grave. To try to talk to her still. But it never felt like she was there. Pa tries, but he isn't good at some things. I suppose a father alone isn't enough."

"I wouldn't know," said Rafe, scowling at the shred of straw left in his fingers. The red blustering face of Thomas Pennington rose before him like a fat jack-o'-lantern. Suddenly he blurted out, "When I have a son, he'll know his father. And he won't be sold away."

"Of course not," she said, looking shocked. "I didn't mean . . ." Her hand was out, across the space between them, nearly touching him. She pulled it back again. "But I wish I could talk to my mother just once more."

"What would you ask?" he muttered, pulling the blanket up around his shoulders, not really caring.

"Did she ever feel this loutish and clumsy, tripping over her feet the way I do? And how did she know when she met my father that he was the one to marry? She gave up being a teacher to come live out here. Oh, and—"

"Hush." Rafe held up a hand to quiet her. "Hear that?"

"What, that thump? The kitchen door, perhaps." But she kept silent. Soft footsteps went from tavern to lane, as if someone were walking out secretly and wished not to be seen or heard. The girl rose quickly and went to the half-open door, looking out. Rafe got up and came to stand beside her.

Someone was walking up the lane, passing the Drummonds' cottage toward the woods, carrying a shuttered lantern. A tall, darkly swathed figure.

"The widow's cape," she whispered. "The blue wool trimmed with braid."

He wondered why Molly cared, why she sounded relieved.

"It's Mrs. Ben." She drew back. "Everyone else in the village most likely is abed."

"Where does she go at this hour?" Rafe asked.

"A few nights ago I followed her." She told him how she'd surprised Mrs. Ben on the beach. "Even though she seems a bit softer these days, I don't trust the woman. Nor should you," she advised. "She'd sell you for a pittance—me, too, if the law allowed."

"But you really think she's out to wreck a ship?"

"I don't know. Perhaps she was the cause of the *Tyger*'s wreck," said Molly. "What else could she be out on the beach for? She doesn't have Janey along this time. But you saw the lamp."

"Maybe," said Rafe, "she goes to signal with it for some other reason."

Molly snorted. "Signal who—out here? All she need do is walk ten steps and tap on anyone's door."

"It could be those pirates. Suppose they chose this island to hide their treasure."

She scowled at him. "Don't even begin, you. I'm not so foolish as that."

He was surprised then. She seemed to think he'd told the stories to make a fool of her. When he'd only done so to make her like him, to make her help. It hadn't occurred to him that he might have insulted her by it.

"All right. But smugglers," he said slowly, "thieves, and murderers aren't fairy tales. Pirates have to hide their gold, if they get any, so it won't weigh them down. They leave it on islands, mark a map, and come back for it later."

"Don't expect me to think some pirate ever chose Savage Island as his treasure trove." She laughed scornfully. Yet her voice was wistful, as if she longed to believe it.

He stood and pulled Janey's old blanket around his shoulders like a cape.

"Where are you going?"

"To spy on the widow. We could use some gold, both of us."

"You're mad," she said. "It's a fool's errand." But she was already rising, putting Ephraim in his pen, following Rafe out the door.

The wind was bitter off the water. They crouched behind a wind-twisted juniper and watched Mrs. Ben, who stood a ways down the beach. She seemed to be waiting for something, or someone.

"Perhaps she's just wondering what sort of weather there'll be tomorrow," said Molly suddenly. "Brr, it's wicked cold out." She tugged at his blanket. "Come on, I need to check on my father."

Rafe shook his head. "Shh. Look out there."

They squinted into the wind and salt spray. In the distance a long, pale shape rode the waves. As ragged scraps of cloud fled across the face of the moon, Rafe saw it was a longboat. Soon he could make out the men pulling at its oars.

"No waterman from mainland or island would be out so late," Molly whispered.

The bow surged forward, keel grating on sand and broken shells. Two men jumped out into the surging shallows. Other sailors backed the longboat off, taking it out to sea once more. Mrs. Ben hurried to meet them.

They drew back into the shadows, but not so far they couldn't see the odd meeting on the beach. "She must be up to some skulduggery," he said.

"All right, then. Come on." Molly led Rafe farther down, toward the surf, until they were almost exposed. "Over here. A bit closer, we might hear what they say," she whispered.

The wind moaned and whined. Sharp beach grass slapped at their faces.

"It's the next thing to freezing down here," he complained.

"At least it's not summer. We'd get eaten alive by mosquitoes and no-see-ems," Molly whispered.

Finally they could make out a sentence or two of the conversation taking place out on the sand.

". . . anchored out," one man said to Mrs. Ben. Then something about a ship that would lie close.

". . . why I called you here," was part of Mrs. Ben's reply. "The letter . . . after my husband died. In . . . papers." Molly inched closer. Rafe squeezed in between her and a stunted myrtle bush.

One man was stout and blocky, the other tall and thin. The fat one had a thick accent. The tall one slurred his words as if he'd had a pot of ale too many.

"Took your sweet time," said the widow.

"No easy task . . . row . . . in this surf," said the tall one. "A long hard pull . . . from ship. Shoals. Wicked treacherous."

Rafe leaned closer, hoping to catch more of the sense of it. He saw the widow fold her arms. "Well, that's your lookout," she said.

The stout one broke in impatiently. "What of the gold? . . . clue where it's hid?"

Gold again, thought Rafe in surprise. *Maybe there is something buried here.*

The wind lulled a moment, and the widow's next words were easy to make out. "An old list . . . found in a tobacco box mentions a treasure. A strongbox . . . plate, gold coin."

She handed over a fluttering, folded paper. The stout man tried to smooth it out while the wind tugged at the corners, as if trying to tear it away. Both men seemed very interested.

"Hid hereabouts. I'm sure of it," insisted the widow. "Wager Ned Savage knows where."

"We'll take him, make him tell," growled the thin man.

She held up a hand quickly. "No! You must let me find out, in my own way."

19

A MYSTERIOUS
NIGHTTIME MEETING

SO I WAS RIGHT, THOUGHT MOLLY. But that didn't make her feel any better.

Now she knew Mrs. Ben's interest in her father had little to do with love or wanting to be a mother to Molly. The only thing Pa still owned, because everyone had deemed it worthless, was the land, the few miles of sand that made up Savage Island. And like anyone who'd heard tales of sudden riches, Molly knew one thing about treasure. If a hoard came to light, who owned it? The master of the ground it was dug up on.

When goods floated in from the sea, whether jettisoned or washed overboard, or left over after a shipwreck, the finder was the keeper. Everyone on Savage Island knew that only too well. Anyone who lived by the sea had dreamed at one time or other of finding a pirate's treasure or a king's ransom floated in off the tide. She'd never heard of a soul who'd been so fortunate, though. Riches for the taking were naught but a fairy tale.

Or so she'd thought till now. And if there really was gold, where had it come from?

"That's right." The tall man was nodding. "A strongbox.

The man entrusted with the strongbox stopped to bury it here. We don't aim to wait till our whiskers turn gray, madam. And we can't come ashore with all these blasted colonials about and start digging holes everywhere."

"It's here," said the widow, in a placating tone. "Ned Savage's spent his whole life here. His family's owned the sorry sand pile for over a hundred years."

"I says the blackguard's only waiting his chance to make a getaway with it," growled the thin man. Molly looked at his beard and his coat. He looked very much like the black-bearded pirate she'd seen with the others who'd just raided the island.

"So you'll marry him quick, and discover the where-abouts," said the stout one to Mrs. Ben.

The wind picked up, and a gust lifted one side of his cloak. Beneath it he wore a fancy uniform jacket and trousers, plus fine tall boots—nothing like the motley garb of a picaroon. But most troubling, his uniform was royal navy blue. A color as known, as feared and hated, as the lobster-red uniforms of old King George's army.

True, Eastern Shore men and even islanders sometimes wore odds and ends from the war, or even captured enemy uniforms. But this coat was sharp-pressed and unwrinkled, appeared clean and new and complete. Could it be that Mrs. Ben was plotting with the British navy, then, right on Savage Island?

The widow pulled her own cape more tightly about her shoulders against the sudden gust. "We split the gold, half and half. Soon as he's recovered from his wound, he'll need only a jug of rum and a reason to celebrate to drink it. Add the attentions of a loving new wife . . . he'll talk soon enough."

"And a bit of cash should keep him happy enough."

"I say we silence him," said the thin man.

Silence him. The widow and these strangers planned to make her father their mark. Then to kill him!

"No, that's not necessary," said Mrs. Ben quickly, her voice rising. "In any case, who would believe his drunken ramblings?"

The two men seemed to be arguing about something. Then the stout one said, "I agree, better with no witnesses. Now, we'll need a priest to marry you . . . but a captain don't perform the ceremony ashore, and this isn't the territory of the Crown."

"A murder will set the law on us," Mrs. Ben protested. "A murder will draw attention—"

"Well, I like it not," snapped the lean man gruffly. His odd accent Molly found part local, yet antiquated. The man wore a shabby frock coat and patched knee britches. But his threatening, spraddle-legged stance, the bullying thrust of his jaw, was frightening. "Aye, you're still the slippery one, Lucinda Makeele," he went on. "It's your misfortune I caught you out. By rights you be my lawful wife still. And I mislike to be cheated."

The widow turned away from them suddenly. Her face looked very white even in the gloom. Molly thought she was wringing her hands.

"Lucinda Makeele," whispered Molly. Was that the widow's full, true name? And she was married to that dangerous-looking man. He had to be the picaroon Wayland Makeele—and he had tried to burn the inn! But if the widow was married to him, then—

"We've no time for this," the other one interrupted, the brass buttons on his uniform winking in the moonlight. "Why *not* just kill this Savage fellow? Dragging more souls in cuts the profit."

"Do you take me for a fool?" said Mrs. Ben quickly, scornfully. Perhaps this bluster sounded like anger to these men, but Molly, all too familiar with the widow's moods, heard the uncertainty in her voice. "It's a small place, we live in each other's pockets. I can't hide a dead husband, the second in a row! After the wedding, he won't bother you."

"No. I've a better plan," said Makeele. "My friend here will press him. Carry him off to the ship for the king's navy. He'll raise no alarms then. And this country will never see him more."

What was happening? Had the widow nodded in agreement? Molly couldn't see.

"If his family raises a stink?" the stout man objected. "It's only the one girl, you said. Perhaps we must silence her as well."

"No, no," Mrs. Ben stammered quickly. "Don't bother. She's lazy as a pig, and homely in the bargain. She'll drudge her days away in some tavern. Ned Savage is known to drink and wager all on the turn of a card. I'll take care of the rest."

"Aye, you'd know much of sham weddings," snarled the tall man suddenly, and grabbed Mrs. Ben's arm. "You hornswoggled that old stoat, Pruitt, right enough. Failed to mention the small matter of me. Your *first* lawfully wed husband."

"Turn me loose, you fool," said the widow, though her voice was shaking. Still Molly recognized the tone. It was the one the widow put on when some disaster threatened, and she must take charge and break a few heads. Molly had heard it before, when there was fighting in the tavern.

Then Makeele, who towered over the tall widow, slapped her. She staggered back a step. He turned his head, spat on the sand. He gave her arm a last rough shake, but at last let her go. "Once a grubbing street urchin, always one," he snarled.

Mrs. Ben brushed at her sleeve with trembling fingers as if to be rid of a spiderweb. "A woman must do what she can to survive. You were no great bargain either, Mr. Makeele. Leaving me to face the law after you escaped the jail."

Molly shook her head. So Makeele was the widow's Norfolk and Williamsburg connection, the one she sometimes vaguely mentioned to impress guests at the tavern. Yet she'd seemed so afraid when the picaroons had attacked. But then perhaps she did fear Makeele *because* she knew him so well.

Mrs. Ben said, "And this part of the bargain you must agree to, Mr. Makeele. That when we have this treasure, we shall be shed of each other for good."

The widow stood with folded arms, back straight, glaring right back at the glowering men. Molly felt admiration for her nerve, despite everything. Then, without another word, Mrs.

Ben spun away from the two and stalked back up toward the lane and the village.

The strangers lingered on the windy beach, heads bent in conversation. Molly grabbed Rafe and pulled him up. "Hurry," she gasped. "We must get back before she misses me."

As they dashed breathlessly up the path again, she could just imagine what sort of looks she'd get from the villagers if she made any wild accusations yet. The widow was perhaps the most respected person on the island, aside from Doc Drummond. And at the moment, all Molly cared about was her father, and the terrible fate—being forced to work aboard a British ship—that might be in store for him.

20

RAFE MULLS OVER SOME UNPLEASANT FACTS

RAFE HAD ASKED MOLLY, when they got back to the inn a few steps ahead of Mrs. Ben, if she'd like him to come in to help keep watch over her father.

All the girl had done was shake her head. She'd barely looked at him. "No, thanks. I'll make sure the widow doesn't come near him."

Somehow her refusal felt like a slap. Though she might not have meant it that way. But it was true he was no part of this white family, even less than he'd been a part of the Penningtons'.

So then he could think of nothing more useful to do than return to the stable, scoop up a pile of clean hay to sleep on; that would do for this night. His old bedstead had been narrow, with a thin mattress, not a feather-stuffed tick like young William's. But still, soft cotton stuffed with corn shucks. And real sheets and a coverlet. Worn, but embroidered all along the hem.

Rafe shook his head at himself. Still conjuring old comforts, as if they made up for the rest. He spread the horse blanket over the straw. Now he was sleeping in a barn. A step up from his sandy bed in a root cellar! How the slaves at Penland would laugh at the idea of living in the Heap. He drew Molly's quilt to his chin. How foolish he'd been. Because he could read and write, and lived in the big house, he'd thought himself better, and been punished. Now, lying first in a damp ship's hold, then a dirty hole in the ground, then a horse stall, he had to admit the real reason he'd run away.

Pride.

He couldn't stand the idea of being one of them, linked by the color of his skin, a mere field hand. To hear what the shirtless, shoeless men and boys would say to see him, the master's favorite, brought so low. He'd been proud. Now he was afraid.

He'd never see his mother again. All he could try to do was escape from here and make his way north. But could he do that, from this island?

Rafe lay back in the straw. "So we share a bed now," he said to the little goat, who was blinking at him in the gloom. "Don't know about you. But I slept in worse."

He reached out and scratched Ephraim's bony head.

He still must remember Molly Savage might turn on him every bit as quick as any other white person. Rafe sighed and rubbed his face, suddenly exhausted. He had deserved the laughter of the field hands back at Penland. He was a slave first and last, and always would be. Until he found his way far enough north to be safe.

Tomorrow he could wake to slave hunters. To being chained, whipped, and sold. He was not like Molly Savage or her father, and never would be. He must never let himself forget that. To forget was dangerous. And so, he was sure, were they.

21

A SAD CASE
OF MISTAKEN IDENTITY

WHEN MOLLY GOT BACK UPSTAIRS TO check on her father, he was tossing and turning in the high narrow guest-room bed. The blanket lay puddled on the floor. And his forehead was so hot she jerked her hand back when she touched it. Gently peeling away the cotton rags covering his shoulder, she recalled how he'd cursed when Doc Drummond had poured brandy into the ragged hole the musket ball had left. Mrs. Ben had been generous then; she'd brought up the good Spanish brandy and handed it over to Doc with no complaints. What a curious and complicated woman she was!

But now the skin around the wound was red and puffy. Molly replaced the bandage, deciding she'd best tell Rafe they had to take Pa to a doctor over on the Eastern Shore. Just before she turned to go, her father opened his eyes. He reached out and gripped her arm so hard she winced.

"Ouch, Pa," she said. "Ease up a bit." But she really was relieved he still had that much strength left.

"Nay, love. You'll not leave me again," he muttered, struggling up on one elbow. She gently pushed him down and wiped his forehead with a damp rag.

In his fevered delirium, he must think Molly was someone else. "Anyhow, I'm not leaving you," she said, to soothe him so he'd lie still and not reopen the wound.

"I may be poorly right now," he muttered. "But soon I'll be up and about. Stay by us. Little Molly needs a mother, and I make a damned poor one."

Then she understood. In the grip of fever, he thought she was her mother, Caroline. She patted his hand, then tried to gently pull away. But he only held on harder, so at last she sat back on the edge of the bed.

"But I'll be right back, er . . . Ned." It felt very strange to call her own father by his first name. "I'm only going to—to check on our little girl."

He closed his eyes, then snapped them open again so suddenly it startled her. This time she thought it was her he saw—Molly. But then he muttered, "She's not . . . not so little now. Fine young maid, almost grown. Though I never . . . tell her so."

He closed his eyes. The hand slipped from her wrist and dropped to the coverlet. For a terrible moment Molly couldn't breathe. She leaned over him, eyes blurring with tears, and lowered her head to his chest. They had said such awful things; had each struck out deliberately to hurt the other. Would she not have a chance, now, to make it up?

He was still breathing, but faintly. The dull thump of his

heartbeat sounded far away, as if he were already leaving her. She rushed to the door, then hesitated on the threshold. What if she left the room, and he got worse? What if—

At last she forced herself down the stairs. Rushed into the stable, out of breath. Woke Rafe and told him how pale her father had looked, his life draining away by the minute.

"The potion Doc Drummond forced down him does no good. And before he left the tavern, Doc talked of bleeding him. But Pa looks as if he has no blood left to spare!"

Molly thought of the various cures she'd seen Doc apply—palsy drops, mithridate, snail water, pokeberry plaster. She'd been dosed herself numerous times with Venice treacle, a disgusting syrup made from pounded snakes boiled with wine and herbs. All children thereabouts were given it for anything from measles to catarrh. But her father needed more than homemade nostrums poured by Drummond's shaky hand.

She pulled Rafe to his feet. "Come on. The widow's abed. Let's hope she sleeps like an old dog full of scraps and won't hear us. I'll go first."

"What for?"

"To get my father to a real doctor, and to safety," she said. "We'll sail across to the shore." She flung open the stable door.

Still the boy hesitated. "All right," he said at last. He pulled a straw he'd been chewing from his mouth. "Did you notice the man in blue, the one who spoke to Mrs. Ben by the water? And his odd speech."

What did that matter now? "Yes, yes, out on the beach," she said impatiently.

"I've heard it before," he said. "He's British, isn't he?"

"Yes, I think so." She recalled that blue uniform coat well enough. But she could only worry about her father now. "We'll talk on the way over. Come quick now."

22

A MIDNIGHT CROSSING

RAFE FOLLOWED MOLLY TO THE TAVERN. They entered through the back door and made quietly for the stairs.

He grasped the stair railing and climbed slowly, as she'd instructed, putting his weight carefully on each step. Praying the old wood wouldn't creak or groan. He heard deep, even breathing from the widow's room. Its door stood partly ajar.

"Don't tread on the middle of that last step," she whispered. "It always gives a fearful squeak."

"I've heard it before," he whispered.

She glanced over her shoulder, looking puzzled. "The step?"

"No, the way they talked, those men. My master had a tutor for his son who spoke just that way."

"Oh."

He supposed she wondered why she should care about anyone's schooling just now. "It's just that they were British. And my master had that tutor sent from London. So perhaps they be spies?"

She paused in the doorway. "But we've no one to report it

to, and surely can't go to the authorities—think what they'd do to you! Please, never mind all that now. I only want to rouse my father and get him out of here."

They reached the top of the dark, cramped stairway at last. What if Mr. Savage had taken a turn for the worse? Rafe wondered. What if he was past all help?

They tiptoed across the floor. A plank creaked, and the snoring across the hall paused for a moment. When Molly gripped his arm, he gasped aloud. But then the buzz of the widow's breathing resumed.

Looking sick with dread, she pushed him ahead of her into the guest room. Her father flinched away when she touched his shoulder. "We're going to get you to a doctor," she whispered. The man mumbled and swatted weakly at their hands. Then he turned his face into the pillow and shut his eyes.

"Mayhap we should go get the doctor and bring him here," Rafe suggested.

"I can't leave Pa alone while we go across and back."

So they tried to move him again, until both were sweating under his limp weight. But he was a large man, it was no use. They finally resorted to deception.

"Ma's outside, Pa," she said. "She's mighty vexed with you, letting yourself get so ill. Now come along. Rafe and I will help you downstairs. Then we'll all go together, get you some medicine to get well."

Her father opened his eyes again. He rose groggily as they pulled on his arms, until at last he sat on the edge of the bed. It was awkward, like moving a huge doll made of stuffed flour sacks. With Molly pulling on one arm, and Rafe pushing against his back, they managed to get him to his feet. He staggered, then shuffled along as docilely as Ephraim, groaning softly now and then from the pain. Rafe braced him up on the left, Molly on the right. They steered him in the right direction when he faltered or seemed about to lose his balance.

As they reached the second landing he lurched against the wall, and what they'd had been dreading finally happened. The even snoring from Mrs. Ben's room stopped, and she called out, "What's that ruckus?"

In a moment she emerged, hair twisted in a long crooked braid for the night, face agleam with some sort of shiny grease. Rafe found it hard not to gape.

"Pa needs . . . a trip to the privy," Molly managed to stammer. "I tried to get him to use the chamber pot, but . . . I called Rafe to help me get him down the stairs."

Mrs. Ben sniffed suspiciously, frowning. Put a hand to her shining face, then touched the twisted rope of hair, as if suddenly realizing how she looked. "Hmmph. He must be feeling better, or he'd be happy with a chamber pot." She looked from Molly to Rafe. "So it seems we shall have our wedding soon, after all."

Then she turned and went back into her room, closing the door behind her.

Rafe's knees nearly buckled with relief. And somehow they got Ned Savage down the stairs and out the door. Then Molly led Janey out of the stable. The mare stood quietly, turning her head and rolling an eye back to watch them sweat and struggle. They finally managed to heave Mr. Savage up onto the horse's back. There he lay against Janey's neck, mumbling like a drunken man leaving the tavern after a pint too many.

"This rough treatment may kill him before he sees any doctor," said Rafe doubtfully.

"We must get him to one before that happens," Molly said stubbornly. "I mean to leave him over there. He'll be safer. Once he's with the doctor, and you're well on your way north, I can find the proper person to tell about what we saw."

The three of them—four, counting Janey—cast a huge fantastic shadow under the half-moon. They slowly passed Doc Drummond's tabby cottage and the other few houses on the lane, expecting any moment to be stopped, for someone to call out. Rafe felt reprieved from doom when they made it into the trees.

At the beach, he helped Mr. Savage slide from Janey's back. Molly gave the horse a slap on the rump and sent her plodding back to the stable. Loading her father into the boat was less easily accomplished. When they reached the thing, which was a large log canoe, Ned Savage balked. "Caroline. Where is she? Where's my Caroline?"

His weak, querulous voice rose, until Rafe felt certain someone might hear. "Please hush, Mr. Savage."

"You said she'd be here," he muttered in the injured tones of a disappointed child, balking at water's edge.

"She is, she is. But, uh . . . on the other shore, Pa," Molly soothed. "We'll take you to the doctor and her now. Just help us get you into the boat."

He climbed in then, and curled up on the bottom boards like an ailing old dog. Molly cast off, and Rafe waded out, pushing the heavy canoe before him until it was floating freely. After he jumped in, she poled them into deeper waters.

The wind was low, the night chill. Molly set the pole aside and wrapped her shawl around her father. Then she raised the lone sail, a nearly triangular piece of canvas.

"He'll be fine," said Rafe. The ripe muck of the marsh smelled familiar to him now, if not exactly sweet. As he looked down over the side, a huge blue crab scuttled under the boat, as if hiding from the moon. "The water's very clear," he said in surprise.

"It is now," Molly whispered. "But next spring it'll cloud up. Be full of life again."

"I won't be here to see that."

She looked abashed. "Of course not. It's a great risk, you going along. Are you sure—"

He nodded and shrugged. As if he hadn't already thought of the danger this trip would put him in.

"I'm afraid you might be seen, and taken," she added.

"Not if you go alone," he said slowly. They had better construct a plan now. "When we land, I'll stay with the boat . . . hide if I see anyone. Don't want to be spotted till I'm far north of here."

She smiled at him. "We'll have to make sure of it."

Then for a while he simply watched her scan the water and adjust the sail to catch the shifting wind. This white girl was nothing like any he'd encountered before. A few daughters of wealthy planters had visited Penland with their parents. They had looked Rafe up and down with curled lips, as if he were a dog in need of a bath. Some had laughed or made rude comments about his clothes and skin and hair. Most of them had ordered him about. Or worse, simply looked through him, acted as if he were not even a live thing, but a footstool or a cushion.

Nor was Molly Savage anything like Kessie, the giggling slave girl a bit older than him who'd washed dishes and scrubbed floors in Penland's huge kitchen. Kessie had caught him behind the pantry door once and kissed him wetly on the cheek, when he was on an errand to fetch a bowl of bread and milk for the always-ailing Will. She'd smelled of fried onions and lye soap, and something else musky and sweet that he couldn't place. He hadn't much enjoyed the sudden wet smack of her lips against his face. And yet . . . he had to admit that afterward he'd felt excited at the prospect of another such encounter.

Molly Savage was not afraid of dirt and mess like the planters' daughters. She didn't giggle or make cow eyes at boys the way Kessie did. She was poor, yet not really like the scrawny pale children in faded dresses and patched britches who sometimes straggled up to the back door of Penland for a handout. He supposed on the surface she was most like those slave girls who herded geese and fed chickens and scrubbed, and scurried about in fear of "mistuss." Except Molly was no fearful, giggling child. She seemed older than her years and afraid of nothing.

He'd like to feel that brave. But then she had the greatest

advantage—a white skin. In the end, how different from the others could she be?

As he watched her steer through narrow passages rimmed with sharp-edged marsh grass and pale, skeletal fingers of driftwood, he began to feel useless. He wished he knew how to handle a boat. Most of what he knew was useless now. As a slave he'd learned to look past or around a white man, never in his eye. How to blend into the background, so he could hear about far-off places he'd never get to see. He'd learned the proper trousers and tie to wear when there were guests for dinner so he could help Will get dressed.

Once, back at Penland, he'd even had to serve at a dinner party. Old Eustis, the serving man, had been down with the quinsy, and lay in bed with a flannel wrapped round his throat.

Mistress had told Rafe he must help Samuel the butler this one night, to serve the many courses at the formal dinner. When he'd asked for instructions, she only snapped, "Merely follow what Samuel tells you, boy," and turned away angrily.

Samuel had certainly given plenty of directions as he pulled on a pair of starched white cotton gloves. And Rafe, who wore none since Eustis's gloves didn't fit him, had concentrated on not dropping hot, heavy soup tureens and brimming gravy boats . . . and on feeling resentful. After the main course he'd stood in the doorway waiting for the next dish to carry or ladle out, even though the guests had already had a half-dozen courses. He longed to slip away and read a book in the schoolroom. Instead he had to stare at the floor while the master and mistress and their guests stuffed themselves on game hens and roast beef and wild rice, and he had to pretend not to be tempted by the delicious smells rising from their loaded plates.

He'd paid little attention to the table talk until Master Thomas suddenly banged the table with his fist, so hard and sharp it made Rafe jump.

"If they wish to abolish slavery in England, sir, so be it," the master'd bellowed. "That's their lookout. But by God we fought them and won. They should keep their limey paws off our goods, on land or sea!"

A discussion about British ways—called high-handed by some and barbaric by others—and the high cost of their shoddy imported goods had followed. But the main thing Rafe had understood was this: There would no longer be slaves in at least one country in the world. All his life he'd been told God wanted slaves to obey their masters, everywhere. That it was His will, and He'd decreed it their lot in life.

Yet there would be no slaves in England.

That being a faraway place, at the time he'd thought it had little to do with him. But if one of those men he and Molly had eavesdropped on was British, spy or not, he must've come from a British ship. And ships eventually returned to where they'd come from.

The plan came suddenly and whole into his mind. He'd only briefly—and not entirely successfully—stowed away on *Tyger*. He'd overheard only a few words of sailor's talk, but perhaps they'd be enough. Perhaps on the way back, if a British ship lay off Savage Island, he could find her and get aboard.

He could offer himself as cabin boy, or whatever sort of hand they needed.

England was farther away from Penland even than Boston. He'd been interested enough after that dinner party to creep back into the nursery schoolroom much later the same night, to find the outline of England in the map book. It was a large heavy volume, and young William had often whined over its colored engravings when he had to memorize and name places.

Rafe knew how much Old Master Thomas hated to travel, even twenty miles from home. He always worried he might be cheated out of a boll of cotton or a flake of tobacco in his absence. And Rafe was far more valuable. Master Tom must've sent slave catchers all over North Carolina looking for him. But surely the master would never come looking for his property all the way across an entire ocean.

23

A FAVOR TO REPAY

A S MOLLY STEERED THEM WEST she thought of Rafe. Or more precisely, of the worry, the reluctance she had noticed in his voice. Yet never once had he suggested they turn back. If he acted strange at times, why, no wonder. Who wouldn't if he was always having to think about being caught and taken back trussed and bound, like an animal on the way to market?

She had to turn her attention to navigating through the sandbars and stands of marsh grass, though. Here and there local watermen had staked leafless branches to mark shoals. If it'd been summer, bellowed frog song would have accompanied them. In fall there was only the silence of the islands about to doze off in expectation of winter. But in her mind, Molly could still conjure the sounds of the warmer season. She could hear the frogs' deep musical croaking counterpointed by the higher-pitched peepers.

Waves lapped soothingly against the sides of the boat in any season. The smell of the marsh was always salt and damp musk and wet earth. Above them stars glimmered, pinpricks in a lampshade of dark, sparkling reflections off the still water, lighting their way just enough. She might actually enjoy this night sail, she decided, if so much weren't at stake. For all three of them.

She lowered the sail and poled as quickly as she could over a sandbar. The wind was from the east, and she could raise the sail again once past Heron and Shipwreck Islands. She was glad those were just humps of marsh grass and mud, inhabited only by herons and crabs. No one would raise an alarm, or ask questions. Once past and in the channel, she would hope for a fair wind to the Eastern Shore.

Her father lay still and quiet in the bottom, but she could hear him breathing. Once or twice he'd moaned.

Finally she handed the pole to Rafe. "Here, take this a while. I want to see to Pa."

He was shivering instead of sweating. Was that good or bad? She knew so little of sickness, except that it often killed the afflicted. Took them away, and left those behind without a mother or wife. Or father.

Without her shawl she, too, shivered in the cold breeze. Though up till now it hadn't been a particularly chill fall, the air was always cooler on the water. Even if she'd had another shawl, she'd pull it off as well and drape it over her father.

A patch of fog drifted by now and then, like an earthbound cloud. At times she could no longer see the opposite shore, though she was certain they were headed the right way. As they rounded Shipwreck, she felt the boat rise on a swell. She glanced over at Rafe. "You can raise the sail now."

The boy hesitated, then reached down and fumbled with

the lashings and lines. Soon all was tangled into a cat's cradle. When the canvas dropped over his head like a shroud, she laughed out loud, then took the line from his hand.

He looked embarrassed. "Sorry. That was clumsy."

She regretted laughing then. Easy to forget that he'd grown up on a landlocked plantation, and had been not a sailor but a stowaway slave. How could she expect him to know about boats? She smiled in apology. "I forget you weren't raised on the water, too."

"How *do* you know we're headed the right way?" he asked.

"Well, there's the moon to go by, and then certain stars. See the Dipper, there?"

"At home, the old slaves called it the Drinking Gourd," he said. "Did you know it can lead you north?"

She nodded. "And there's a feeling you get after a while. I can just tell."

But after a bit, as the little boat pressed on, she felt less sure. The water was rougher, as if she were headed seaward instead of west to the Shore. Once a swell broke over the bow and soaked them all. Finally she lowered the sail and jerked the tiller hard to the left.

"What's wrong?" asked Rafe.

"We're a bit off course, maybe," she said. They were in the open stretch between the islands and the Shore. A storm now, even a squall, would be very bad in this small boat. Aside from a few low patches of fog, a few scraps of cloud, the sky had been clear when they'd left. But a low bank of fog had moved in, and it clung to the surface of the broadwater. Dark and fog meant she no longer had landmarks to go by. They sat drifting in a damp wrapping of mist as Molly looked around.

To the north, above the low-hanging fog, a faint dark shape hulked where there should be nothing but open water.

"That isn't right," she murmured. There was no island there.

Then she heard, faintly, the dull ringing of a heavy chain. So it was a ship of some kind. As they drifted closer, a long bowsprit pierced the fog, loomed over their canoe like a huge needle.

"Those men on the beach," she whispered, nudging him. "One said they were anchored off the island, that it had been rough getting in."

That still didn't tell her who they were. But as they drifted alongside with the current, Molly saw the ship flew the colors of a British merchant, a Union Jack in the corner of a red background. And yet . . . overhead, square ports pierced the sides. Covered now, but she could see they were gun ports.

"It's a man-o'-war," she whispered. "Pa's described such to me. The geezers in the tavern are always jawing on about them, thinking they've seen one coming over the horizon. I thought they were just old fools full of hot air and brandy, dreaming up something to gossip about."

"It looks fair solid to me," said Rafe.

Voices came from above them, then a rattling clank.

"We have to get away from here, quickly," she whispered.

"They mustn't see us. Take the pole. I'll tack back toward the islands. When we hit water shallow enough, pull like mad for shelter. Go back round toward Shipwreck Island."

After they rounded the bend of Shipwreck, she told him to stop poling. They ducked in behind a stand of rushes and reeds just as a new craft approached the ship. This one flat as a griddle cake, with a boxy structure on top.

"Look at that raft," said Rafe. "Like one I saw the morning the pirates came ashore."

As Molly watched it approach the ship, she felt stiff, and even colder. "It'd be a good craft for ducking down creeks to hide, to slip away from the law. Especially if your name was Makeele, and you hated your countrymen who won the war."

"So picaroons don't fear hailing a British ship?" asked Rafe as a figure waved from the raft and gave a loud halloo.

"No, because they're Tories still, loyal to the king of England. That's why they skulk about the swamps and inlets like marsh rats. Come out only to raid and burn and loot the homes of honest folk. They think it's their due—revenge for losing in our Revolution."

"What now, then?" asked Rafe. But he was still watching the raft and ship. The look on his face was strange. Not worried— on the contrary, he looked too interested. Almost . . . eager.

"We can pole around the island," she said. "We've got to cross open water, head west toward the Shore. But we'll wait here a bit longer. At least we're concealed."

As they watched and waited, two men boarded the ship. Others stayed behind on the raft. Molly took the pole at last, and they backtracked around the island, then set out again for the Shore. "Hear that drunken laughter? Bet they're the same ones raided the island."

She caught herself listening for the telltale bleat of a goat. But surely poor Miranda had long since been killed and eaten by the pirates.

Molly poled out until the sandy bottom sank away, then hoisted the sail. Ahead lay the dark tree line of the Eastern Shore. She had only to guide the tiller and man the sail while Rafe cradled her father's head in his lap.

"He's less fevered now," he said, tucking the shawl around her father's shoulders.

At long last the canoe scraped bottom again, and Molly jumped out to beach it. She recognized this place—the same one she'd landed at with her father a few times, on errands for the widow. It sported only a tumbledown fishing shack, nailed together from driftwood and old planks, squatting near a thick hummock of spartina grass.

"Let's draw up here. Then you can hide, should someone come by."

They shoved and pushed together, beaching the boat well above the high-water line. It was a difficult task with the limp weight of her father still in the boat.

Rafe looked around skeptically. "Not a house or a barn in sight," he said. "Much less a doctor."

"No, but Eyre's Landing isn't far," she said. "A doctor lives near there. We came for him once before, when Ma . . . when my mother was sick." She shivered again, in the damp wind.

The sawbones had not saved Caroline Savage, nor old Ben Pruitt, or the others who'd succumbed to the terrible coughing sickness. Perhaps he could do nothing for her father now. But she had to try.

"I've been thinking." Rafe sat back on the gunwale. "I could say I'm your father's slave. That I brought him here for a doctor, if anyone comes by."

Molly had been so caught up in her own worries, she'd nearly forgotten the dreadful risk Rafe was taking. "Anyone *we* know knows Ned Savage hasn't the means to keep a slave. No, you'd better just hide. In that shack over there."

Somehow she couldn't meet Rafe's eyes when she said, "No one but Pa has ever risked so much for my sake before. Do you think . . . maybe we're friends?"

"I suppose we are." But he, too, looked away, as if suddenly interested in the sand beneath his bare feet. He added, almost unwillingly, "Perhaps we've got things in common, despite our different skins."

Molly smiled. "Maybe that's not so much a difference as we've been told, then." She drew a deep breath. "Someday I'll repay you, Rafe. And I swear I'll help you get away north, law or no law. After Pa's well, you can surely count on his help, too. He always says a Savage never forgets a favor, and never lets a debt go unpaid."

It was an odd thing to say, she supposed, when he'd lost them so much, even grandfather's tavern. But at the moment she didn't care. He was her father, and she still believed, despite his flaws, that he was a good man. That he would agree, in the end, that helping the boy mattered more than some laws set down by rich men, far away.

"I just . . . I'd better set off to find that sawbones," she said. Then she turned and dashed off down a narrow path through the scrubby, salt-stunted bushes.

24

TAKEN BY SURPRISE

AFTER SHE LEFT, Rafe went to check on Mr. Savage. The sick man still slept, muttering from time to time, even striking at the air as if he fought an enemy. He was shivering again. So Rafe tucked the shawl more closely around the man, then sat with his back propped against the boat. Soon the damp sand soaked his trousers. And no matter how he shifted, the gunwale of the canoe dug into his back, hard and splintery. At least it would keep him awake. He'd decided not to hide in the shack yet, as Molly had suggested. The waning night was clear, the land flat, and his view long. Surely he'd see if anyone approached from a distance.

It would probably be some time before the girl returned. He hadn't felt this tired since he'd been on the run from Penland. Then he'd spent night after night running, walking, then running again. And spent the days hungry, his stomach gnawed hollow. His eyes stretched wide and sleepless by the fear someone might spot him curled like a frightened animal beneath bushes by a road, or burrowed like a field mouse into some farmer's haystack.

He shifted, slid down the side of the boat a bit. And closed his eyes, just for a moment.

Sometime later he heard a stealthy noise, the crackle and snap of a twig, perhaps. He sat up with a jerk and realized he'd dozed off. But for how long? The moon was low in the west, and a pinkish light was glowing in the east, over the water. Ned Savage still breathed, and still lay quietly in the boat. Rafe reached over the gunwales and felt the man's forehead, for reassurance.

"I pray you'll be well soon, sir," he said.

"Mayhap you won't be so lucky your own self," growled a deep voice behind him.

Rafe froze, then turned slowly. Before him stood three men dressed in ragged knee britches and dirty white shirts. One, a tall, thin fellow, also wore the ragged remnants of a cream satin waistcoat, stained with darker patches. They reeked of old sweat, and surely had bathed in rum. Their smell even overpowered the salt and decayed fish smell of the marsh.

The tall man, obviously the leader, grinned at Rafe with blackened stubs of teeth. "What we got here, lads? A little darky out all alone. Tell your name, boy!"

Rafe hesitated only a moment. "William Pennington, sir," he said loudly but politely, careful to keep his eyes downcast. The same way you would with a mad, bristling dog.

The man strolled over casually, as if they were meeting on a village street. He looked Rafe up and down, and curled his lip. "Fine fancy name for a nigra whelp. And who," he said, aiming a kick that rocked the log canoe, "who might be this layabout who sleeps so sound and rudelike when he's got company?"

"He's my . . . my father, sir," said Rafe. "Master Thomas Pennington." Then clamped his lips tight with dismay. Now why had he said something so foolish as that? Sweat prickled under his shirt. Well, no way to take the words back.

"If he's your da, I'm the bleeding queen of Spain!" snarled the man. He grabbed Rafe's shirtfront and dragged him across the sand, holding him so tight his nose was pressed into the man's filthy shirt. The smell of stale sweat and spoiled food and alcohol fumes was even worse close up. It made Rafe gag even on an empty stomach.

"No, you're right . . . sir. I only . . . *think* of him as my pa," he said quickly. "I work for him, apprenticed bricklayer by trade. And a freedman."

"Not no longer you ain't," said the tall man. He belched loudly and let Rafe drop to the sand like a sack of kindling. "From here on, you be the goods of a loyal subject of His Majesty King George the Third. Property of Wayland Makeele, the Pirate King of Virginia."

25

RUNAWAY . . .
OR *STOLEN* AWAY?

THE SUN WAS JUST LIGHTENING THE SKY in the east, and Molly had slowed to a walk on the unpaved road that led to Eyre's Landing. Limping from a cut on one foot and out of breath, she could run no more. She figured she had gone about three miles. Just ahead lay a lane leading to a small farm. On a board tacked to the front gate was scrawled *Nottingham*. She hung on the gatepost a moment, breathing hard. This place she recalled, too: a tidy whitewashed brick house and summer kitchen, set amid fields and pastures where black and white sheep lay about, fenced in with peeled saplings. Of course, she and her parents had passed it in a hurry, back when the sickness had struck the island. When her mother lay so pale and thin, barely breathing, in the back of the wagon.

That had been five years ago, yet she remembered clearly. She'd been not quite eleven and, practicing her letters, had spelled out and pronounced the name on the gatepost aloud. For her mother had always told her to read new things each time she had the chance. Even a word as brief as that signpost had been a relief, because for a moment it had taken her mind off the terrible fear that her mother, who lay in the back of the wagon, was already dying.

By the next day she knew that fear had been justified. And they'd passed the farm again, from the other direction, to take the body of Caroline Savage, wife of Ned, mother of Molly, back to the island to be buried.

She caught her breath and shivered; the wind cut through her sweat-soaked dress. In the field a sheep bleated. Then a rooster crowed, as if challenging her right to travel his road. The farm looked so orderly—a paradise of ordinary life. The neat shell lane was a long white invitation to step along it right up to the tidy whitewashed house with black shutters.

It looked nothing like the life she'd become used to.

But Dr. Henderson did not live there. He was outside town, on the far side, not at this seaside farm. So after a moment Molly pushed away from the gate and went on. Soon the lane widened to a clay road rutted by wagon wheels. A half-dozen buildings lay ahead.

Eyre's Landing was a small village with perhaps a hundred and fifty souls living in its cottages and on surrounding farms. As she passed, a yellow dog barked at her from someone's front steps. There was a blacksmith shop, and through its open door the forge glowed. The crackling fire looked warm and pleasant. Just inside the doorway a black man with heavily muscled arms yawned, then sipped from a steaming mug. He nodded at her, staring curiously as she passed. She wished she had a mug of something hot, too. Though it felt wrong to think of her own thirst when her father was so desperately ill.

But she'd had nothing to eat or drink since the afternoon before. Hard to believe so much had happened in only a few hours.

Soon the modest houses gave way to countryside again. After a half mile or so she turned in at the doctor's place, a white clapboard two-story with a squat brick chimney, surrounded in front by a low picket fence to keep out wandering livestock. A fat orange cat with a bent tail rushed ahead of her, purring, trying to rub her shins. It twined around her legs, meowing, as she knocked at the big front door.

When no one came, she knocked again, harder. At last she heard footsteps and braced her arm against the door frame, trembling with fatigue.

A short, round woman in a gray dress and sparkling white apron and mobcap wrenched open the door. She looked down at her, frowning, dusting floury hands on the apron. "And who might you be, miss, come pounding so hard, so early?"

Suddenly Molly was aware of how dirty she must look, caked head to toe with sea salt and road dust. Her hair was snarled and windblown, a wild myrtle bush compared to this woman's neatly coiled gray bun. Yes, she must surely look a fright to any decent folks. But her father lay dying in an open boat, and she would get help for him somehow, even if she had to kidnap the doctor and march him all the way back.

"I—I'm Molly Savage. My father was shot by picaroons. I've carried him all the way over from Savage Island in the boat. I'm afraid he might . . . he might . . ." She bit her lip and looked away, trying to calm herself. But she couldn't stand it any longer. Her lower lip trembled, and she began to sob.

"Well, why did you not say so right away?" The woman clucked, patting Molly's shoulder as she drew her gently into the house. "Doctor's awake. Just had his breakfast, you're in luck. He'll be in good spirits and won't bite your head off."

She led Molly into a dining room, then through to the kitchen. A gray-haired man in a starched shirt and black coat sat at the table, wiping his mouth on a napkin. He looked only a little surprised to see her.

"Here now, dear," said the woman, "sit yourself down and tell Doctor your troubles. I'll get a bit of biscuit and bacon. How about a nice cup of hot milk? Poor thing, you look done in."

Molly sat and told the doctor, between bites of hot crumbling biscuit and sips of milk, about her father's wound. When Henderson turned to issue orders to his housekeeper, and Molly thought neither one of them was looking, she tucked a biscuit into her pocket for Rafe.

"Please, may we go now?"

"Of course," said the doctor. "I know your father. He once sold me the best pan fish I've ever tasted. But that was after your poor mother . . . ah. Well, let's go. And take all of Mrs. Morey's biscuits you like, my girl." He patted her shoulder.

Molly was too tired to blush or refuse politely. So she only said, "Thank you," and tucked three more biscuits in her pocket.

"Mrs. Morey," called the doctor, slipping on his coat. "Have Lucas hitch up the mare."

* * *

Though the doctor's carriage moved much faster than Molly could have, it still seemed hours before they finally jolted back over the rutted track down to the shore. The boat still lay beached, as Molly recalled. But Rafe was nowhere in sight.

He must've heard us coming, she thought, *and hid himself back in the bushes, or inside the shack.* That was good, for though Dr. Henderson seemed a kind man, Molly assumed his black servant Lucas, who'd brought the buggy around, was likely a slave. Even kindly folks, as slave owners, would frown on helping a runaway escape his lawful master.

The doctor climbed down and walked over to the boat. Stooped, hands on knees, he said loudly, "Good morning to you, Ned Savage. Been years since we last met."

Her father opened his eyes to slits. "Aye," he whispered through dry, cracked lips. "I was in a sight better shape then. Brought you . . . a fine mess of pan fish. Flounder. Was my wife who had need . . . of you . . . before that."

"I still regret I couldn't save her. A lovely woman. But we lost a good many that year." Henderson bent lower and looked him over carefully. Tapped his chest and listened against Ned Savage's shirtfront as Molly stood anxiously waiting.

The doctor hesitated in his examination, as if he'd just thought of something, and looked back at her in surprise. "How did such a slight girl as you get such a big, heavy man here all alone?"

She stared at him mutely, not having concocted a story for this question. But all she saw was concern in his eyes, so she mumbled, "He was not so sick when we started out, sir, and could still walk a bit." What a skilled liar she'd become! But lately it seemed she must pile one untruth on top of another merely to survive.

But my mother and father never prepared me to deal with pirates, she thought. *Or British spies, or unjust laws. They always said people were good at heart.*

Why did they not tell me the true nature of the world?

Now that the doctor was looking after her father, she began to worry again about Rafe. They'd agreed he'd conceal himself when she returned, but—

"Molly."

At her father's voice, she turned. The doctor was putting a new dressing on. *Pa looks paler than ever,* she thought in alarm.

He motioned her to come closer.

"Pray give us . . . a moment, sir," he said to the doctor. Henderson nodded and stepped back. She knelt and took her father's outstretched hand.

"Listen close, Moll. Some foul pirates, picaroon scoundrels . . . may be taking the boy to Makeele himself. Came upon us a short while back—no, don't bother to look to the shack or the woods! Your friend's not there. The fiends seized him. I fear they mean to sell him off."

"Oh no!" Molly whispered, biting her lips hard so the doctor wouldn't notice she was upset. Their plan had been too dangerous after all. It was her fault. "What should I do, Pa?"

He closed his eyes and sank back, exhausted. "I don't know,

princess. Just wanted you to know the poor boy was faithful. He didn't desert me, but was dragged off by those scum."

Molly rose and stepped back as Dr. Henderson returned and put the final touches on the clean bandage. He praised Molly for the neatness of the first one. She was too upset to tell him not she but Doc Drummond had done it.

"I shall have to take Mr. Savage back to my place," said the doctor. "He's too weak to go home now. My housekeeper will feed him on beef tea and fresh eggs. I wager he'll be fit in a week or so."

Only a week. But he'd be out of Mrs. Ben's reach that long, at least.

"And how will you get home?" asked the doctor, smiling. "Would you care to stay as well? We've room to spare. Surely Mrs. Morey wouldn't mind an extra hand about the house."

"Thank you, sir," she said. "But I must get back. Can you tell me, is there a—a constable or magistrate hereabouts?"

"Yes. Mr. Leatherbury, in Eastville." He glanced at her father again. "I doubt you'll find much satisfaction, though, if you want justice done the pirates. Picaroons are a plague no magistrate has yet managed to control."

"No, it's for another legal matter . . . about our tavern. Something to tell him," she said, thinking of Mrs. Ben and her connection to the pirates. "I'll make a small payment on your bill, sir. It's all I have at the moment, but later . . . is Eastville far?"

"Well, yes. About eight miles. I'd take you now, but I have

patients to see, and must go first to Town's End. If you'd care to ride along, I could carry you there this evening."

This evening? That would be too late to help Rafe. Perhaps too late to stop whatever deviltry the British and pirates were planning as well. "Is there a market there—I mean where they sell slaves?"

Now the doctor stared, as if she'd lost her wits. "A slave market? No, not between here and Norfolk. Whatever would you need—"

"I only . . . was curious. I've never seen one."

Norfolk. In her little boat, that would take days. She might as well try to rescue Rafe from the moon. She sighed and dropped into his hand the four pennies she'd kept hidden in her pocket—the ones she'd never given Francis Ley for the onions. So even that small start on their freedom was gone. But what good was freedom for a girl who'd just lost her only friend?

26

A DEN OF THIEVES
AND LIARS

WHEN THE PIRATES SURROUNDED HIM, Rafe had been afraid to move, or speak. If they didn't kill him, he'd supposed they would sell him. Perhaps send him south, to one of the terrible rice plantations where so many black men and women died of malaria and overwork. Perhaps it would be best if they killed him.

Then he recalled what Molly had said—that the pirates and the British were working together. Was it possible this wasn't the end, but a roundabout way to freedom? Still, he had to be careful what he did, what he said to these ruthless devils. And how he said it.

He look a deep breath and recalled to himself the speech of the field hands back at Penland, for he suspected it wouldn't do to sound too educated here. He threw himself at the feet of the largest pirate. "Praise God. You come to deliver me, Marster!" The pirate's boots were mud-caked, and the leather reeked of unwashed feet and whatever manure they'd just tromped through. *No matter,* thought Rafe, clenching his teeth. *It'll be the perfume of paradise if these stinking boots lead me to freedom.*

The pirate squinted down, slack-jawed. "Get up, boy. What ails you?"

"Old Marster always say Captain Makeele a good man, never mind what lies them rebels spun 'bout him. That he lift up any man, no matter what color or the size of his purse, if he do swear to the king."

"You know of Makeele?" said the pirate doubtfully, scatching his stomach beneath his dirty shirt.

"Who don't?" Rafe tried to look astonished.

"Hmm." The pirate eyed him. "And what d'ye think he'd do with a black-skinned mooncalf but sell his hide for rum?"

"Put me in his navy, sir," said Rafe. "I strong and willing. Can tell stories to keep the men happy when they's got nothing to do."

"Let's be gone," said one of the other pirates, who were shuffling their feet and glancing nervously about. "I says we kill the sick rebel and be gone, afore some 'citizen' sees and raises the alarm."

"No call to waste good powder on him," said Rafe, trying not to seem too concerned lest they not believe his story. He only hoped Mr. Savage would understand what he was trying to do. "Marster soon be done for. He been sick for weeks. His family away, got no one to look out for him. Only me."

"Well, there's the boat." A fat yellow-bearded pirate pointed out to their leader. "We ought—"

"Old scow leak like a busted bucket," said Rafe quickly, scornfully. "We ain't be here now if it stay afloat. Only carry us far as round the point, to find a doctor. Then we gots to put in here or swim."

"Ah, devil take him and his boat," the tall pirate had said. And they'd marched Rafe off to a big raft hidden in a cove. They'd blindfolded him with a greasy rag and shoved him down to the hard, splintery deck.

It seemed they floated on for hours. At first the rocking of the raft made Rafe feel sick, though there was no food in him to lose. After a while he got used to it and began to feel hungry again.

At last the raft scraped bottom and lurched to a halt. The men grunted and cursed as they dragged it up on shore. Someone jerked him to his feet. He stumbled along as best he could, tripping over roots he couldn't see thanks to the blindfold.

Finally he heard other voices. Dogs barking. And, unexpectedly, the squeals of children at play. He felt warmth nearby, heard the crackling of a huge fire, just before someone shoved him down again.

When they took off the blindfold, he was sitting on the ground near a roaring fire where two toothless women, their greasy hair pulled back and dirty skirts tucked up round their knees, boiled laundry in a huge black kettle. Rafe wondered whose clothes were being washed. None of the men had smelled as if theirs had ever encountered soap and water. Off to the side, three sooty-faced children wearing only ragged shirts, along with a mangy yellow dog, stood staring at him.

"He's awake," said the smallest. "But Da'll whip you for taking off his mask."

"It's no mask, Jemmy," said the largest boy scornfully. "It's a blindfold. And he be the black devil who come to eat you."

The littlest shrieked and ran to hide behind a tree. But the middle-size child, a girl, only looked Rafe up and down and giggled. "Go on, Ty. He ain't black. Only a sort of brownish color." She squinted back at her playmate and grinned. "Your face be blacker'n his, from all the dirt."

"Here, you little devils!" A man with a vest but no shirt came out of a ramshackle cottage. "Leave off playing with the bloody captive."

He came over and stood Rafe up again. "Come on, then."

"Where you taking me now?"

The man laughed, showing pegs of brown teeth. "Only to meet your new master. The master of us all," he said, grinning. "Cap'n Makeele."

He jerked Rafe forward, toward the hut. Inside, the man shoved him to the floor, which was of hard-packed dirt. A dozen pirates were arguing around a table, pointing at some sort of map or papers.

Rafe was so tired and weak with hunger he could barely follow their words. Until he heard one say, "Off this knob of sea grass, called something like—"

"It's, er, let's see . . . Savage Island, Sawney," broke in another pirate.

"The devil it is! I know me directions—"

"Shut your holes, the both of you," growled a deep voice.

"Captain Makeele, your honor!" cried one man.

The arguing pirates suddenly slunk back like cowed dogs. A

tall, thin, ugly man in a brocade waistcoat and scuffed black boots strode into the room. He was tanned like leather, his long face a map of scars. He wore a cutlass and several long knives were tucked into his belt. He glared round at everyone, eyes glittering so, he might've had the fever. When that gaze paused on him, Rafe felt a chill. He understood why the others all stepped back. He wanted to get out of the way, too.

Makeele said, "We'll meet the ship in open water . . . *there*." He jabbed a dirty-nailed finger like a knife at the map. The other pirates quickly nodded.

"And what about the boy here?" said one meekly.

"Oh, he'll play his part." The captain smiled at Rafe, but his bared yellow teeth weren't friendly. "We're short warm bodies, since that last raid on the same bloody island lost us Dan and Billy and Samuel. He'll man a skiff with you and Sawney."

Both muttered and aimed dark looks at Rafe, but didn't argue.

Makeele sat on the one chair. A woman, younger and better dressed than the hags Rafe had seen doing laundry, came in. The pirate snatched a mug from her hand, and she backed out again, looking at the dirt floor.

Makeele took a long pull, then wiped his mouth on a stained lace cuff. "Now don't trust the blackie with firearms. But it seems he can sail, no? So we'll go ashore, take any likely goods, and burn the houses. A strike back at the white master. You'll like that, boy. Eh?"

"Yes . . . yes, sir." Rafe nodded, trying to look eager. He was glad the pirates hadn't seen his clumsy wrestling match with the sail on Molly's log canoe. Perhaps they were just short-handed, but they seemed to be almost accepting him as one of them. And if they were set to meet with the British man-o'-war, he might still have a chance to join it.

But he'd not figured on being a pirate—a farm-burning, goods-thieving, bad-smelling outlaw. Now he'd be doubly hunted, by slave catchers as an escapee, and by the law as part of a gang of cutthroat thieves.

Unless . . . well, he'd have to bide his time and see what he could do to improve his ever-changing lot in life.

"Thank you," he said, bowing as he'd seen the others do. "I be a loyal man, a big help to you, Cap'n Makeele."

27

MOLLY HAS
A BETTER IDEA

DR. HENDERSON'S SLAVE, LUCAS, helped her father out of the doctor's wagon. The big man half carried him into the house and laid him on a bed off the kitchen. Then Molly sat down with a plate of ham and biscuits and fig preserves, the best she'd ever tasted. Yet the food was sawdust in her mouth. She couldn't really enjoy the salty chunks of ham or the sweet brown figs, for thinking: *What can I do about Rafe, about Mrs. Ben?*

She couldn't wait much longer to tell someone about the widow's plan. She had the rest of the islanders to think about. What would happen to them if the British came ashore? Perhaps they'd want revenge for their allies, the picaroons. Would poor old Doc and Hank Blodgett be taken captive, pressganged into the king's navy? They were too old to survive such treatment.

Then there was Ephraim. Just a goat, true, but the closest thing she'd ever had to a pet. Perhaps she was foolish, but she couldn't stand the thought of him ending up on Mrs. Ben's table.

But with her word against the widow's, and no proof in hand, why would the local officials believe her story about the ship lying off Savage Island?

She raised another piece of biscuit, but stopped her hand halfway to her mouth. She'd just thought of someone who *would* believe.

The old soldiers.

They'd fought the king's men alongside her father, when he'd been barely more than a boy. A number of veterans lived right here on the Eastern Shore. Some nearly as young as Ned Savage, and still strong. Some older, like Hank and Doc. These men never doubted the British would be back; they talked of it constantly. She wouldn't have to work hard to convince them of what she'd seen.

Perhaps her best chance was the Ley farm, home of Francis's family. It was not far from Town's End. The doctor had said he was going there, so she could ride along. Francis might be glad to see her for other reasons, but that seemed a minor problem now. She knew the Leys. They'd at least listen. Surely Mr. Ley, a respected farmer, would know whom to talk to.

The doctor finished his lunch and picked up his bag. Molly thanked Mrs. Morey for her good food.

" 'Tis no bother," said the woman. "Only wish you'd stay a bit longer, girl."

Molly hugged her ample waist, then mounted the carriage's passenger step. The doctor leaned out and gave her a hand up into the two-wheeled gig. The carriage was dusty, the leather seats cracked, but it all seemed very fine to Molly, who'd only ever ridden in an open farm cart or on Janey's bare back on the beach at home.

Dr. Henderson urged the gray horse into a trot. They bounced along the rutted sandy lanes so rapidly Molly felt dizzy. She was not used to going fast, except occasionally on the water, when a gust caught the sail. The doctor pointed out various sights as they passed, mainly other farms. She saw dozens of woolly sheep grazing in flat emerald-green pastures. Any number of dark-skinned slaves spreading manure or planting. It was past the season for corn or oats, or to be tying up what little tobacco was grown here, so Molly didn't know what they were planting. Dr. Henderson was only too happy to tell her.

"That'll be winter rye, now."

She nodded, beginning to wonder after a while why he'd become a doctor instead of a farmer, since he seemed to know all about growing things.

He also kept up a running commentary of who owned which farm or sawmill or woods, and how well or poorly they did. She let his words rumble above her tired head, the steady murmur washing over her like warm waves. He seemed happy if she simply nodded from time to time, which was good, since she was too worried to keep up a real conversation.

At last they turned into Town's End, a hamlet of neat white homes and a few stores.

"Here I must check on two ladies who have expectations," said the doctor gravely, reaching back for his leather bag.

Molly was first puzzled, then realized he meant the women were soon going to have babies. She felt her face heat up with embarrassment. Of course no one would ever speak of such things outright.

"Oh. Well, I'll get out here, sir," she said. "It's not far to my friends' farm. I can walk the rest."

"Wait," said the doctor. "Mrs. Morey would flay me if I forgot." He handed her a clean, bleached flour sack from the floorboard. "A little salt ham, some biscuits, a jar of wildflower honey, and some dried apples, I believe she said."

"Oh my. Thank you," said Molly. It was a feast. How kind these people were. She couldn't imagine Mrs. Ben giving strangers at her door anything better than a taste of shoe leather as she booted them off the steps. "You've been very good to me."

The doctor cleared his throat. "Well, well, don't mention it. Don't worry about your father, child. He'll be fit again soon. We'll take care of him."

She made her way out of town, toward the water. Round a bend in the lane was the gate to the Ley place. The farm sat on a point, on a large marsh, overlooking lush grass and water. She saw the sloops the Leys used to ferry vegetables up and down the coast and over to the islands for sale. Someone was mending nets by one; it appeared to be the broad-shouldered figure of Francis's father, Baxter Ley. Molly went on past the house, toward him.

But when he turned to look, she saw it was not Mr. Ley but young Francis, her would-be suitor. When had he gotten so broad in the shoulders? As she drew closer, he set the net down and grinned. Despite her tiredness, Molly also noticed his beaming face didn't look quite so spotted as before. And that she felt somewhat happier to see him than when they'd last met over a bunch of onions. Unfortunately, his four pennies were gone for good.

"Molly!" Francis looked overjoyed. "But . . . what brings you here, and over land, too? Surely you're not alone." He frowned, cocked his head until he looked so much like a puzzled heron—so much like the old Francis—she laughed. Some things, at least, remained comfortably the same.

"It's good to see you, Francis."

"But you must be done in, you've been traveling far." He took her elbow gently, as if she were delicate. Molly let him lead her into the big white farmhouse with black shutters and high-peaked windows.

"Look here, Ma," Francis called, steering her through a muddy entrance hall, its floor deep in big dirty boots, with woolen capes and jackets hung two and three deep on pegs. She'd forgotten how many brothers Francis had. As she came into the kitchen, she was greeted by a fat tail-wagging hound and a burst of the most wonderful smell of bread baking. Francis's stout, red-cheeked mother turned from the stove. "Bless my soul, if it isn't Miss Molly Savage!"

In no time they had her boots off and drying by the fireplace, her feet on a hassock, a mug of mulled cider in her hands, a plate of cake before her. And they were both talking at once, asking about her father, her health, the tavern, even the weather on the island. Molly answered briefly and quietly, determined to catch her breath and get her thoughts in order.

Then Mr. Ley and three of Francis's brothers and even a couple of unmarried uncles crowded into the room, all asking questions, too. At last she was able to explain about her father's wound, the pirate raid, and her midnight sail to the doctor. The assembled family gasped and elbowed one another, and shouted in astonishment. Together they all made so much racket Molly was sure her ears would ring for days.

But she didn't yet tell of the British. And she did not mention Rafe.

"Ah, what a time you've had of it," his mother said, shaking her head. "I tell you, I never did like that sharp-nosed woman, not since she married poor old Ben Pruitt, God rest his soul."

The mention of marriage seemed to set her off in another direction.

"Which reminds me. Have you got a hope chest together, poor motherless girl? Aye, it's early, but never too soon to plan ahead. You'll be needing a dozen sheets and at least twenty towels and forty napkins stitched and hemmed. I suppose your poor departed mother taught you to make candles and soap and brooms, and to weave cloth and dye it. But can you brew a decent keg of beer? My Francis likes his—"

"God's teeth!" Molly exclaimed suddenly.

A hush fell over the assembled family. Mrs. Ley pursed her lips, clearly astonished to hear such language from a girl.

"Oh, I'm sorry. But I must tell you now," said Molly. She took a deep breath. "I'm not here just to visit. Mr. Ley?"

Baxter Ley lowered his eyebrows, looking suddenly serious. "Tell away then, girl. I'm listening."

"There's a British man-o'-war anchored off Savage Island, and a spy consorting with them. I think they plan to take the island first, then come on to the Shore."

"But what brings 'em here now?" said Francis's oldest uncle.

"I think it might be the redcoat gold," said Molly. "It's an old tale, true, but the men I saw on the beach spoke of treasure. What else could it be?"

Silence fell in the room. She glanced from one shocked face to another, afraid they'd laugh and say, "Oh, pish, Molly. You had us going there for a moment." Or, "Tut, girl, you're imagining things." And then turn their backs and go on with their own affairs.

Instead Simon Ley, Francis's uncle, gave a whoop that sounded oddly joyful. "I knew it," he cried. "Knew the limey blaggards'd be back!"

Mrs. Ley sighed and rolled her eyes.

After a wild moment, as the boys jumped about and shouted, Baxter Ley broke in. He looked somber, not joyful. But then Mr. Ley had actually been to war, like Molly's father, and knew what it was like. "Quieten down, you rowdies," he snapped. Then, to his wife, "Don't just sit there, woman. I'll get my musket while you pack some victuals. If we must, then we'll send 'em packing again." He sounded resigned, not elated at all.

Francis and his father and an uncle soon were laying out muskets and powder and knives and sharpening bent and rusted swords. Francis's younger brothers shoved and taunted one another, whining and begging to go. Instead they were sent to the neighbors, to carry the summons to arms.

Francis sidled over to Molly. "I'll fight those redcoats for you," he said. "You'll b-be proud of me."

Molly didn't know what to say. She should've known these people, the ones who understood what it was like to work hard and scratch out a living on the water or from the land, would come to her aid. Unlike a magistrate, which she'd always imagined as some soft-bellied, bewigged fellow who sat all day puffing a pipe, then eating himself into a stupor. Though of course she'd never met one.

"I owe you much, Francis," she said, thinking not only of the money for onions. She hadn't the heart to say it, but she doubted any act on his part could change her mind about a future wedding. He was just plain gangly Francis the vegetable seller, an old friend. She smiled at him, though. He was tall and kind, not so bad-looking, after all. Some girl would be lucky to have him for a husband one day.

But that girl wouldn't be Molly Savage.

Before dark she was back in the canoe, headed for Savage Island. But not alone. With her came a flotilla of long boats, canoes, and skiffs with men pulling hard on the oars. Francis had insisted on riding with her. She was too tired to protest when he took over the tiller.

Poor Rafe! She'd wanted to ask what to do about him as well, but Mr. Ley owned three slaves himself. Not knowing how he would treat a runaway, she kept silent. But what terrible things must be happening to the boy right now, at the mercy of pirates? She imagined him beaten, tortured, killed.

Of course, she'd also heard picaroons forced captured men into their crews. When they fought back the redcoats, she might see Rafe on the other side! If she spotted him then, maybe he could be set free. Poor as it was, that was her only plan. For she had no more idea than anyone else where the pirates might be hiding. Up a creek on the coast, on a bay or sea island to the north or south. Up in Maryland or around the point near Cape Charles, in the Bay. Tangier Island was supposed to be their main outpost. But it was foolishness, if not sure death, for anyone not of their tribe to approach that den of cutthroats.

Francis said, as he took the tiller, "Isn't this thrilling? We missed the big war, but here a battle's coming up before our eyes."

"People get hurt in battles, Francis," she said. "I'm not looking forward to that. But what else can we do?"

He nodded somberly, as if he agreed. But his eyes still glowed with excitement.

Baxter Ley's calling out of the militia had assembled at

least forty men, some old soldiers her father's age. Many older, with a few of their grown sons. They wore homespun shirts and felt hats and wool vests and heavy boots caked with soil and manure. They carried old but well-oiled muskets—and a variety of other weapons: flintlock pistols and pitchforks and knives and old cavalry swords.

These farmers did not look as impressive as the British navy, with their fancy blue-and-white uniforms. But fashion hadn't won the war against England. These men knew the woods, fields, and waters—all the hiding places of their land, better than anyone. She hoped that advantage would work once again, for that stealthy ship might hold many more fighters than this straggling little force.

Mr. Ley hailed the boats behind him. They all hove to, to hear what he had to say.

"Now we split up," he shouted. "Martins and Nottinghams and Killmons and Tankards go with me. The rest of you pass around the lee side of the island. Put in at the cove there. Hide your craft as best you can. Then sneak through the woods to the Hog's Head Tavern. Wait out back, and keep out of sight till you see my signal. Then we'll give the limeys a load of shot that'll send them flying back to England!"

Recalling the size of the man-o'-war, Molly closed her eyes. How would they do that? The British even had cannon on board.

But all the men cheered, and Ley said, "Well then, boys, pass the word on!" Then he and his group split off from the rest.

She'd worried that a lookout from the ship would spot

them, especially if it was still light when they arrived. But Mr. Ley had reassured her that in daylight the British would be unlikely to anchor close to shore, or they, too, might be spotted. She hoped he was right. If not, she'd never get a chance to help Rafe.

She listened to Francis prattle away as he steered. What romantic notions he had. She began to wonder what the British might do to a girl captured in the midst of a battle. Clearly nothing nice, especially if they learned it was she who'd brought the militia down on them. In such a case, she might never see her father again. She could feel the weight of what they were about to do bearing down harder every minute, and wanted to turn back. Or to hide. But she'd be ashamed to do that, with so many fearless men all around her.

No. She'd show them a young woman could be brave, too. No matter what it cost.

A lone longboat was pulled up on the beach when they finally passed the Heap and rounded the bend of Savage Island's north shore.

"That doesn't belong to anyone in the village," Molly told Francis. He brought them in close as he could, then Molly dropped the sail. She tied up the canoe at its usual place, a fallen oak tree that lay across the beach.

"Come on," said Francis. Other boats were pulling up by then, men piling out and wading through the shallows to shore. He motioned to them all to follow. Then he and Molly made their way into the woods and down the winding lane to the village.

28

THE SHORT CAREER OF A BLACKAMOOR PIRATE

BY SUNSET RAFE WAS STILL PULLING HARD at the oars of his skiff, along with two pirates. One was a skinny graybeard in knee britches and a ragged dress shirt with flapping cuffs. The other, a stocky young fellow with tight-curling red hair and a clumsily embroidered eye patch. They'd both been content to let him do all the rowing. He felt as if his arms had died a thousand strokes back and would soon fall from their sockets. So when the island finally came into sight, he felt a mixture of relief and dread.

At least, he thought, *Molly and her father are safe on the far shore.*

He'd kept a sharp lookout as they'd crossed the broadwater between the peninsula and these outer sea islands. But he'd seen nothing resembling a warship. Only the ragtag flotilla that surrounded him. And he'd heard only their drunken hullabaloo of laughing, blustering, and cursing, mixed with Captain Makeele's shouted orders, called back from boat to boat.

Was the man-o'-war late, or hove to on the other side of the island? Perhaps it wasn't coming at all.

Rafe glanced over his shoulder at the nearing shape of Savage Island again. An odd glow rose above the treetops. His companions noticed it at the same time. They pointed, then called out to the nearest boat.

Makeele, two sloops ahead, bellowed, "Ahoy, men! His Majesty's navy has beat us to the game. Let's join in before they take more than their due, eh?"

The sea rats cheered, clearly eager to get ashore and see what this treasure their masters talked of so often might be. *They want their share,* thought Rafe, *like everyone else. But my idea of great reward is different.* Somehow, he had to find that British ship and get aboard. Whether he'd stow away this time or board her openly would depend on what he learned after they landed. In any case, he'd make sure to escape this dirty gang at the first opportunity.

The skiff scraped bottom, and his surly boat mates jumped out to steady it. Rafe shipped the oars and climbed out to help beach the skiff. Nearby lay a longboat, very much like the one he and Molly had seen the officers arrive in when they had talked with Mrs. Ben on the beach. So they were indeed already here!

If only he could slip off in that longboat. Tired as he was, he'd pull all night for the ship if he had to. He'd beg them to take him along when they returned to their country. For now, he might at least hide in its bottom until the British returned. But the redheaded picaroon was already pushing him roughly into the woods. There didn't seem much chance of freedom at the moment, surrounded as he was by Makeele's whole gang.

One by one the pirates either beached their craft or anchored out and waded ashore, muskets and swords held high and dry. His keepers—as Rafe was beginning to think of them—prodded him into a run, toward sounds of shooting and commotion and shouting.

"Onward, lads," called Makeele behind them. "We'll meet no resistance from a pack of soft islanders. Mere babies and skirts and dotards!"

They were halfway to the village when the woods suddenly came to life. The very trees seemed to reach out leafy arms to do battle. Musket shots rained down from above. Every bush came armed with knives, swords, pitchforks, hoes, even iron skillets. As Rafe halted in confusion, the pirate ahead of him was jerked up by his heels to dangle in midair.

A trap! All around him, confused pirates tripped and danced and howled, thrashing blindly in the dark, besieged on every side by an angry yet invisible mob.

Rafe didn't try to run, for he could see that had done the pirates no good. Instead he dropped to the ground and rolled under a bush, then wriggled in deeper on knees and elbows, calculating his odds of doubling back to the longboat. Wondering if it would be better to hide for a while first.

Several picaroons thundered past his hiding place, retreating. Armed men Rafe didn't recognize were hot on their trail. These pursuers had smeared their faces with dirt or lampblack; their eyes looked frighteningly white and large above soot-darkened cheekbones. Their bloodcurdling cries sounded more beast or demon than human.

Soon any pirate not wounded or killed was hightailing it back to their landing beach, the defenders close behind.

Rafe didn't know whether to laugh or cry. His dirty picaroon captors had been beaten at their own game. Yet he . . . well, *he* was right back where he'd started, hiding on the very same island. Still he felt some renewed hope. For if he only kept still and out of sight, perhaps he might get away after all.

29

OLD SOLDIERS
RISE AGAIN

MOLLY POUNDED ON DOC DRUMMOND'S DOOR. "What in thunder?" he said as he opened it. "Ah—it's you, child! Mrs. Pruitt's been looking everywhere for you. Says your dad's suddenly gone, too. Real mysterious! The man looked far too sick last I saw him to be making any voyages."

"I took him across to the Shore."

She decided not to mention Dr. Henderson. It would annoy Drummond to have his treatment second-guessed, and they needed him on their side. "He's a bit better, Doc, and had some business to attend to over there. But now you and the rest of the villagers are in danger."

Doc squinted. "Eh? What's that?"

Molly took a deep breath. The fastest way to get him moving wouldn't be with long-winded explanations. "The *British*, Doc. You and Hank were right. They've come back. A man-o'-war's lying just off the island right now!"

His gnarled hand gripped her shoulder so hard she yelped. "The yellow dogs!" he shouted. "Well, why'n't you say so in the first place? Wait there, I'm going for my musket, and—"

"Can't linger; got to tell the others," said Molly quickly. "I've called men from Town's End and Eyre's Landing to help. Baxter Ley's in charge. This is Francis, his son."

Doc nodded to the boy. "If an old soldier like Ley's in on it, things must be right serious." He disappeared into the house. Molly and Francis ran to the next cottage.

In the same way, she roused Hank Blodgett and his wife, then Tim the netmaker, and one by one, all the others. Even the little gray-haired widow, Mrs. Meeker, came out with a blackened skillet in hand. When Molly tried to persuade her to stay indoors, the old woman shook the cast-iron pan at her.

"The lobsterbacks killed my Jake," she said fiercely. "I've an old score to settle."

Francis told everyone to meet in the woods behind the inn. To go quietly, to stay in the trees and out of sight. Then he headed behind the cottages, too, so they might slip that way unnoticed. Suddenly Molly stopped. As she turned back, he caught hold of her arm.

"Where are you going? Did we forget someone?"

"Ephraim," she said.

Francis frowned and crossed his arms. "And who might he be?"

Molly laughed at his sullen expression. "*He* is a very young billy goat."

"Oh, now. It's too dangerous to go up there on your own. Come along with the others. I'll help you get the goat later."

Molly didn't care much for this new, bossy Francis, but she pretended to agree. Then, while he was directing the islanders and trying to calm Mrs. Meeker, who was still waving her frying pan about recklessly, Molly slipped away.

Not get Ephraim indeed, she thought. She wouldn't leave the goat to the same fate as Miranda. Francis would just have to understand.

She kept to the shadows under the trees, then darted into the stable. There was Ephraim, munching hay. He bleated when she came in and trotted up to nuzzle her pockets. She fed him a bit of the crumbled biscuit she'd taken for Rafe.

"See, I've come for you," she whispered, then scooped him up. Ephraim had ever been a talkative creature, so she gently grasped his muzzle with one hand to stifle any inquisitive bleating. Over the open top half of the stable door, the yard appeared empty. The tavern showed a faint glow in the downstairs windows. Molly stepped out into the yard, intending to cross to the woods again. But she was as curious as Ephraim. So instead she sidled along the stable wall, past the kitchen, and under that lit window. Then she raised up on her toes just enough to see inside.

Several men were in the back, behind the taproom. They weren't sitting and having a pint, though. One man was rifling through the old pie safe, another was tossing papers out of her grandfather's desk, and a third was tapping and prying at the wooden paneling. Though he wasn't in uniform now, Molly recognized one as the short, stout officer she'd seen on the beach with Mrs. Ben. The widow didn't seem to be with them, though.

They were clearly searching for something. But if the redcoat gold had simply been hidden in there, her father and grandfather would surely have found it long ago. Of course, these men didn't know that.

As she watched, Ephraim squirmed and struggled, then gave a muffled bleat. She shushed him with more biscuit and took a firmer grip. When she looked up again, the stout officer was no longer in there. Well, she shouldn't linger, but go on and join the others.

As she turned away, a hand clamped hard on her shoulder.

"Where are you sneaking with my property, girl?" The widow's fingers tightened and she pulled Molly around to face her. Ephraim struggled free, and leaped from her arms. He ran off into the woods.

"Too bad you're a thief as well as a busybody," said the widow, holding Molly so she couldn't follow Ephraim. "Lieutenant!" she called. "Help me with this spy."

The officer stepped out of the back door. He took Molly's arm roughly, his hands even harder and stronger than Mrs. Ben's. Though she struggled and kicked at his booted shins, he dragged Molly up the steps and through the kitchen. His breath was thick with rum and fried onions. The man might look soft and stout, but he was strong. He held her out of striking range effortlessly, so all her blows landed on thin air.

Inside, the four other men turned to stare. "What've you caught, Llewellyn?" a thin blond man with a mustache asked Molly's captor. "Some local wildcat?"

"Nay, a scruffy little colony rat," the stout man said. They all laughed.

"But does it talk?" said a dark beardless fellow with huge muttonchops but not much chin.

"She will soon enough," said Mrs. Ben. Her tone changed, became softer, placating. "Now, girl, tell me quick so things will go easy on you. What were you doing lurking out in the yard? And where have you hidden your father? We believe he has something that belongs to King George."

Molly refused to look at the woman or to answer her. She wouldn't tell anyone about Pa, no matter what they did to her. She hoped the others would come soon, though; not liking the way the British navy men looked at her. She felt small, alone, like a calf singled out for slaughter. *At least Ephraim got away,* she thought bleakly.

"The little rat remains silent," said the chinless man thoughtfully.

"Put that poker to heat in the fireplace," said the stout one.

The chinless fellow hesitated a moment, but at last did so.

"Now, what do you think I'm going to do with a heated poker, my girl?" said the stout officer. "Make hot toddies for us all?"

"No," said Molly unwillingly. She couldn't help glancing at the fireplace. It was burning low. Red-hot coals glowed at the bottom.

"That's right. I have different plans."

Mrs. Ben looked alarmed, then disgusted. "You go too far, sir. What good is the girl to us, truly? We'll be about our business and gone before she can tell anyone."

"You said her father may know the whereabouts of what we

want," the officer reminded her. "In point of fact, she may know herself."

"He doesn't know a thing!" cried Molly. "And even if he did, he wouldn't tell you."

Startled by her outburst, the man holding her loosened his grip for a moment. She jerked away.

"Wait!" Mrs. Ben grabbed for her again, and Molly pulled away. Her back struck the edge of the table behind her. The oil lamp that always sat on it tilted, and they all paused to watch, horror-struck, as it teetered for a second. Then the burning lamp righted itself.

Lord have mercy . . . this dry old place would go up like a tinderbox, thought Molly, after the near accident. The relief on all the faces that ringed her was plain.

But then she thought, coldly, *as little as this inn means to me now, if it would stop them, even that would be worth it.*

This time she lunged deliberately for the lamp. Both the stout Llewellyn and Mrs. Ben reached out to push her away, but Molly managed to brush the lamp's base with her outstretched fingers. With one last lunge, she slammed a hip into the table and it went over, lamp and all.

In the shocked silence that followed, she thought, *What've I done?*

No time for regrets, though. For after a brief moment, the spilled oil caught, spreading flame like a blazing carpet of hot flowers over the floor planks.

"God's mercy. Water!" cried Mrs. Ben. "Get water, you great fools!" The fat officer made another grab for Molly, who dived beneath the legs of the upturned table. The heat of the spreading blaze came even through the heavy tabletop. Suddenly everyone was running around—to the kitchen, outside to the yard pump. Molly backed away on hands and knees, toward the window. She rose and hammered at the sash, trying to force it up, but the old back windows had rarely been opened in all the years they'd existed. This one groaned and screeched up a few inches, then stuck fast. She could put her head out and gasp a breath of clean, smokeless air. But that was all.

She stopped trying to open it, expecting hands to close on her any minute, to haul her to her feet. But she didn't turn away and run because she'd just noticed something outside. What would ordinarily be a most peculiar sight.

Mrs. Blodgett and the Widow Meeker were standing at the edge of the woods in nightgowns and bonnets, hair and hat strings flying in the breeze. With them were Hank Blodgett and Doc Drummond, who had a musket on his shoulder. Doc was pointing, gesturing toward the tavern.

They must've seen the flames through the windows, she thought. So her sacrifice had been for something after all.

With a chorus of shouts, the island people all burst from the woods, running full-tilt toward the Hog's Head. She could hear them through the window, men and women both, howling and whooping and shrieking. Had she not known them all by daylight as reasonable, quiet folks, it would indeed have been a frightening sight.

Perhaps they think the fire is the sign to attack, she reasoned. At least now she might be rescued before she roasted alive. For out in front and leading the charge was Francis Ley, and just this once his long, long legs were proving a great advantage.

The British sloshed pans and kettles of water onto the blaze, but it was clearly too little and too late. As they ran back and forth, cursing, Molly edged along the wall toward the tavern's front room. She might slip out that way while everyone was distracted by the fire. But when she entered the bar, Mrs. Ben was there, clearing the cash box of coins from the evening's business.

When she noticed Molly, the widow cried, "This is all your doing, you miserable wretch! Why must you meddle?" She stuffed the coins in her apron pocket and leaped up, chasing Molly toward the back again. The room was filling with smoke. The British had apparently given up fighting the fire and fled.

The widow looked around frantically. "Well, don't stand there gaping! Do you plan to simply watch, or get out of here with your skin?" In the firelight, Mrs. Ben's face twisted with fear; tears ran from her eyes. Now that she was at bay, the woman seemed smaller, weaker, almost tragic. Or perhaps . . . perhaps she'd never been the terror Molly had always imagined. This was such a freeing thought, she laughed out loud. The widow backed away, staring as if Molly were mad.

Voices clamored in the yard between stable and inn, and sounds of shouting and screaming and fighting. As the widow hesitated, the floor flared up in a wall of fire. She rushed back into the big tavern room. Molly followed, gasping and coughing. As they entered, the front door flew open, and a blue-coated officer raced inside, pursued by a pack of armed islanders. He must've been taken quite by surprise, because he still carried a teakettle from the kitchen.

Hank threatened the man with a pitchfork, and little Mrs. Meeker raised her deadly skillet. But then she saw the widow. "Here she is. Here's Lucinda Pruitt. The spy in our midst!"

Mrs. Ben gasped, pushed past Molly, and ran for the door. She was faster than Mrs. Meeker, for her legs were longer, and could easily outdistance the smaller woman.

But Ephraim had returned as well. He stood in the doorway, his plaintive cries adding to the confusion. Mrs. Ben stumbled over him and fell into the yard, then scrambled up on hands and knees.

Francis Ley came around the corner. When he spotted Mrs. Ben, he shouted, "What've you done with Molly Savage?"

"Stop her, Francis," Molly cried from the doorway.

Before the widow could pick herself up, Francis tackled her from behind. Then he sat, pinning her firmly to the ground.

The islanders and a few of the Eastern Shore men who'd joined the fight marched three Britishers, hands tied behind them, around to the front of the flaming building. The uniformed men looked stunned at being suddenly in the custody of country farmers and angry women. At last Francis let Mrs. Ben up, so Hank and Tim the netmaker could help him tie her up securely.

"Well, madam," said Doc Drummond. "What d'you have

to say for yourself? Seems you've betrayed your country and hornswoggled your neighbors."

The pale, trembling widow pressed her lips together, unable or unwilling to speak in her own defense. She only shook her head. Behind her, with a roar and a shower of sparks, the burning roof of the Hog's Head collapsed.

"You won't get away with this," shouted Llewellyn, the stout officer. "Our reinforcements will soon be here."

"Good," said Francis. "We'll have a grand welcome waiting for them, too."

"She's not just a spy. She may be a wrecker, too," said Molly. She then told everyone of the widow's midnight walk with horse and lantern. "You recall that ship, the *Tyger*, which broke apart? I think she's to blame."

The islanders stared at Mrs. Ben in horror, then muttered darkly among themselves. Mrs. Meeker stepped forward, skillet hanging loose in her shaking hand. "My only son died in a shipwreck off the Carolina Banks," she said. "Killed by a conniving devil like yourself, leaving me alone in this world. Oh, shame, shame on you, Lucinda Pruitt!"

"It was an accident!" cried the widow, tears streaking her face as she struggled against the imprisoning arms. "Dear Lord, I never meant to wreck anyone. I was told to give a sign to these men when it was safe to come in. I was only following orders, showing a light when I had information of such things as the—"

She stopped short, apparently realizing she'd just confessed her role as spy in front of a dozen people.

"Following orders? As if that's an excuse for murder!" Mrs. Meeker spat at the ground by Mrs. Ben's feet. "Damn you to Hades, Lucinda Pruitt!"

The widow looked round at them all, her face ghost-pale, her long black hair tumbling from its wooden combs. Her gaze stopped at Molly, desperate and imploring. With those dark locks curling around her face, with her eyes so wide and frightened, she looked softer, younger. As if she could actually be hurt. Perhaps she'd shown this other side to Ned Savage, when Molly was not around. If so, it might explain why he had seemed to see her somewhat differently.

The widow's face crumpled in grief. She began to cry.

"Do you think I don't see those men, hear them in my dreams? I didn't mean—it was only that stupid treasure . . . oh, I was forced into this by *them*." She pointed to the officers. "I feared for my life. The pirate Makeele, surely you've all heard of him?"

"Aye, quite recently," said Doc Drummond drily. "Go on."

She turned in a slow circle, appealing to the surrounding islanders, whose faces were tinted orange by the flames of the burning tavern. Who looked to Molly, once again, as daunting and fantastic as they had on the beach, the night of the shipwreck.

"The man's a fearful brute!" cried Mrs. Ben. "A demon! When I was but a girl, he forced me into marriage. He forced me to . . . I cannot describe to you all the things I've suffered. Aye, since I was younger than you," she said to Molly. "I escaped this monster only when he was jailed for pirating. But he's out again, and wants treasure, has threatened force to make me do his bidding."

The villagers looked unimpressed. But Molly felt a pricking of sympathy, despite her dislike. She knew how it was to feel as helpless as a marker in a game. Perhaps so many terrible, nameless hurts had somehow twisted the woman, had made her hate-filled and desperate.

She'd never imagined the widow might've suffered once, too. That something in the past might have sharpened her words and make her outlook so grim and mean.

But she also remembered the poor drowned sailors on the beach. And Rafe was still missing. Was pity for the widow's past enough to justify, or at least to forgive, these wrongs?

"What is this wonderful treasure," Molly demanded, "that can make picaroons join their old allies again and attack innocent folks?"

Mrs. Ben shook her head. "That, I know not. Only that these men spoke of it as a great loss to England. Something to do with the time of the royal governor's rule."

The chinless officer glared round at his captors scornfully. "It's the property of King George, you bloody traitors. Governor Dunmore's seal, his mace and signet, saved from a filthy insurrection by true loyalists. Lay a dirty paw on one piece, and we'll hang you all."

"Quiet, you fool," growled the stout lieutenant.

"Come, Llewellyn. This ignorant rabble must be taught a lesson. Must understand who are the real masters here!"

The islanders and Eastern Shore farmers looked at one another, then back at the British officers. Then they staggered and shouted with laughter, falling about in amusement at this empty threat.

"If a neck be stretched anytime soon, it won't be a patriot's," said Blodgett. "Well then, men . . . and ladies. Keep a sharp lookout. Where limeys tread, can their thieving pirate henchmen be far behind?"

Everyone dispersed as Baxter Ley assigned lookout posts. Hank and Doc led Mrs. Ben away.

Francis came up to Molly again. He leaned and put his lips close to her ear, his breath stirring her hair, his voice at once intimate and uncertain. "I'm going to j-join my father and the other men," he whispered. "I'll make you proud of me yet."

Before she could say a word, he vanished into the woods.

30

FRANCIS TAKES
A PRISONER

RAFE HUGGED THE GROUND until all noise of the fighting died away and was replaced by the normal sounds of the woods night life. The ghostly calls of hunting owls, the rustle of four-footed animals in trees and bushes, the trills of nightbirds. And the uncomfortably close rustlings of some sort of unseen creatures that he hoped would not feel moved to bite or claw or sting him. Did snakes live on islands? He hadn't seen any yet, but still . . .

He waited, until certain he was alone. Then he cautiously squirmed out from under the thick, thorny branches, adding new scratches and scrapes to those already crisscrossing arms, legs, and belly. He pushed up on hands and knees to rise.

"Stop where you are, filthy p-pirate," said a low voice.

Rafe froze, then turned his head slowly to look up. A lanky, trembling, white-faced boy held a musket trained right on him. The fellow was perhaps a little older than Rafe and didn't look all that strong. He acted very nervous. But none of that mattered, for he held the gun.

"Don't shoot," said Rafe quickly, for he feared with the

boy's shaking hand, the accidental jerk of a finger would fire the musket of its own accord. "I'll go along with you."

Clearly no use to insist he wasn't a pirate.

The tall boy motioned to set him onto the path, and they marched back toward the village.

"Ho, Dad! Got me a blackamoor buccaneer!" his captor shouted as they emerged into the clearing.

"Good work, lad! Truss the fellow up and stow him in the stable," said the boy's father shortly, turning to confer with other men again.

They passed the familiar shingled cottages, but Rafe stared straight ahead. For just up the lane, the Hog's Head Tavern was burning to the ground. Nearly all that remained was the privy and a decrepit smokehouse. And the stable, where several wounded men lay about or were propped against its wall. Wayland Makeele was not among them. Again, Rafe felt glad Molly Savage was across the water, safe. Imagine how she'd feel when she saw what was left of her home. He supposed he must've slowed down, for the boy prodded him with the gun barrel.

As they approached the stable Rafe was just beginning to notice, over the ache of his exhausted arms, that he had a good many deep cuts and bruises, too. His old broken ribs hurt again. He wanted nothing more than to drink a bucketful of cool water and lie down.

As they reached the stable, a familiar figure came out. A

thin red-haired girl, face and dress streaked with soot, hugging a small white goat to her chest.

"Rafe!" she cried. She set the goat down and ran toward him. Francis scowled anew at this, but Rafe didn't care. Neither of them could ever imagine how glad he was to see Molly Savage again.

31

KNOW THINE
ENEMY

OLLY WAS SURPRISED and thankful to see Rafe was unharmed . . . or, from the look of him, at least not too badly hurt. She wondered by what miracle he had landed back here on the island. But when she came forward to find out, Francis stepped between them.

"Watch out, Moll," he said importantly. "He's my prisoner. Found him hiding after that fray in the woods."

"Your prisoner? Don't be silly, Francis, this is only—" But then she stopped. How could she safely explain Rafe's presence on the island?

Francis looked at her curiously. "Surely you don't know him?"

"I only meant," she went on more slowly, "that he looks a good deal like . . . like one of Captain Arnold's younger darkies. A slave from their farm I've seen once or twice."

"Well, then. There you have it," said Francis. "Clearly he's run off and joined Makeele's band. I simply caught him up here. His cowardly brethren ran off and left him."

Molly hovered as Francis tied Rafe's hands. She followed them as he pushed the boy into the empty stall next to

Janey's. The stable was full of prisoners, British and pirate alike. Mrs. Ben had been taken under guard to the Blodgetts' shed and locked inside.

Francis shut the stall door, then turned to Molly. "Come on," he said. "I need to see about what we'll do with these prisoners. And you can't stay in here."

Surely this was the chance to help Rafe, as promised. She wanted to ask him what he thought best to do, but it was impossible with Francis listening.

"Of course not," she said. "Only . . . just let me get Ephraim settled and fed. I'll be right along."

Francis hesitated. "I can't leave you alone here. Not with the likes of these."

"Francis Ley," said Molly sternly, folding her arms, drawing herself up to be as tall as possible. "Are you telling me your pa and his men don't know how to tie a knot? And that you can't either? I suppose next you'll be telling me I don't know how to feed a goat all by myself."

Francis reddened. "Of course not. They're trussed like hogs. But—"

"Well then, go about your business and I'll do the same. Since the inn has burned, this stable and goat and horse are all Dad and I have left in the world. And he's not here, so I must look after things." For it had occurred to her that since Mrs. Ben was to be sent to the magistrate, at least the stable and livestock might be theirs again.

Someone outside shouted, "A frigate sighted, lying off the island!"

"Aye," called another excitedly. "'Twas coming in. But it's only standing off now."

Francis picked up his gun. "They must've noticed the f-fire, and all. I'm going to see what's up. V-very well, then, Molly Savage," he stammered, then shook his head. "What a stubborn girl you are. Ma says so, too." He pointed at her. "But mark me. I'll be back in a few minutes to see all is well."

Molly repressed a sigh. "Thank you, Francis," she said, trying to sound meek.

"But here's my gun," he added. "I know you can shoot well enough. Don't hesitate if any of these rascals gives you trouble." He pressed it into her hands, then rushed out.

As soon as he'd left, Molly sat in the straw beside Rafe. "What happened?" she asked quietly, so the other captives wouldn't overhear. "You're all bloody and bruised! Here, I'll untie you."

"No. Best not. Not yet."

Then he told how the pirates had come on him as he watched over her father, and taken him prisoner. He described the fearful Wayland Makeele and his rough headquarters, though he could not say where it was, thanks to the blindfold. Then he recounted the long trip back to the island and the surprise attack that had greeted them. "So the picaroons are routed. But I didn't see Makeele after that."

"Nor I," said Molly. "He must've turned tail and run when they were attacked in the woods."

Rafe looked skeptical and shrugged. "No doubt. But the ship has come back."

"And what will we do?" she asked. "Seems every time we plan to free you, you become ever more trapped."

"That's true. But I have a plan. Listen," he said. "There was a longboat pulled up on the beach. . . ."

He told her of his idea of taking it out and joining the British ship, as crew or stowaway.

"But, Rafe," she protested when he'd finished. "They're our mortal enemies."

"They're *your* enemies," he pointed out. "But if, in England, there are no slaves, then I could truly be free."

She was listening to him well. She wanted to help, of course. But help him escape to the British?

"But then . . . you'd be my enemy as well," she whispered, all too aware of the prisoners not far from them.

"I'd never be your enemy," he said quietly. "No matter where I live. You saved my life and hid me away. Every day I expected you to betray me—to be like all the white people I'd ever known. But I was wrong."

She nodded, understanding all too well. She could not explain exactly when it had shifted, what was between them. It was true—you couldn't know a person by the whole of their kind, or simply by how they looked.

But she must put this lesson away for the time being, and try to think of a better plan. He wasn't safe here, and she'd heard the law even let slave catchers follow an escaped slave up north. So perhaps he was right—there truly was nowhere in the States he could be safe.

"All right. I'll help you do it," she said at last. "First, I must convince the village men not to take you across to the mainland with the other captives. If they believe you're Captain Arnold's property, as Pa claimed before, they wouldn't deprive him of the right to punish his own slave."

Molly stood and dusted straw from her skirt. "Francis or someone else might be looking for me. I'd better go now."

When she finally found Doc and Hank, they were poking gingerly through the still-hot ashes of the tavern. Looking for any stray bottle that might've escaped the blaze, she supposed. By their long faces, they hadn't had much success.

She explained that Rafe had been taken hostage by mistake, when Francis thought him one of the pirates.

"You recall, he was stranded here not a week ago," she said to Doc. "After the picaroon raid."

Drummond rubbed his grizzled chin whiskers. "Sure, I recall the young darky fella . . . I think . . . don't I?"

Hank nodded solemnly. "Aye, ye do."

Molly pressed on. "He told me the pirates seized him while he was out hunting for Mrs. Ben."

"They've been known to do such as that and worse, the swine," said Hank.

"Captain Arnold will surely want to come himself to get the boy back," she said.

"No doubt of that. We'll send word," said Hank. "Right after we take the prisoners ashore to gaol."

The last thing Molly wanted was for them to tell the Arnolds about Rafe. Imagine their puzzlement when they counted heads on the farm. . . . But she could think of no good reason to discourage them at the moment. At least the boy might gain enough time to get out of slaveholding territory.

But now it was growing late, and she felt so weary she was swaying on her feet.

Mrs. Meeker came up and laid a hand on her arm. "You're a brave one, no mistake, little Molly Savage," the widow said, though she had to peer up into Molly's face to do so. "Come along now to my cottage. You can wash up and rest."

"Oh, but—"

"Now, you can't sleep in a barn, child. With a pack of pirates, and a young nigra boy, and those blasted British in there? 'Twouldn't be proper."

All around, exhausted men and boys were bedding down on horse blankets and coats, since there were too many to lodge overnight in the cottages along the lane. Soon they'd be up again, hauling the prisoners to Eastville. And Molly could do nothing for Rafe till then, with so many about to witness it.

"Thank you, Mrs. Meeker," she said at last, feeling the tiredness she'd been too busy to notice until then settle in her bones. Against her will, she yawned. "It's kind of you to offer."

They cut through Doc Drummond's tiny yard on the way to the Meeker cottage. When she saw the shed, Molly remembered Mrs. Ben had been imprisoned there. As they passed the ramshackle building, she was sure she heard muffled weeping.

"What will they do with the widow, in Eastville?"

"Why, what they do with any traitor, I imagine. Shoot 'em. Or hang 'em," said Mrs. Meeker with some satisfaction.

Molly hadn't imagined that ending to the story. She glanced over her shoulder, at the shed. Her steps slowed.

"Oh, don't waste your pity on that one, dear," said the widow. "She's told enough lies to dig her grave." Then she looked thoughtful. "I didn't mean to upset you. Forgot what a soft spot you have for all critters, large and small. Anyhow, dear, they don't hang women. Not usually, these days."

Molly supposed Mrs. Meeker was right. But what if she wasn't? She was surprised at the bit of sympathy she was beginning to feel for a woman she'd always assumed she hated. One who'd always seemed to hate her. Though at odd times it was true Mrs. Ben had spoken up for her. Like the night before, when the officer had threatened to brand her with a hot poker . . . well, she supposed she hadn't really known her at all. Now it seemed she never would. As Mrs. Meeker said, the woman had told so many lies. Now who could say what the full truth was?

Of course, Molly thought with a pang of guilt, she, too, had told a few lately. Believing, of course, that she had good reason. To help herself, or others she cared about. To spare folks trouble or pain. Yes, she'd had her reasons—but perhaps the widow had thought the same.

32

FINDERS, KEEPERS

NEXT MORNING Baxter Ley and the other old soldiers marched their captives down to the beach, to load them onto fishing boats and off to justice in Eastville.

"You'll answer to King George for this outrage," protested one, stumbling along in the sand. "And for kidnapping His Majesty's servants!"

"Oh, be still," said Mrs. Ben, straggling hair blowing into her eyes, her black dress streaked gray with soot and ash. "You and your secret treasure!"

Molly stood at the edge of the water, watching as they settled the widow in the stern of a log canoe. A few days earlier, she might've felt triumphant to see her enemy brought low. But somehow, this morning it wasn't a satisfying sight. She felt relieved, yet a bit sad.

Francis came up to stand beside her. "Molly." He shyly touched her arm, then drew his hand back. Looked down, as if worried she was angry, and kicked at a shard of whelk shell. His cheeks were flushed.

"Are you leaving, Francis? Maybe you could check on Pa for me, and tell him I'll be over soon to fetch him home."

"I will. But I don't see why you aren't coming now." When he looked up again, his face was puzzled. "What's left for you here on the island but a pile of ashes?"

She hesitated, wondering which words would best show she wasn't being foolish or stubborn. "Well, first, it's my home, Francis. The only one I've ever known. The island's been our family place for ages. Grandfather thought highly enough of that old tavern house to move it all the way from the south end, way back when it nearly washed away. So I can't take such things too lightly."

He nodded slowly, regretfully. She knew he understood. The notion of home was a powerful thing, to anyone. "Yes, but—"

She raised a hand to stop him. "But that's not all. Second, Pa and I will own what's left, I hope, after being servants so long in our own place. Of course, we don't know for sure; perhaps it will all be taken from us. So I want to feel it *is* ours again, at least for a little while."

Francis nodded again, but less unwillingly. "That makes sense. But I can't help wishing you weren't so attached to this island."

Francis no longer looked foolish and gawky. After all, he'd fought bravely. But she still had to laugh, recalling the sight of him sitting on the widow as if she were a sack of meal.

"What?" he said anxiously.

"I was just remembering the way you tackled Mrs. Ben yesterday. You appeared like a hero and did exactly right. And for that alone I could kiss you, Francis.

"Though I won't," she added, when he looked hopeful again. "But"—she took his hand—"I see you're no foolish boy at all, but a brave, kind man. And I'll always remember that I owe you much."

He reddened again, but Molly was glad to see he took the rebuff fairly well.

Then Francis surprised her. "Maybe I'll collect that debt someday, Molly Savage," he said. "Unless you decide to even our accounts first." He grinned, then made an about-face and went off toward his father's sloop. She watched him go, surprised. *Well, well,* she thought. *I really haven't given Francis enough credit by half.*

After the last boat pulled away, she walked back up the path. The familiar woods, the birds trilling from unseen perches high in oaks and loblolly pine, the rustle of leafy branches like a taffeta dress sweeping the floor—it all seemed even quieter since the rush and shouting of the night before. She'd have liked to linger, to sit on a cushion of pine needles and just do nothing for a while. Now she could, without worrying if the widow was on her trail, or if she'd said or done something that would bring grief to herself or her father.

"I'll be back soon," she whispered to the trees, to the small creatures going on about their lives all around her. But at the moment, she had one more task left.

A few islanders were out puttering around their cottages and yards, fixing smashed shingles, hanging fallen shutters, repairing all sorts of damage done the night before. She waved to Doc, who held a hammer and a mouthful of nails. And to Mrs. Blodgett, shaking the ash from her curtains and rag rugs, while her grown daughter sat on the front stoop, bouncing the baby on her knees.

Molly figured it best to wait until folks went in for a mid-day meal before she risked sneaking Rafe from stable to shore. The British longboat still lay on the beach, pulled up on the sand above the high tide mark, not too far from the Heap. She'd need to put together some provisions for him, and a cask of water. Somehow.

The ashes of the inn were nearly cool. And in them she saw no sign of any legendary treasure, no melted puddles of gold. Aside from a rough, square foundation of soot-blackened orange brick, not much was left at all. The kitchen chimney and the tavern-room fireplace, a few iron blacksmithings from doors and windows. Funny, she felt no great regret for the loss yet. But then she'd had so little of her own up in that tiny attic. One old dress, too small. A wooden comb, minus three teeth. An extra pair of woolen stockings, much mended. Over the last few years the tavern had come to seem as if it did indeed belong to Mrs. Ben. Whatever happened, she and her father would manage.

She thought she understood a bit better, as well, why he'd balked at leaving. The unknown was frightening. Even so, she knew that grown-ups made mistakes, too. They were not all-seeing, or even as powerful as she'd always thought.

To pass the time, she began to sift through the ashes, picking up an occasional still-warm hinge, a blackened brass door-knob. *Might as well scavenge what I can,* she thought. Ephraim took a dim view of this poking about. He perched on a pile of brick near the blackened foundation, bleating at her.

After a half hour, she stood and stretched to ease her aching back. She'd made a little pile of finds. No gold, of course, despite the tales. Not even a tiny melted nugget. Clearly nothing of value had ever been hidden in the tavern walls or floors or ceiling. She wasn't fated to swan off like a great lady in a golden boat, that was for sure.

"Ah, well. A small heap of not much, but it's all ours," she said. "Not treasure, but perhaps still worth a few pennies."

Something about houses and treasure was still nagging at her mind. And heaps of things. A heap of what . . . or was it *the* Heap? The place where the inn *used* to stand.

Hank and Doc had talked of treasure. Her father had teased her silly about it. He and her grandfather had once looked and looked through the Hog's Head, in vain. The old story of that legendary night might still claim that two Englishmen had come to the inn, then argued and fought. That one had died, and the other run away. The fire had proved one thing—there was no treasure concealed in her family's old tavern, and probably never had been.

But . . . what if it had never been hidden in there at all?

Where else would a frightened man on the run, a stranger desperate to hide out till he could steal a boat or even swim out to a waiting ship, hide something valuable?

Oh, for mercy's sake. Why hadn't it occurred to her before? Molly snatched up her skirts so she wouldn't trip, and ran down the path toward the water.

At the Heap, outside the old root cellar, she eyed the sunken foundation on which the Hog's Head Inn had stood before the big storm all those years ago, when her own father was but a boy. It'd taken thirty strong men to move the house inland, Pa had told her, rolling it on huge logs rafted in over the broadwater. They'd knocked apart the foundation, too, all but the lowest course, because bricks were valuable.

But before the Revolution, *this* was where the tavern house had stood. A man seeking to escape an island must head for the water. But if he'd been forced to hide for a bit . . . or perhaps, the most desperate measure of all, to swim for freedom—well, then, he couldn't carry anything at all.

She picked up a flat piece of driftwood and began digging in the damp heavy sand inside the foundation. But after sweaty minutes of this work, and only a middling-size hole to show for it, she stopped. It might take years to find the right spot. The treasure—if indeed there was one—could've been buried anywhere.

Or could it?

The Hog's Head had never had a basement, in either location, just a hog crawl space not even big enough to sit up in. Dig deep almost anywhere on the island, and you struck water, either fresh or salt. It would've been impossible for a man to squeeze underneath the building, much less take along a shovel. The old root cellar was shallow, but still too damp to keep any foodstuffs there for long.

The root cellar. The ramshackle structure old as the original house. The men who had moved the tavern hadn't bothered to also move that hump of timbers and earth. Because it covered a floor that was nothing but . . .

Sand. Soft sand, good for digging.

She did just that for the better part of an hour, using the driftwood and then the end of a broken, rusted pick she discovered on the edge of the Heap. Trying first a front corner, then a back one, then the middle. Sweat ran in her eyes. Her shoulders ached. Her skin prickled, too, for somehow she expected any moment to turn up a skeleton wrapped in bits of rotting blue uniform cloth. That was silly. The British sailor was long gone, either drowned or back in England. Still, the image wouldn't leave her, thanks to all the ghost stories she'd grown up on.

It began to feel as if she'd always been there, digging, digging, and would never get any farther. But at last the point of the pick went *whock* as it struck something.

Molly froze, her breath stopped halfway. It couldn't be a rock . . . there was not a stone or pebble to be had on the island, only sand and some clay. She wiped trembling, sweat-slick hands on her skirt. Took a better hold on the pick, trying to ignore the blisters on her palms. She dug on, deeper, until she uncovered the top of a dark box. She had to reach out to feel the rough surface, the raised grain of wood under her fingers, to convince herself it was real. Then, forgetting all her aches, she dug even harder, until she could work the pick under one edge and pry the chest up from the damp, hard-packed sand.

It was of some blackened hardwood, old oak or maybe teak, with rusted bands of iron holding it together. There was a latch, but no lock. Set in what looked like hammered silver in the lid was a carved, fancifully scrolled, and badly tarnished letter *D*. The fine work certainly fit for royalty. Or for . . .

"Dunmore," she whispered. "*D* for the old devil himself, the king's governor, Dunmore."

It could've been a treasure chest, except it was small. Still, her heart drummed hard as she fingered the latch—as if this could be a dream or a spell that one wrong move would break. She grasped it. The rusted hinge resisted, but she forced it up. Sand fell away in a fine shower as she lifted the lid.

Inside, on a bed of damp, stained velvet, lay three things: a gold ring, a gold seal, a satin pouch with drawstrings. And beneath them some other, larger items, wrapped in flannel. Staring in awe, Molly sat back. This hoard was not what she'd imagined. Gold coins, yes. But these odd things . . . she prodded the ring and seal cautiously with one finger, the metal cold to the touch. They looked official, important. What had the plump British officer said?

Your father has something that belongs to King George.

When her find didn't vanish into thin air, she lifted the pouch carefully, with both hands. The drawstrings had rotted from salt and damp, and when they parted the bag gaped open, spilling its contents in a gleaming shower.

Redcoat gold.

"It *is*," she whispered. A heap of thick, heavy-looking, round gold coins lay scattered inside the box where they'd landed. A couple had hit the edge and bounced off into the sand. She picked one up, gently polished it with the hem of her skirt. And looked at the graven picture, a profile of a sharp-nosed man wearing a crown. On the other side sat a woman in a helmet and long, flowing gown, holding a sort of three-pronged spear. Molly turned it over again, then dropped it on the pile and counted up the whole golden hoard. Surely it was enough to pay off all their debts and have much left to spare!

She scooped the coins back into the pouch and pushed it into her pocket. Then she picked up the gold ring. Heavy, flat on the face, it had no jewels set into it but was engraved with the figures of a lion and a unicorn. She turned it over, then tried it on one finger, but it was far too large and slipped wrong side around. She tucked it and the seal into her other pocket, then picked up the last items, wrapped in flannel.

These, at least, were not gold at all. One part was shaped curiously like a fancy doorknob, along with several sections of ornately carved rod, and all was tarnished the dull black of never-polished silverware. They were threaded at each end, and she soon had screwed them together into a long staff, something like a fairy-tale scepter. She had no idea what on earth it might be used for, but it looked important. Assembled, it would be much too large for her pocket, so she took it apart, wrapped the pieces in the cloth again, and set them down.

She put the box back in the hole and kicked sand over it again. Then she picked up the heavy bundle containing the staff and looked around the root cellar. There *had* been treasure hidden on Savage Island, as Hank and Doc had joked— as Rafe had insisted there should be. But even he had never guessed he'd been sleeping over the trove the whole time!

She ran up the path again, no longer tired or sore-muscled. As she reached the first cottage, her excitement began to fade. She slowed and looked behind her. Would anyone notice how her pockets sagged and guess what she'd found? She pulled the folds of her skirt protectively around it and walked more quickly.

I must hide it, she thought feverishly. *Right away.* The weary, unpleasant feeling persisted. If anyone saw and asked, she calculated, she could say this was coin put away by her great-grandfather. But who would believe that?

It bothered her to think that even though Mrs. Ben was gone, and she, Molly Savage, was free, she still needed to concoct tales. She slowed her steps. How terrible to suddenly fear and mistrust the same people who'd come to her aid the night before. How silly to think Doc or Hank or little Mrs. Meeker would wrestle her to the ground and rob her! True, she'd once or twice been robbed of her finds, like that nice painted tray, by scavengers. But she was sure they'd come from elsewhere, not the island.

She'd never had to look sideways at old friends before, to scheme against them. Was that what riches did to folks?

She walked to the stable slowly, so as not to attract attention, though no one was about. It was hard to have to hide how happy and excited she felt. Still, the gold was theirs! She could pay their debts. Perhaps build a small inn to serve travelers. Or just a little cottage that would not take half so much work to keep up as the tavern had. After toiling years for Mrs. Ben, she did not feel like doing more sweeping and dusting and scrubbing than necessary.

Now the second-most exciting part came. She *could* tell Rafe.

She looked around, then laid the bundle containing the silver staff behind a crate by the stable door. It was so bulky, she'd never be able to hide it in a pocket.

She found the boy sitting in the straw, trussed hands wrapped around a mug, clumsily drinking. Water spilled and ran down his chin. An empty tin plate lay beside him.

"Here, now I can untie you," she said breathlessly. "I wanted to come sooner, but folks were about. And I have wondrous news."

He rubbed his wrists when they were free. "That's better. Though I was getting good at two-handing it. What's your great news?"

Molly hesitated. She told herself that was only because she wanted to prolong the pleasure of knowing—to keep it just her secret, for a bit.

"We'll need to find you some provisions," she said quickly.

"And then we must make our way to the beach. Those fishing today are already out. The others are in for a meal, so this is a good time. If we wait until evening—"

"It may be too late," he finished for her. "But what news?"

She pretended to sigh. "I'm afraid someone, perhaps Captain Arnold, may come to look at you and stake a claim, whether it's true or not."

"Yes, yes," said Rafe, as if that danger were of no importance. "But, Molly, what—"

Suddenly she didn't wish to wait any longer; it was too exciting. "Close your eyes."

Rafe looked puzzled, but did as she ordered.

Molly reached in her pockets and took out the pouch carefully so the coins wouldn't clink and give the surprise away. She left the gold ring and seal in her pocket and spilled the hoard into his lap.

"Now—look!"

Rafe opened his eyes, then looked up again, startled. He whispered in awe, "Have you taken up pirating yourself?" as he lifted one heavy gold coin and examined it.

Molly laughed, though she was dismayed to realize she minded that he was handling her gold. The wonderful find of which she already felt so possessive.

"I don't know what to say," he said, then frowned. "Oh, what happened to your hands?"

Molly turned them from backs to palms, looking down as if they belonged to someone else. They were bleeding, torn, pocked with blisters. She was still too excited to mind the pain, though no doubt they'd hurt like the devil later. She was so aware of the ring and the seal, still concealed in her pockets, that she felt their weight through the material of her skirt. She did not bring them out, only smiled and watched the boy fondle and count each disk of gold.

Then she told him all about the finding of the secret treasure of Savage Island.

As they prepared for Rafe's departure, she couldn't think of a way to beg food without arousing suspicions. They'd wonder why she'd want to take it with her rather than sit and eat in a warm kitchen.

Then she remembered the sack of biscuits and honey and other victuals. The one Dr. Henderson's housekeeper, Mrs. Morey, had given her the day before, and that she'd dropped when the lieutenant had dragged her into the tavern. She looked around the yard. The sack was still there, battered and sooty, stepped on by many feet, but its contents still looked edible.

"What luck," she said, and quickly returned to the stable. She tossed the sack to Rafe, along with a jacket abandoned on the ground. "Go now, through the woods. But wait for me halfway along the path to the beach."

"Not at the Heap?" he said. "I'd have spoken more kindly of the place had I known its secret."

She peered out over the half door. "All seems clear, now."

He slipped out of the stable, along the sidewall, and made a dash for the woods. Molly waited, heart thumping, expecting any minute someone would cry, "Runaway!"

No sound but the song of the birds, the rustle of leaves in a sea-sent breeze. And the faint, receding patter of bare feet. So in a moment, she, too, set out casually up the path, as if only out for a walk, the little goat trailing along behind. It felt like nothing had changed as she strolled the familiar path.

Then Rafe was rising from under a tree, standing to meet her. And it was time for him to go on to . . . who knew what fate.

She pressed the sack of provisions into his hand. He was wearing the abandoned jacket, which was heavy and warm but too large for him. "Look," he said, "I found an old bottle, dropped by a pirate, perhaps in the fight. It'll clean up nice, and I can fill it from the spring."

"Good idea," she said. "You'll need water, and . . . and . . ." Her voice trailed off. She couldn't think what to say next.

Rafe hesitated, then stooped to hug Ephraim. "Take care, old friend," he said to the little goat, who licked his cheek. That was why, surely, it looked so damp when he stood again.

It would be much too forward to embrace him. The fact that she, a white girl, had even thought of reaching out in such a way to a black boy would shock the lives out of most folks she knew. So instead she tucked four gold coins in his pocket, for the journey. He looked at her, and she at him. She hoped her gaze told him enough of her gratitude.

She'd just opened her mouth to say good-bye out loud when a large grimy hand with black-rimmed fingernails closed hard on her wrist.

"I'll take that," growled a deep voice horribly close to her ear. "Though 'tis a touching scene, Mistress Savage, I do swear. Makes me want to weep into me hanky. If I had one."

Molly choked back a scream that was scraping her throat trying to get out. Ephraim bolted off, bleating in alarm. And Rafe . . . Rafe seemed frozen in fear, or horror, as the shaggy, dirty man who had hold of her reached out and fished in his coat pocket, taking all the coins.

For he was a dreaded picaroon—a house burner, kidnapper, goat stealer, nailer of hands to barn doors—and even bigger and taller than her father. Thin, yet far more muscular beneath the knee-length damask waistcoat and torn lace shirt. His clothes were blotched in places with dried blood, probably from a wound beneath the dirty rag tied around his head. His greasy hair hung in twisted coal-black ringlets, and he was bearded to the eyes. He had a leathery, tanned face, cracked and seamed like an old boot.

But his eyes were the worst—cold, pale blue—and in them Molly saw only amusement. There would be more kindness, mercy, and sympathy in the flat, unblinking gaze of a water snake. Then the pirate laughed, the hot gust of his stinking breath like old meat. His few teeth were yellowed and crooked. One looked as if it had been filed to a point.

She flinched away, but he only reached out and dragged her close, until her face was pressed into his waistcoat. He grasped Rafe's jacket, too. A stench of unwashed man and raw, reeking rum made her feel sick. This terrible ogre had said her name; he actually knew her. But when she looked up into his smirking face she didn't recognize him.

Rafe clearly did, though. "Cap'n Makeele," he whispered. And though the boy's face looked calm—or maybe blank with fear—his voice shook.

"Aye, the same," said the pirate, and now that Molly knew who had hold of them, all hope drained away.

33

THE PIRATE KING
RETURNS

WAYLAND MAKEELE PICKED UP RAFE and shook him the way a terrier would if it was determined to snap a rat's neck. So one of the pirates had escaped—the worst of the lot. By the leaves and twigs caught in the tangled black hair and beard, the picaroon chief had been hiding in the woods, biding his time since the day before. Rafe was grateful he hadn't spotted Molly earlier, when she was coming back up the path, carrying her treasure. When he got a glimpse of her pale, shocked face, the girl seemed to be praying. Rafe said a quick prayer himself. *Please let me think of a story so good, this devil will let us go.* For no one knew where they were, or was likely to miss them. They'd made sure of that.

"The patriots . . . they took us hostage, sir," said Rafe suddenly, trying to make his voice sound earnest and outraged. "The traitors to the king and . . . and to you. It was a fearful fight! Most all lost or captured. This girl . . . she's been helping me escape to . . . to return to warn you."

The pirate raised an eyebrow. "Is that so." His mocking tone sent a chill through Rafe. "Then we all go along in one merry group, don't we?"

He shoved Rafe ahead and, gripping Molly's arm, dragged her in their wake. "'Tis real heartwarming to know I have loyal followers yet," said the man drily, giving Rafe a shove that knocked the breath from him. "And that you'll no doubt be happy to row me all the way back to camp."

Rafe thought frantically. There was no reason left for Makeele to let them live. They would tell the islanders about him. How could they escape? Molly's father would never have allowed this to happen, but he was ill, and far away. Crusty Mrs. Ben wouldn't let a pirate push her about, even if she had to scratch, claw, and pinch him to death. Even the lanky, weedy boy Molly had called Francis might think of something.

Desperate, Rafe craned back to look at her.

She looked hard at him, too. Then suddenly she lowered her head and sank her teeth into the bare dirty wrist showing below the pirate's tattered lace cuff. When the man pulled it away and howled in pain, Rafe jerked hard against the fist gripping his overlarge jacket. He lifted his arms and slipped clean out of it.

"Run!" he heard Molly cry as the pirate roared in renewed pain. She must've bitten him again, Rafe thought as he bolted blindly into the woods, not daring to look back and see if she was behind him. He ran as fast as he could, but even so Makeele's cursing, his thudding footsteps seemed close behind. The first promising hiding place Rafe saw was a thick, gnarled oak with a warped trunk. He grabbed the lowest branch and vaulted up.

Makeele drew closer, and Rafe held his breath. He pulled

back a leafy branch and looked down. Below was Molly, with the pirate pounding close behind. As he ran Makeele drew a long-barreled horse pistol from his coat and leveled it at the girl.

But she was jerking desperately at the shawl flying around her shoulders. She tugged the knot free and then, as the two passed beneath Rafe's hiding place, she wadded it up and threw it. The bulky shawl caught the pirate square in the face. He stumbled, clawing at the cloth, then tripped over a root, fighting the length of dark cloth like a human enemy all the way to the ground. He got up again, cursing, and lumbered off. Rafe leaped from the oak, and a soft bed of leaf mold and pine needles broke his fall. He, too, scrambled up and after Molly, but unlike Makeele, he had seen which way she'd gone.

"Wait," he gasped as he finally caught up. "It's only me."

She stopped. "You make a good assassin," he said. "But we'd best run back to the village for help."

"We can't," she gasped. "Think what Makeele might tell them about you. You'll be imprisoned again, or sent to the Arnold Plantation, or—"

"But we can't stop him alone. He's too big. He has a gun and a knife and will be glad to use them."

When she opened her mouth as if to argue again, a shot rang out through the woods. They both gasped and dropped to the ground. A long moment of silence, followed by a new round of piratical cursing. But the crashing, the thudding of heavy footsteps, had ceased.

Rafe tugged at Molly's arm. "I don't know what this means, but there's no time to argue."

"No, wait," she said. "Listen. He's not running after us anymore."

He frowned. "But I still hear him shouting. What do you think—"

But she was lifting her skirts, gathering them, and running. Not away, but *toward* the pirate's hoarse cries. Rafe stared after her. Had she gone mad? Giving up at last, he followed.

"Keep down," she whispered as he caught up. They crawled the last few feet through vines and sand and briars. And there they finally saw Makeele, the dreaded pirate king—swinging like a smoked ham, by his heels, from a tree.

"A snare the old soldiers set," she said. "One that the other pirates missed!"

Makeele revolved slowly and heavily from the noose, arms flailing, as the branch overhead creaked ominously. He waved the pistol menacingly, but couldn't reach his pouch to reload.

"The village will be out here soon enough after that shot, and all this shouting." Molly nudged Rafe. "Come. We must get you off, and headed for freedom."

34

FAREWELL,
AND A NEW BEGINNING

MOLLY FOUND THE BAG OF PROVISIONS and water jug lying in the path where they'd dropped them. She and Rafe hurried down to the beach, where the longboat still lay beached at water's edge. He rinsed and filled the bottle at the pond, and used a knot of wood for a stopper. So then he had all he needed. There was no call to linger and every reason to go.

How different he seemed now than when he'd washed up on the island. First he'd been a curiosity, and a mystery. Then gradually he'd become a burden, and even a danger. But now she simply saw a boy her age, ready to make his own way and see how far he could get. She'd understood Rafe in the beginning even less than she'd understood Francis Ley.

". . . so if I see no ship out there, I'll head on north, keeping offshore," he was saying. "I'll travel mostly by night. That way, perhaps no one will see me."

She nodded. "I suppose that'd be best. And rowing, well . . . you aren't much of a sailor, yet."

He smiled. "Too bad you haven't time to teach me. I'll try to send word from where I end up . . . if you want to hear."

"Yes, please do," she said. But delivery of letters between

the still-new States, and especially to Savage Island, was very haphazard. The long, hard journey Rafe was about to undertake most likely meant she'd never see him again. Even if he did survive and reach freedom.

How sad that made her feel.

And he looked sad as well. "When I first ran, and lay in thickets during the day hiding, or traveling roads at night, I thought someday I'd go back. To free my mother. But I think now that won't happen."

If her own mother were held captive in some place she could reach in this life, she thought she'd go anywhere, do anything, to see her again. But then, she was not a runaway slave, hunted on sight by anyone who wanted to collect a reward.

On impulse, she thrust her hand into her pocket and took out the coin pouch and ring and seal.

"Here," she said, handing him all those things. "I think any British ship will welcome you if you come bearing these. Keep the coins, though, and then perhaps you can go back one day, after all. To free your mother."

Rafe looked at her in disbelief and shook his head. "But I can't take all—"

"You can, and must. I don't want them." Strangely enough, it was true. Surprising how much better she felt when all the redcoat gold—the heavy gold disks, the thick carved ring—no longer weighed her down. Besides, there was still the strange-looking staff hidden near the stable. Whatever its use, it was solid silver. Surely that alone would pay off their debts. It would be more than enough for her and her father.

"I can't ever repay you," he said, shaking his head again, but with less conviction.

"Someday, if it's ever safe, come back. And bring your mother to visit us. That would be payment enough. Now please, go!"

He took the oars, and with a few strong strokes shot safely across the Bandy.

Molly waved, keeping her hand upraised until her departing friend was only a speck on the horizon. Then she turned back through the cold, darkening woods. Toward the village that was still home. From the lane, she heard a murmur of raised voices, the tramping of many feet. The villagers were headed into the woods to investigate the latest ruckus. Later they'd be wondering how a captive runaway, a slave and a pirate, had escaped from her stable. Lord, would she need yet another story?

Perhaps she'd just let what they found in the woods, wiggling like a fish on a hook, be explanation enough: One young scalawag pirate escaped; his older comrade and liberator not as lucky. Molly smiled ruefully. She might otherwise have a good deal of explaining to do, and didn't look forward to it.

But soon she could also take the log canoe—now her own boat once again—and sail across to bring her father home. She could go out when she liked and catch oysters and crabs. Then sell them or eat them, as the mood took her.

And if she saw young Francis when she went over to the Eastern Shore, or over a boatload of vegetables, she could repay him those four pennies, with interest.

While Rafe was setting out on a long-delayed journey,

Molly felt she'd just finished one of her own. She might one day leave the island, too, but felt certain she'd always return. Her mother was buried here. This was the land her great-great-grandfather had chosen for generations of Savages to be born, to live, and to die on. Surely no other place, in the New World or the Old, could ever offer a better treasure, or a truer home.

AUTHOR'S NOTE

THE TREASURE OF SAVAGE ISLAND IS FICTION, but Molly and Rafe's story was inspired by historical places and events. You won't find Savage Island on maps, but eighteen real barrier islands much like it lie off the Virginia coast. Before and after the Revolutionary War, some were inhabited, though only by hardy souls. Such islands have always been plagued with harsh winter winds, raging nor'easters, and clouds of insects in summer. They are lonely and remote in all seasons.

Islanders would have been wary of strangers, for good reason. There really were pirates called picaroons, who were feared along the mid-Atlantic coast and around the Chesapeake Bay. Picaroons were British Loyalists who refused to swear allegiance to the new United States, during or after the Revolution. They attacked farms, plantations, and villages and ransacked merchant ships on orders from the last royal governor of Virginia, Lord Dunmore. He tried to make as much trouble for the people of Virginia as he could. *The Virginia Gazette* said he had "perpetuated crimes that would even have disgraced the noted pirate BLACKBEARD." When the war turned against the British, the unpopular Dunmore fled on a man-o'-war back to England.

When people depart in a hurry, they leave things behind. I chose a silver mace as one of the buried items for Molly to find because it was the traditional symbol of royal authority that an official like Dunmore would have carried. I based its description on one I saw in a museum in Norfolk, Virginia. This mace was made of pure silver, carved with leaves and scrolls and topped with a crown and cross. It was over three feet long, assembled. When the British bombarded and burned Norfolk in 1776, Loyalists hid it from the American patriots, burying it in a garden. I wrote about what might have happened if they had tried to take it back to England.

A peace treaty was signed with England in 1781, but by then pirating had become a family trade for some Loyalists. They still raided ships and even abducted their crews, for experienced hands were scarce. Joseph Wheland, the real-life picaroon on whom the character of Wayland Makeele is based, was notorious for kidnapping seamen on the Bay. The navies of Maryland and Virginia were too small to deter picaroons, and their raids went on well into the nineteenth century. It took fifty years, and the help of the French fleet, to wipe out these pirates.

Another worry for Eastern Shore residents was that the pirates' old partners, the British, still were sometimes sighted off the Atlantic coast, despite the treaty ending the war. Many Virginia residents, especially those who had served in the Revolution, expected them to return.

In the novel, Molly suspects Mrs. Ben of being a ship wrecker. Before and during this time, wreckers plied their deadly trade along the Atlantic coast, especially off North Carolina. They really did use lights hung around a horse's neck to lure unwary ships aground. Some were rumored to murder survivors to avoid being punished for their crimes.

Both the British and the Americans recruited African-Americans during the Revolution. Both sides were desperate for seamen, and blacks had already served in British and state navies, and on merchant vessels, north and south. Before the war, Dunmore issued a proclamation offering freedom to any slave who would serve King George. Many British vessels gained men who knew local waters well enough to be pilots. Some were runaways, others slaves of Loyalists; others were freemen pressed into service. If Rafe had boarded a short-handed British man-o'-war, he probably would have been made to serve. Many sailors were teenagers and some were even younger.

It might have been better than being dragged back to North Carolina. Runaway slaves were severely punished. Still, some were helped to escape by free blacks and sympathetic whites, especially Quakers who felt slavery was morally wrong. A girl like Molly would have had little extra food or clothing to offer to a boy like Rafe. But she might, in some way, with food or money or by providing a temporary shelter, have helped a slave on the road to freedom.

—LENORE HART